Eli

A major new film from
Working Title/Polygram

A novelisation
by Tom McGregor

based on the script by
Michael Hirst

First published 1998 by Boxtree
an imprint of Macmillan Publishers Ltd
25 Eccleston Place London SW1W 9NF
and Basingstoke

Associated companies throughout the world

ISBN 0 7522 2459 X

1 3 5 7 9 8 6 4 2

A CIP catalogue record for this book is available from
the British Library.

Typeset by SX Composing DTP, Rayleigh, Essex
Printed by

Prologue

'Is the Lady Elizabeth aware of our intentions?'

Thomas Wyatt looked up in surprise. 'But of course. Why do you ask?'

The other man ignored the question. 'And she knows that we are obliged to act now, not later as intended?'

'Yes. Pickering has ridden to inform her.' As Wyatt spoke, he looked down at the papers in front of him – missing the expression on his companion's face. 'Word has arrived from Leicestershire', he continued. 'And from Devon.' A small frown creased his brow as he read. ''Tis a pity they're fewer in number than we are, but that paucity should be matched by the Government troops who . . . '

'But we haven't received word from Lady Elizabeth herself?'

Irritated now, Wyatt looked up again. 'Have we not already had enough of the Inquisition? But no: she has not replied to my letter.'

The other man paused before replying. Then, at length, he nodded in approval. 'Good. We would not want proof of her complicity. Letters have a habit of . . . of falling into the wrong hands.' As he spoke, he looked at his own hands. They were capable, strong and, for an aristocrat, strangely workmanlike. And they were empty. Then he leaned over the table and grasped Wyatt's arm in a warm, conspiratorial gesture. 'You're right, Thomas. Enough of the Inquisition', he said with a smile. 'Our success will rid ourselves of them – and of all things Spanish.'

Wyatt, too, allowed himself a smile. 'Is that how you see the Queen's future husband? As a thing?'

The other man laughed. 'Oh . . . worse than that. A noisome thing, perhaps?'

'Which would mean,' finished Wyatt, 'that this marriage is a match made in heaven.'

Beneath the table, the other man gripped the arms of his chair, willing himself not to betray his excitement. That he had put the words into Wyatt's mouth mattered not a jot. Later they would be extracted, under duress, probably under torture. Wyatt had insulted both Queen Mary and her betrothed – treasonable crimes in themselves. Better still, he had admitted to informing the Queen's sister about the planned rebellion. A pity she had not replied. A letter from Elizabeth, an indication of her compliance, would secure a fate for her as grisly as that in store for Wyatt, for it would be sure to fall into the wrong hands: the hands that were gripping the armrest.

But, thought Wyatt's companion, one couldn't have everything. It was victory enough that he had infiltrated Wyatt's band of traitors. He looked again at the bowed head opposite him. A pity, he mused, that such a learned man, such a capable soldier should allay himself to such a dangerous, doomed cause. A great pity that he should choose the path of treachery. But perhaps that path had been chosen for him. Feeling a first – albeit faint – twinge of pity for

2

the man before him, he let his thoughts wander to Sir Thomas's father. Wyatt the great poet had – in a supreme irony – been felled by romance. And a romance with none other than Anne Boleyn; witch, adulteress and second wife of Henry VIII. And mother of the thorn in the crown of Mary's reign – Princess Elizabeth.

Perhaps it wasn't surprising that Wyatt the son should follow in his father's footsteps. Like father, like son. And like mother, like daughter. Anne Boleyn had lost her head on Tower Hill. Her daughter would follow suit.

Wyatt's rebellion against Queen Mary was over almost before it began. Enough of the Queen's men infiltrated the camps in Devon and Leicestershire to ensure that retaliation was swift and severe. Wyatt's and his men in Rochester, although also infiltrated, were more successful: they marched from Kent to London and forced their way into the city. But that was as far as it went. The Queen's army was waiting for them – and cut through them like a knife. Most of Wyatt's men were killed on the spot. Wyatt was not: he was taken to the Tower of London, there to endure incarceration and months of torture whilst his captors tried to prise from him the names of other collaborators. There was one name in particular they wanted. And it was the one name Wyatt persistently refused to divulge: that of Princess Elizabeth.

Chapter 1

There were many at court who nursed the suspicion that Queen Mary was going mad. Her appearance did little to disabuse them of this notion. Her disconcerting stare, born of short-sightedness, had taken on a manic intensity. Her teeth, like her eyebrows, had all but disappeared, lending her a faintly ghoulish appearance. And her conversation, never dazzling at the best of times, was almost exclusively limited to two topics: love and religion.

The topics were connected. The latter had always been an obsession with her: her primary concern since ascending the throne the previous year had been the restoration of the Catholic faith. In that she had succeeded, using force where necessary. All over England, Protestant heretics were burned at the stake; a lengthy, agonizing and near-barbaric form of execution. It was, in part, this appalling demonstration of Mary's increasing religious intolerance that prompted Wyatt's rebellion. But it was her engagement to Philip of Spain that had ignited the fire of its brief life.

In July 1554, Mary married Philip, heir to the throne of Spain and son of the Holy Roman Emperor. The match meant a reunion with Rome, an alliance with a great dynasty and, crucially, a union that would provide Mary with a Catholic child – the succession would then be secured. Mary's child would be heir to the throne – and its existence would banish the threat of Elizabeth for ever. For as Mary's rule had progressed, so had her intolerance of her half-sister.

An intolerance that, combined with her religious zeal, begged doubt of her sanity. The severity with which she had dealt with Wyatt and his conspirators was unparalleled: the heads of every man even suspected of collusion in the revolt were still rotting on stakes all over the capital city.

Mary's hatred of Protestants was equalled only by her love for Philip. The intermittent, paternal affection of her father apart, Mary had been a stranger to love for all of her thirty-eight years. Now she was making amends for that. She doted on the short, fair, slightly distant creature she had married.

The affection wasn't reciprocated however. Philip's indifference to Mary sometimes bordered on disgust. He hadn't been over-enthusiastic about the match in the first place, and didn't regard marriage to the ruler of a small, insignificant and impoverished country as much of a coup. The fact that the ruler was physically unprepossessing and eleven years his senior didn't help at all. Yet the fact that she *was* a ruler was vital to Philip's interests. In time, he would make her crown him King of England. In time, he would make her go to war with France to further Spain's interests. In time, she would do his bidding.

But for the time being, Philip preferred to avoid his wife as much as was possible. She still doted on him, yet now she had only one topic of conversation to regale him with: Princess Elizabeth's involvement in the Wyatt rebellion. 'It must be *proven*', Mary kept reiterating. 'The bastard daughter of Anne Boleyn will *not* inherit the throne of England.'

It didn't seem to occur to Philip that, in avoiding his wife's bed, he was compounding the issue. If Mary became pregnant, Elizabeth would be far less of a threat.

Mary's courtiers, however, were obliged to endure her incessant rantings about her sister's guilt.

The Duke of Norfolk heard more than most. Though England's greatest noble, a Privy Councillor and a powerful force in the land he was, nevertheless, Her Majesty's subject. And on this day, as on many other days, the object of her wrath.

'Are you going to tell me,' snapped Mary the minute he walked into her Audience Chamber, 'that she's *still* pleading illness?'

Norfolk bowed. 'Her household begs that she would benefit from more time before embarking on an arduous journey.'

'The journey from Hatfield is *not* arduous.'

'No, Your Majesty.'

'And what of our physicians? Did we not send them to examine her for ourselves?'

'Yes.'

'And?'

'They deduce that she is indeed ill – but that she is perhaps just well enough to travel.'

'What's wrong with her?'

'It appears that she is suffering from watery "vapours".'

'Hah!' Mary leaped up from her table and pointed a fleshy finger at the startled Duke. 'Then she is pregnant!'

'Your Majesty . . .'

But Mary had the bit between her teeth, and wasn't about to let go. 'Bad blood will out,' she exclaimed. 'A bastard will beget a bastard. And it is well known that my sister is a "spirited creature". For this if nothing else we can ensure that she is sent to the Tower.'

Norfolk remained mute as he watched his sovereign pace the room. The physicians, he knew, suspected that the 'watery vapours' suggested an inflammation of the kidneys rather than a pregnancy. Yet he also knew that Mary was obsessed by the idea of children. If her own stubbornly refused to arrive, then she would imagine other people's.

'So,' Mary muttered to the room in general, 'she is with child.' Then she rounded on Norfolk again. 'And what more of her involvement in the rebellion against me?'

Here Norfolk was on more positive ground. 'We have intercepted a letter from Antoine de Noailles to the King of France. It reads that Princess Elizabeth was aware of the conspiracy and was assembling her supporters in readiness.'

That news, to Mary, was even more inflammatory than the pregnancy she had invented. Her beady eyes were now positively gleaming with triumph. She rounded on Norfolk. 'Then we will accept no further delay. She *must* be brought to the Tower!'

Norfolk knew perfectly well that Elizabeth had

assembled no supporters – but that fact would contribute little to her defence. That the news was contained in a letter from the French Ambassador to Henry II was, on the other hand, a bonus to her accusers.

'Send word to her,' continued Mary, 'that we will hear no more of illness. Tell her that, while we regard her health with sisterly concern, she will be as well looked after in London as at Hatfield. Tell her,' she finished, 'that Her Majesty commands her presence.'

A slow smile spread across Norfolk's handsome features. Any sisterly concern, he knew, had long since evaporated. And ordering Elizabeth's presence was, at last, a summons to arrest.

But as he turned to leave the room, Mary's attention turned away from thoughts of Elizabeth's arrest – towards those of her pregnancy. Then, her brow furrowed, she herself turned to her ladies. 'The Countess of Lennox', she announced. 'Bring her to me.'

The order was addressed to no one in particular – Mary didn't regard her maids as people in particular – but it was obeyed by the eldest. And she, like the others, knew exactly what it meant. While none of them would have dared to speak during the audience with the Duke of Norfolk, all of them had listened. They had listened to particular interest to the news of Elizabeth's 'watery vapours'. The Countess of Lennox, possessor of the loosest tongue and the sharpest ears at court, would know exactly who had caused those vapours.

*

When Margaret Douglas, Countess of Lennox, arrived in Mary's apartments, it was in some trepidation. Usually ebullient even in Mary's dour presence, she was, today, of a different demeanour. She was frightened. While that particular emotion was now commonplace under Mary's reign of terror, the Countess's fear was of a different colour. She wasn't scared that Mary had discovered any secret Protestant leanings, but that she had found out about her new *sobriquet* – and the identity of the woman who had bestowed it upon her. For, in whispered voices behind closed doors, the Queen was now known as 'Bloody Mary' – and the author of that title was the Countess of Lennox.

But the Countess should have known her sovereign better. Such was Mary's absorption with her husband, her religion and her half-sister, she remained blissfully unaware of the bloodiness of her reputation in her own court. And even at the best of times, she had little time for gossip – unless it related to her obsessions.

'The Lady Elizabeth,' she announced as soon as the Countess entered the room, 'has recovered her health.'

Margaret Lennox paused before replying. Mary was in the habit of making sudden pronouncements designed to wrong-foot her courtiers. An expression of delight on the Countess's part may lead to a burst of rage about the fact that Elizabeth was now able to plot against her – yet Margaret could hardly profess herself disappointed that Elizabeth was well again. To confound the issue, Elizabeth, like Mary herself, was a cousin of Margaret Lennox – all three were grand-daughters of Henry VII.

When she did reply, the Countess opted for a diplomatic evasion. 'I have heard,' she said, 'the air in Hertfordshire is renowned for restoring the spirit.'

'Pah!' Mary let out a derisive snort and glared at the other woman. 'I have heard nothing of the sort. The air in Hertfordshire appears to favour malingerers who choose not to accept my invitations.'

Margaret Lennox suppressed a smile. 'Invitation' was hardly the word she would have used.

'We have not seen our sister Elizabeth for some time', continued Mary, in a deceptively conversational tone. 'Nor are we aware of the company she keeps.' Her next words, and the question mark at the end of them, were left hanging in the air – and at the corners of the toothless, sly smile she bestowed on the other woman.

Again Margaret paused before replying. 'I . . . I too am unfamiliar with The Lady Elizabeth's household.'

'I'm not referring to her household', snapped Mary. 'Tell me about her guests.'

Feeling herself to be on increasingly uneasy ground, Margaret tried to stall again. 'I . . . I am unaware of any guests she may entertain.'

'That is not what I asked. I don't care what you may or may not be aware of. I want to know,' she said, stepping closer, 'what they're saying in court.'

Margaret knew defeat when she saw it. Any more prevaricating on her part and Mary would start to make threatening noises about dismissal from court; banishment to the wilderness.

'There has been some word,' she said with a sigh, 'of Robert Dudley.'

'*Dudley*?' The shriek echoed through the room. 'Dudley? I had heard of Courtenay – but *Dudley*?'

Mystified by Mary's extraordinary reaction, Margaret merely nodded.

Then Mary's eyes narrowed. 'Which Dudley?'

'Lord Robert, I believe.'

'Hah!' Another shriek, this time even louder. Then Mary clapped her hands together and, to Margaret's even greater astonishment, began to laugh. Cackles and shrieks were Mary's trademarks – laughter, in the current climate, was all but unknown. Yet there was no mirth in the sound. The laugh was almost wicked, and carried with it an unmistakable note of triumph. Protocol demanded that Margaret wait for, not ask for enlightenment. It was a long time coming.

'My sister Elizabeth shall not be lonely when she comes to London', said Mary as her laughter subsided.

'Lord Dudley is here?'

'Here. Yes. Or, more precisely, there.'

'There?'

'Yes. In the Tower.'

It was only as she made her way back towards her own apartments that Margaret Lennox realized the full import behind Mary's words. Desperate to rid herself and indeed her country of Elizabeth, she had never found a means to do so. Now, it seemed, she had several.

Elizabeth's direct involvement in the Wyatt rebel-

11

lion – real or illusory – was one. Given enough time, those hostile to Elizabeth would be able to furnish some sort of evidence against her. Thomas Wyatt, given enough torture, may even provide it for them.

And now, in the shape of Robert Dudley, Margaret Lennox had just unwittingly provided Mary with another string to her bow of antagonism. Another reason to suspect Elizabeth of plotting to overthrow her.

For that was what the Dudleys did. They plotted against kings and queens. Three generations of Dudley kingmakers – Lord Robert's father, grandfather and brother – had already lost their heads in dangerous games of self-aggrandisement. Mary herself had ordered the execution of two of them. And now Robert was in the Tower, awaiting trial for his part in the Wyatt rebellion.

Everyone close to Robert Dudley would be treated with the utmost suspicion. Especially the lady who was closest of all.

Chapter 2

Elizabeth *had* been ill. For the past five years she had suffered from one ailment after another. Doctors came and went, diagnoses and treatments differed, but Elizabeth knew there was a common thread running through all her maladies: stress. And now, although recovering from her latest infection, she was under greater stress than ever before.

So were those around her. Kat Ashley, unofficial governess, guardian angel, confidante and friend, had been with her mistress for more than half of Elizabeth's twenty-one years. There was very little she didn't know about the clever, mercurial creature whose life she would defend with her own. There were few thoughts behind those deep green eyes that she could not read. And there were very few letters whose contents Elizabeth did not share with her.

Sir Thomas Wyatt's letter had been shared. Then it had been burned. Both women knew enough of the machinations of Mary's reign, clandestine as well as overt, to be aware of the dangers of keeping it. It had been easy to destroy the letter: impossible to consign its contents to oblivion.

'If Wyatt succeeds,' Elizabeth had told Kat, 'then I am to be placed on the throne. If he fails . . . '

'Then you shall remain where you are.'

Elizabeth had laughed at that: a laugh that carried

no trace of humour. 'No, Kat, I shall not – as well you know.'

Kat did know that. Appeasing Elizabeth with platitudes was a habit to which she sometimes reverted in times of crisis: she sometimes forgot that Elizabeth was no longer a child, but a highly educated and highly intelligent young woman.

'If Sir Thomas fails,' said Elizabeth, 'they shall send for me. They shall question me about my knowledge of Wyatt's plans . . . '

' . . . knowledge that you shall deny.'

'Kat!' Elizabeth's green eyes blazed. 'I'm not a child! I can deny the letter: I can hardly protest my ignorance of a plot that, by all accounts, is becoming less secret by the day.'

Kat gave her mistress a shrewd, penetrating stare. 'Whose accounts would those be, madam?' Kat was constantly amazed by the way her mistress, supposedly in self-imposed, semi-retirement from court, kept herself abreast with current affairs. And usually via the most controversial channels.

'Sir Nicholas's', answered Elizabeth. 'He visited but the other day.'

Kat almost forget herself; she all but rolled her eyes heavenwards. Sir Nicholas Throckmorton was possibly the most controversial courtier of them all. By entertaining him, Elizabeth was playing with fire.

'So', continued Elizabeth, suddenly becoming agitated. 'If Sir Thomas succeeds, he intends to put me on the throne. If he fails, I shall be called to London. I shall probably be arrested, I may well be imprisoned in the Tower. Then,' she finished with dramatic flourish of her beautiful hands, 'I shall be found guilty and I will lose my head.'

'Madam!'

'And do you know what it is about this affair that upsets me so?'

'I . . .'

'It's not even that I may die, Kat! It's that there's *nothing I can do about it*.' As she always did when she was vexed, Elizabeth began to pace the room. 'There is absolutely nothing I can do to dictate what may happen to me.'

'Madam, I think . . .'

'I am a pawn, Kat. Nothing more, nothing less!' Stopping at the great mullioned window that gave on to the Hatfield park, Elizabeth paused for breath. 'Is it not strange,' she added in a smaller, wistful voice, 'that bad news always comes to me here, at my favourite home?' Pressing her face against the cool of the glass, she reflected on the momentous news that had been conveyed to her at Hatfield. Seven years previously, it had been the news of her beloved father's death, then of her poor brother's unhappy accession to the throne of England. Then, in turn, the news of his death the previous year – and the beginning of Mary's reign.

Behind her, Kat's shrewd eyes looked to the window. 'Forgive me, Madam, but you seem contrary to your optimistic nature. You seem so sure that Sir Thomas will fail. Why?'

Elizabeth remained silent and still. Then, slowly, she turned from the window. 'Because,' she all but whispered, 'my sister is still not secure on the throne.

She has her spies about her. They fan from her court all over her realm. And I have no doubt they are already acquainting themselves with Sir Thomas and his rebels.'

'You cannot be sure of that.'

'Perhaps not. But I can be sure of one matter.'

'What, madam?'

'I can be sure,' sighed Elizabeth, 'that my sister the Queen will not have forgotten what the Dudleys did.'

Silence enveloped the vastness of the room. Kat would have liked to demur, to assure her mistress that Mary would have forgotten. Yet that was impossible. Mary would never forget. She would never forget what the Dudleys had done.

The day after her anguished outburst was the day Elizabeth fell ill.

Her recovery was not aided by the news of Wyatt's failure. Nor was it abetted by the repeated requests from Whitehall. Various – and increasingly curt – epistles requested that Princess Elizabeth leave Hatfield at once for London. Elizabeth countered these requests with letters, alternately pleading, effusive and unctuous, to her half-sister. It was only her illness, she protested, that prevented her from travelling.

And her terror. News had reached her of Mary's near-hysterical reprisals against the Wyatt conspirators. Severed heads on stakes; heretics burned alive on fires that took hours to consume their victims; brutal raids on even the most distant relatives of the rebels. And there was no immunity from suspicion at the

Palace of Whitehall. Several courtiers were questioned about their involvement – and Sir Nicholas Throckmorton was arrested for treason.

That last event reduced Elizabeth to tears – and increased her fear. Sir Nicholas was as innocent as she of any involvement in Wyatt's rebellion. Her fate was drawing inexorably closer; the web was closing around her.

It settled, finally, the day after the Queen's doctors came to Hatfield. For in their wake came the Earl of Sussex at the head of a troupe of the Queen's soldiers.

Norfolk had not been idle.

And nor had Elizabeth. The minute the doctors had pronounced her fit enough to travel, she knew that further procrastination on her part would be in vain. Worse, it would be construed as an admission of culpability. If she had nothing to hide, her accusers would ask, then why was she hiding?

After the doctors had delivered their verdict, Elizabeth ordered her ladies to pack her trunks. We will not delay further', she later explained to Kat. 'Better to leave now, in willingness, than to wait for a hostile escort. For that,' she added with a sad sigh, 'is undoubtedly what will happen if we stay. And I don't think I could bear the ignominy.'

But bear it she had to. the Earl of Sussex arrived exactly an hour after she had issued the order to pack.

It was Kat who heard the clatter of the horses' hooves as they cantered up the avenue. Curiosity gave way to horror as she flew to the window and identified the procession for what it was: a hostile escort to convey her mistress to London. Elizabeth's efforts to preserve her dignity were both in vain and too late.

'Madam?' Tentative rather than alarmist, Kat turned to her mistress.

Elizabeth had been watching almost disinterestedly as her maids folded her clothes. Her expression didn't change as she looked over to Kat.

'Madam . . . I fear our preparations are in vain.'

'They have come, then?'

Surprised by Elizabeth's seeming lack of fear – or even surprise – Kate merely nodded.

Elizabeth turned back to her ladies. 'So. This is it. I have tried my sister's patience too far. But,' she said, managing to muster a smile for the benefit of the other women, 'perhaps the Queen shall grant me an audience before . . . before . . . '

Before taking me to the Tower – words Elizabeth couldn't bring herself to articulate.

Kat knew perfectly well what Elizabeth was thinking. Desperate to distract her, she stepped forward and gestured towards the gowns laid out on the bed. 'You haven't changed yet', she said, again in tones that suggested she was talking to a small and wilful child. 'I think something simple would be suitable . . .'

Elizabeth smiled. 'When have I ever been known to wear something complicated?'

This was true. Elizabeth rarely dressed in the finery that befitted someone in her position; she seemed indifferent to jewels and frippery. Her style of dress was perhaps unusual, but it wasn't unattractive. Blessed by nature with the Renaissance high ideal of beauty, her natural attributes were sufficient to draw attention to herself. Fair of complexion, with delicate

18

eyebrows and her mane of light auburn hair, she was also tall, slim and possessed of a regal poise. And then there were the hands. Always the hands.

Kat now tried to press one of those dresses into Elizabeth's hands. To her intense surprise, Elizabeth recoiled in horror. 'No!' she shouted. 'Not that one!' She turned to her youngest maid. 'Quick, another! That one – the yellow.'

The maid did as she was bid. 'But madam,' protested Kat. 'The white would be more demure, more suitable for . . . I mean . . . It would be more . . . '

'White,' snapped Elizabeth, 'is what my mother wore when they took her to the Tower!'

A stunned silence greeted her outburst. Elizabeth *never* spoke of her mother. Not even to Kat. She had been two when Anne Boleyn, branded a witch and adulterer, had lost her head on Tower Hill. Nearly twenty years had passed – twenty years of silence from Elizabeth on the subject of her mother. She undoubtedly knew every salacious story about her father's hapless second wife – she had just demonstrated knowledge of her mother's attire on the day she was beheaded – yet she never sought to confirm nor deny them. She had, until now, remained mute on the subject. Just as she had remained silent on the subject of marriage.

'Yellow', sighed Kat, eventually breaking the agonized silence. 'Yellow it be then.' Her words, however, were almost inaudible. As she spoke, Sussex and his men stormed through the entrance to Hatfield and into the Great Hall below. The sound of their heavy boots echoed up the stairway and through the open

19

door of Elizabeth's room.

But she was not in her room when they found her. For a moment Sussex assumed she had taken flight: a notion he contemplated with wry amusement rather than alarm. She would not get far. Further, by taking such an action, she would be digging another inch of her own grave.

She had not fled. She had chosen to spend her last moments of freedom in the chapel, praying, for possibly the last time, the prayers of a Protestant.

Sussex paused a few feet into the room. Behind him, the soldiers lowered their eyes. Abashed to be storming the house of God on such a mission and, furthermore, carrying swords, they were reluctant to step into the room.

Sussex had no such compunctions. A smug, self-satisfied expression spread over his face as he watched Elizabeth at prayer. He stepped closer. 'I see the Lady Elizabeth's adoption of the Catholic faith was, as rumoured, an artifice.'

Still with her back to him, Elizabeth bit her lip. She had, under duress, paid lip-service to her sister's faith – yet she had never believed it.

But nor, she remembered, had many others. Slowly, she turned to face Sussex. For a moment she didn't speak. Nor did Sussex – but he did draw an involuntary breath. He had forgotten quite how striking she was. Even *in extremis*, under what must be appalling strain, she looked beautiful, serene, and utterly composed.

'My Lord Sussex.' Elizabeth inclined her head. 'We are all worshipping the same God, are we not?'

No, thought Sussex. This woman is a heretic. A bastard. A threat to the State and to the Queen. Annoyed with himself for being affected by her beauty, he glared at her with overt hostility. And when he spoke, there was venom in his voice. 'Princess Elizabeth,' he sneered, 'you are accused of treason. You will accompany me to London.'

To his intense annoyance, Elizabeth barely reacted. Then, to his greater fury, a small smile began to play at the corners of her mouth.

'How very inconvenient for you, my Lord,' she murmured before brushing past him and heading out of the chapel. Inside, she was quaking – yet she would be damned if she would betray that to Sussex. She knew that her greatest strength was her ability to face adversity with a fighting spirit. That was what she would show to her captor.

Her weakness lay elsewhere – in her heart. And what Sussex didn't know was that her heart was already breaking. Not on account of the fate she was about to suffer, but on account of others who suffered with her. Elizabeth knew beyond a shadow of a doubt that the man closest to her had already gone the way of Sir Nicholas Throckmorton and others of her circle. She knew that Mary and the Duke of Norfolk would not have sent Sussex to fetch her unless the rest of the suspects had been captured.

Elizabeth had predicted the failure of Wyatt's rebellion. Now she knew that the rest of her predications had been accurate. Mary would not have forgotten the events of a year ago. She would already have incarcerated Robert Dudley in the Tower. What

Elizabeth didn't know was whether or not she had already sentenced him to death.

To Elizabeth's surprise, Sussex and his soldiers did not take her to the Tower. That in itself was enough to ignite a flicker of hope. The flicker grew into a flame when she realized their destination was to be the Palace of Whitehall.

'So,' she said as they entered London and headed east, 'my request for an audience with the Queen has been granted?'

Sussex didn't even bother to reply and, with a weary sigh, Elizabeth sank back against the cushions. Conversation was anyway beyond her. Almost from the moment they had begun the journey, she had begin to feel extremely ill. Her complexion, always pale, had turned sallow, and the light had left her eyes. Yet she hadn't uttered a word of complaint All she had done was request that Sussex open the curtains of the litter. Sussex had agreed with alacrity – he did not want his prisoner to be sick all over him.

Yet, by the time their retinue reached London, the open curtains were serving a two-fold purpose: they were enabling air to reach Elizabeth – and they revealed to the crowds thronging the streets both Elizabeth's identity and the state of her health.

Mindful of his duty, Sussex leaned forwards and closed the curtains. Elizabeth had always been popular in London – far more popular than her half-sister the Queen. The last thing he wanted was for the people of London to know that she was being escorted, ill and against her will, through the streets.

That, as far as he knew, was the only reason they were going to the Palace rather than the Tower. If Londoners saw the Princess being taken to the latter, they would assume the worst.

It was one thing for Mary to burn her subjects in public, to show severed heads on stakes; quite another to parade her prisoner sister through the streets. Mary still had a reputation – of sorts – to consider.

Elizabeth's health, and the supreme effort she had made to appear proud and defiant in Sussex's company, began to take their toll when they reached the huge, rambling Palace of Whitehall. Her spirits began to sink and, again, the terror took its hold. A further blow came when the members of her Household, apart from six ladies and two gentlemen attendants, were dismissed upon arrival at her apartments. It marked the start of the slow, inexorable process of stripping her of her dignity and, ultimately, her freedom.

In the late afternoon, safely ensconced within the Palace and away from prying eyes, she was formally arrested. It was Sussex, again, who was sent to her. Yet the smug expression he had worn while contemplating her in the chapel at Hatfield had almost completely disappeared. He looked, if anything, uneasy. Yet he spoke with authority – words that cut through Elizabeth like a knife. 'Princess Elizabeth,' he announced after the briefest of bows, 'you are arrested for treason. I am commanded to take you hence, from this place . . . to the Tower.'

He could have been forgiven for thinking Elizabeth

hadn't heard him. Again she didn't even flinch; not even by the flicker of an eyelid did she acknowledge his words.

'Madam . . . ?'

'I heard you. When are we to leave? Now? Or do we go under the cover of darkness?'

An hour ago, Sussex would have replied in the affirmative. But that was before the Queen had been informed of her sister's arrival.

'So,' Mary had almost spat, 'her procrastinations have been in vain.'

'She insists that it was illness, not procrastination that delayed her arrival.'

'Yes.' Mary fixed Sussex with a beady eye. 'We know all about that. But she wasn't too ill to travel, was she?'

That, thought Sussex, was a moot point, one that he sensibly ignored. 'She has repeated her request,' he ventured, 'that you grant her . . . '

'An audience?' The scorn was etched deep in Mary's face. 'I have heard all I need through her letters. We have no need for her here. She must be conveyed to the Tower.'

'But it is not yet dark! The people . . . '

'She will go in daylight. Tomorrow.'

'Tomorrow?' Sussex was stunned.

'Yes.' Mary bestowed her most ghoulish smile on the Earl. 'Tomorrow is Palm Sunday. There will be no people about then, will there? They will all be in church. All of them. No one will be around to see their beloved Princess Elizabeth being taken to the Tower.'

Sussex smiled in return. How fitting, he thought. And what a sweet irony. For if anyone was around to witness the journey to the Tower, they would surely be burned at the stake. Not on account of what they had seen, but because of the simple heresy in not going to church.

Now, standing in front of the condemned woman, Sussex explained in gleeful detail that she would be taken in a barge in broad daylight to the Tower of London and that none of her adoring public would be around to see her.

Yet when Palm Sunday dawned it heralded another, bitter-sweet irony. For even if Londoners had been foolish enough to parade beside the river, they would not have been able to see Elizabeth. For the day was heavily overcast: great grey clouds hung low over the city and, as Elizabeth was led through the Palace garden and down to the river steps, the heavens opened, drenching her and sapping what remained of her spirits.

In spite of the fact that there would be few, if any, witnesses to her indignity, the actress in Elizabeth had planned a symbolic protest; a dramatic playing out of a role as the victim of a cruel injustice. But as she was bundled into the barge, it was all she could do to remain calm. Sussex had made great show of dismissing her already sparse retinue: only Kat Ashley and Isabel Knollys remained with her. And Isabel was already crying. Elizabeth couldn't even summon the strength to comfort her.

Twelve armed soldiers accompanied them. So, to Elizabeth's surprise, did the Earl of Arundel.

Although a Catholic and a stalwart supporter of Mary, he had, in sharp contrast to Sussex, always been kind to her. But today he seemed too embarrassed to speak to her. He positioned himself a few feet away from her and stared fixedly ahead. Beside him, Sussex kept casting sidelong glances at Elizabeth. Surely she would break soon, he thought. The misery of the day, matched by the hopelessness of her position, was bound to reduce her to tears.

But Elizabeth stayed silent as the barge pulled away – and remained so for the duration of the journey. Even as they passed in full view of stakes carrying rotting, severed heads, she kept her poise. Only when the massive, forbidding walls of the Tower of London loomed out of the mist did she begin to shiver.

But when the vessel slowed down and the oarsmen guided it to its berth she cried out in alarm.

'No!' she shouted. 'Not that gate! Anywhere but that gate! Please!'

'Madam! Restrain yourself, I beg you. It is simply the most convenient way to the Tower by water.'

Elizabeth whirled round and glared at the Earl of Arundel. The notion that he could still be her ally was cruelly dispelled as the barge floated closer to the Traitor's Gate.

'Sir,' she snapped, 'I'll thank you not to take me for a fool. I think we are both aware of the fates of those who have passed through this gate before us.'

Arundel curbed a smile. This, he thought, was more like it. The flash of anger from those sparkling eyes; the defiant straightening of her shoulders – this was the Lady Elizabeth he knew.

26

He leaned forward and whispered in her ear. 'Madam, it is done. We are nearly there now. And our . . shall we say unfortunate choice of gate is merely to ensure your safety.' But even as he spoke he regretted his words. Elizabeth was no idiot. She must know, as he did, that entering the Tower by way of the Traitor's Gate was quite deliberate. It was the gate through which her mother had been escorted to her incarceration and her death.

Then Arundel noticed that his charge was shivering. Her simple dress, he belatedly realized, was no barrier against the chill and the damp mist that hung over the water. 'Madam,' he said, 'you are cold. I beg you, take my cloak.'

Elizabeth silently cursed herself for showing weakness. Yet it was true; she wasn't just cold – she was freezing. And scared. She looked at the proffered garment; longed to drape it over her shoulders. Instead, with a look of scorn, she pushed it away.

But Arundel was looking at a cold, lonely and frightened girl barely out of her teens – not a captive and aloof Royal Princess accustomed to giving commands. He leaned further forward and, ignoring her protests, draped the cloak over Elizabeth's shoulders. 'Accept it, then,' he urged with a smile, 'for my sake.'

Elizabeth did so. A moment later there was warmth in her voice as well as in her body. 'Thank you,' she murmured with a smile of gratitude. 'I shall not forget this kindness.'

But how long, thought Arundel as the barge nudged against the walls of the Tower, will she have to remember it?

27

Kat and Isabel, standing protectively behind her, shuddered at the sight of the waterside gate. Lit by torches mounted on spikes, it looked exactly what it was – the gateway to a prison. Then, as the boatman cried to the gatekeepers, Elizabeth glanced up. An involuntary gasp escaped her lips as she saw, through the swirling mist, five more spikes positioned further up the Tower. Their burden spoke of a fiery rage greater than any flames. Five shaven heads rested squarely on the spikes; five gruesome faces stared blankly down at her.

Elizabeth stumbled backwards and, fearful that she might lose her balance altogether, grasped Kat Ashley's arm. At the same time, all the torches on the barge were extinguished as Sussex, well aware that Elizabeth was reeling from the sight of the heads, called out to the gatemen, 'Open the gates for the prisoner!'

A moment later, shrouded by the damp mist and descending darkness, the barge slipped silently through the Traitor's Gate and into the heart of the Tower of London. And as it did so, Elizabeth breathed a sigh of relief. Her brief, grisly sighting of the heads above her had been shocking in the extreme. Yet it had also left her with hope: the head of Robert Dudley wasn't among them.

The cavernous gloom of the interior, however, sapped Elizabeth's spirits once more. Stone steps streaked with mud rose from the quay and gave on to a walkway lined with soldiers. Dear God, she said to herself, do they really think I'm going to escape from here? What sort of threat do they think I pose? Then, in the light of a flickering torch above her, she picked out the pinched, pock-marked face of Sir John Gage, Constable of the Tower. He was leering down at her, triumph blazing from his beady eyes. And his smile said more than any words could convey – Elizabeth posed no threat whatsoever: this show of power was but a reminder of how utterly defenceless she was.

The barge bumped against the stone steps, rising and falling against the swell of the water. 'Prisoner to the steps!' shouted Sir John.

'Ship oars!' shouted someone in the barge.

Elizabeth looked around her. No one, it seemed, was prepared to help her alight from the barge. Sussex and Arundel were now on the other side of it, giving orders to their soldiers. Her ladies were gathering her belongings as best they could, scrabbling about in the crowded vessel. And above her, Sir John Gage was looking on in delight, relishing her humiliation.

Elizabeth squared her shoulders and took one unsteady step forward. With the next step, she reached the stone stairway – and with the next the mud and slime swirled round her dress, as if trying to drag her backwards and into the water. Yet Elizabeth managed to retain her balance and mounted the steps with as much dignity as she could muster.

His face alive with malice, Gage greeted her at the top. 'Come, Madam', he smirked, gesturing towards the dark passageway that led to the bowels of the building.

Elizabeth glared at the little man. Once more anger quelled her fear and, with ill-disguised contempt, she waved him away. 'No', she said. Then, to the alarm of everyone present, she sat down on the stone wall beside her. 'No,' she repeated, 'I shall not come with you.'

This wasn't quite what Gage had in mind. He had envisaged leading a cowed and terrified girl into his fortress. Instead, he was faced with a haughty, resolute princess who refused to do his bidding. Completely wrong-footed, his face now puce with fury, he glared down at her.

Then Arundel leaped off the barge, hurried up the steps and bent down to Elizabeth. 'Madam,' he whispered, 'you cannot sit here. It is not seemly.' And, he thought, it is also heart-rending.

'I would rather sit here,' replied Elizabeth, 'than go with you to a worse place. For God knows,' she added with venom, 'what you mean to do with me!'

Arundel sighed and shook his head. Nothing, he wanted to say. He had no quarrel with this woman. He was merely doing the Queen's bidding. But before he could compose a reply, Lady Isabel Knollys burst into tears again.

Forgetting her own plight, Elizabeth reached out to her. 'Don't cry, Isabel. Please don't cry. I need your strength now – not your weakness.' Then she glared defiantly at the fuming Gage. 'I am innocent, Thank God. *No one* has any cause to weep for me.' Then, gripping Isabel's arm with a renewed and surprising strength, she rose to her feet and looked down – for Gage was an inch smaller than she – at the Constable of the Tower. 'I will go with you now.'

Beside her, Arundel breathed a sigh of relief. So,

unexpectedly, did one of Gage's soldiers. He sank to his knees and looked with near-reverence at Elizabeth. 'God preserve your Grace!' he exclaimed.

Almost apoplectic with rage, Gage rounded on the young man, raised his fist and struck a vicious blow to his face. 'God damn you!' he screamed. 'You will not utter such defiance in this place!'

Elizabeth remained impassive. Yet, inside, she felt a warm glow. If one young man, unknown to her, should show such loyalty, then might there not be others?

But that warm glow was extinguished a few moments later. She allowed herself to be escorted in Gage's wake, down the dank passageway and then up another flight of steps, out on to Tower Green.

Suddenly Gage turned and smiled at her. 'This,' he said, 'is where your mother lost her head.'

Chapter 3

'What on earth,' bellowed Norfolk, 'is that God-forsaken noise?'

'Bells, sir.'

'I know they're bells, damn you – but why are they ringing?'

Norfolk's manservant, pristine in his yellow livery but quaking in his boots, reached for his master's cape. 'I think, your Grace,' he stammered, 'they're . . . they're ringing for the Queen.'

'You think.' Norfolk bristled with disapproval as the trembling young man fastened the garment around his shoulders. 'You think. But you don't *know*.'

'No, your Grace.'

'Why don't you know? What have you been doing all morning?'

'I've been . . . I have been preparing your Grace's attire, sir. And breakfast. And . . . '

'And if you'd been a little quicker about it then you would have had time to find out why the bells were ringing, wouldn't you?'

'Yes, sir.'

'You will be quicker next time.'

'Yes sir.'

Then, without having once looked at the young man he was addressing, the Duke of Norfolk strode out of the room. His hunting dogs, more fortunate than the manservant only in that they were mute, rose and followed him.

The manservant, one William Mason, exhaled deeply. He supposed he should be grateful that he was in the employ of the greatest noble in England. But sometimes he wished the great man were possessed of a little more nobility.

Norfolk's temper didn't improve as he walked at his usual breakneck speed through the rambling warren that was Whitehall. The Palace was in any case one of his least favourite places. 'One thousand four hundred rooms,' he was prone to declaiming, 'and you can't find any of them.' Today, matters weren't helped by the fact that at every corner he turned, the cacophony intensified.

Norfolk may have been incapable of finding any of the Palace's rooms, but he knew his way round its corridors. And, in one of them, he ran into the Palace Chamberlain. 'Who gave the order,' he barked by way of greeting, 'for the bells to be rung?'

Trotting in order to keep abreast with the Duke, the Chamberlain cast a surprised look at his companion. 'Why – the Queen herself did, your Grace.'

Norfolk stopped dead in his tracks. 'The Queen?'

'Yes. The Queen.'

'And why would the Queen do that?'

The Chamberlain was as taken aback as the Duke had been a moment before. Surely, he thought, Norfolk would know.

But the look on Norfolk's face indicated that he didn't know. It also indicated that the Chamberlain's continuing good health may well be contingent on his being informed.

'Your Grace,' panted the little man, 'the Queen gave the orders to announce that she is with child.'

'*What?*' Norfolk stopped dead in his tracks. 'With child? The *Queen?*'

The Chamberlain shared Norfolk's incredulity, yet wisely declined to share in its expression. He nodded gravely. 'Yes, your Grace. The Queen is expecting a child.' Then, unnerved by the expression on the other man's face, he lowered his eyes.

'They should,' snapped Norfolk, 'have made enquiry of me before they rang the bells!'

The Chamberlain bowed his head. 'Yes, your Grace.'

'And is this why Her Majesty has called for members of the Privy Council?'

'I believe so. Some of the Council are already . . .'

But his furious Grace was already stalking off down the corridor. An impressive figure at the best of times, his forbidding presence was enhanced by his anger.

A few moments later he reached the Queen's apartments. Brushing past the guards to the antechamber, he stormed into the room and glared at the assembled company. The six young ladies-in-waiting, who had been gossiping in low voices, became suddenly mute. All of them curtsied. Five of them lowered their eyes immediately; the sixth, Lettice, looked long enough to be able to gauge Norfolk's mood. Then she too bent her head.

But if she sought to avert Norfolk's attention, her efforts were in vain. He walked up to her and drew

34

her brusquely to one side. 'They say the Queen is with child. Is this true?'

Still Lettice looked down. 'Yes, your Grace', she mumbled.

Norfolk sighed, exhaling deeply. A distant and rarely heeded voice in his head told him that a less bombastic attitude may elicit more information. With a tenderness that belied his annoyance, he reached out and cupped Lettice's chin in his hand. The gentle upwards pressure left Lettice no option but to raise her head.

'I ask you again, Lettice,' Norfolk's steely blue eyes bored into her, 'is this true?'

'There are ... there are symptoms,' said Lettice. 'The Queen has ceased to bleed. Her ... her breasts have produced some milk and her stomach is swollen ... '

'And yet?' The evident doubt in Lettice's tone was matched only by that in Norfolk's mind.

Regretting her transparency, Lettice didn't reply for a moment. She knew she was being disloyal to her mistress – yet the information was hardly private. the Queen had no privacy. And besides, Lettice had a certain amount of sympathy for her disillusioned sovereign. 'It is a mystery', she said at length. 'The King has not shared her bed for many months. He appears to have a repugnance for it.' Then, half-coquettish and half-accusatory, she added, 'As lately your Grace has for mine!'

Almost involuntarily, Norfolk's jewelled hand tightened its hold on Lettice. Then, as a slow, lascivious smile spread across his face, he lowered it.

Without uttering a word, he let it brush gently against her breast. Lettice held her breath – and his gaze. But she could feel her heart betraying her – as could Norfolk. Lettice wondered if Norfolk knew the real reason for the pounding in her breast. She wondered if he was aware that she feared him more than she desired him.

Abruptly, he broke away from her. As he turned, the smile disappeared. But the expression in his eyes remained the same: cold, flinty and superior.

He strode to the door that gave on to Mary's bed-chamber. It was guarded, as ever, by two soldiers, their battleaxes held out to form a barrier across the threshold.

Norfolk was one of the few people for whom the barrier was automatically lowered. Bowing and with-drawing the axes, the soldiers opened the door to Mary's inner sanctum.

A sweet, cloying smell assailed Norfolk's senses the moment he stepped into the room. He wrinkled his nose in disgust. He hated this room; loathed the excessive paraphernalia of Catholicism with which Mary surrounded herself. It wasn't the religion that rankled with Norfolk: he and his family had never embraced the Church of England that Mary's father had founded. It was her total immersion in her faith and its offshoot of complete intolerance that Norfolk found distasteful. Yet in order to preserve his head, he never remarked on it – just as he never revealed that he held the entire Tudor dynasty in disdain. As far as he was concerned, they were upstarts.

While large and filled with mirrors, Mary's bedchamber was oppressively dark in atmosphere as well as appearance. Not even the flickering candles could cast much light – or even life – on the occupants of the room. The irony of Mary's celestial surroundings, thought Norfolk, was that they created a stygian gloom.

Checking himself, remembering to walk slowly towards Mary's bed at the far end of the room, Norfolk cursed under his breath as a dwarf scuttled out of the shadows. Resplendent in a miniature version of a court jester's attire, she leered grotesquely up at Norfolk, stalling him in his tracks. Then, giggling, she ran back whence he had come.

'Ah!' called a voice from near the bed. 'His Grace the Duke of Norfolk has arrived.'

Norfolk didn't miss the note of condescension in the voice. Reaching the bed, he responded by bestowing a small and somehow equally condescending bow towards the dapper little individual who had spoken. Philip of Spain, now King Philip II of Spain and, in titular name only, King of England, glared back.

Norfolk acknowledged the others standing beside the bed with a curt nod. Such were the shadows cast by the drapes surrounding the bed that they appeared more ghost-like than real.

But they were all real enough. Stephen Gardiner, Bishop of Winchester and now Lord Chancellor; a zealot whose fervour matched Mary's. The Earls of Arundel and Sussex and, to Norfolk's intense displeasure, the Spanish ambassador, Bishop Alvaro de la Quadra.

And, on the bed, Queen Mary I of England, two

dogs and a monkey.

'What say you?' rasped Mary, stroking her simian companion.

Norfolk bowed low – partly in an attempt to compose himself after the shock of Mary's appearance. Every day now, she looked increasingly unkempt. He was accustomed to the teeth and the eyebrows, but now her hair seemed to be falling out as well. The wisps that remained were scraped back from her forehead. Death's Head, thought Norfolk with a start. But as he straightened, he couldn't help noticing the very visible signs that heralded a new life: Mary's stomach, covered like the rest of her with only a thin shift, was visibly distended.

'Your Majesty?'

'What say you, Norfolk?'

'About what, Madam?'

'About our sister Elizabeth.'

Before Norfolk could reply, Stephen Gardiner bent towards the bed's recumbent occupant. 'For the security of the State, Madam, she ought to die.' Gardiner made no attempt to disguise the relish in his voice. Of all the members of the Privy Council, he was the most antagonistic towards Elizabeth and the religion she practised. Having been incarcerated in the Tower for his opposition to Henry VIII's doctrinal reformation, he was now violently opposed to Henry's bastard daughter and the heretic Protestantism she would no doubt be bent on perpetuating. 'For as long as Princess Elizabeth remains alive,' he finished with a flourish, 'there will always be plots to raise her to the throne.'

The flourish was infinitely more dramatic than the

import of his words. Norfolk, Arundel and Sussex were unimpressed by his statement of the obvious. Proof of Elizabeth's involvement in those plots was what was required – not the existence of them. Elizabeth had now been incarcerated for two months – and no proof was forthcoming.

Mary, however, seemed pleased. Then she turned to Alvaro de la Quadra. 'Ambassador?' She seemed to have quite forgotten that she had been soliciting Norfolk's opinion.

De la Quadra glanced at Philip. The Spanish monarch remained completely impassive. Small and insignificant though he looked, he was far from stupid and was well aware that he was widely held as the catalyst for Mary's reign of terror. He was also well aware that if he kept away from State affairs, his detractors could not cite him as the power behind the throne. In public, he kept quiet. In private, he briefed his ambassador to act as his mouthpiece. And this, although Mary's bedroom, was effectively a public forum.

'I agree with his Grace the Lord Chancellor', said de la Quadra. 'She is a heretic. She must never be allowed to succeed.'

Mary nodded, rather less enthusiastically that de la Quadra had hoped she would. The word 'succeed' was an ill-chosen one.

The Earl of Arundel, dismissive of Spanish platitudes, stepped forward. 'The point is, there is not yet enough proof to bring her to trial.'

Norfolk nodded. That, he knew, was the nub of the matter. Mary's religious fervour may have got the better of her, but, fundamentally, she was guided by the lodestar of her conscience. As much as she desired Elizabeth's execution, she could not order her death without either proof or a confession. While still blissfully unaware of her rapidly decreasing popularity, she was well aware that Elizabeth was loved by the people.

Norfolk articulated her doubts for her. 'There is no need for a trial, as long as Your Majesty can prove her guilt.'

Mary flashed him a nasty look. 'It is not *I* who need to find the proof, my Lord Norfolk.'

'But if she is found guilty *without* a trial,' protested Sussex, 'we ourselves might be condemned. She has many friends in Parliament. And,' he added with contempt, 'among the London rabble.' Like many other courtiers, Arundel was appalled by what was referred to as Elizabeth's 'common touch'. In the past she had been known to descend from her carriage and approach the masses, even laughing with them and accepting nosegays from their filthy hands. Princess Elizabeth's behaviour, he thought, was deplorable.

But he had spoken too hastily. Mary needed no reminding of Elizabeth's popularity. 'Friends!' She shrieked. 'Amongst the London rabble! Bah!' Suddenly incandescent with rage, she swiped at the bedcovers with a gnarled, white-knuckled fist. In the process, she hit the monkey who, with a wide-mouthed scream, bounded off the bed and scrambled off into the shadows. Beside Mary on the bad, the dog raised his hackles.

Again, Norfolk was consumed with distaste.

Unusually disposed to matters of hygiene, he found Mary's menagerie revolting. And, for that matter, Mary herself.

'My sister,' she screamed, 'was born of the whore Anne Boleyn. She was born a bastard. She must *never* rule England ... ' Then, as she glanced at her husband, her anger abated. 'But she will not', she purred with a crooked smile.

Philip, as startled as the other occupants of the room, offered a weak smile in return.

'She will not rule,' continued Mary as she patted her stomach, 'because of this, our most happy condition, for which we both do thank God.'

At the mention of the deity, a nun appeared from the furthest recess of the room. A priest, too, materialized from seemingly nowhere.

Mary was in full flow now. She leaned over for her unwilling husband's hand. With visible distaste and, as if dissociating the hand from the rest of him, he allowed her to place it on her stomach. 'Yes', said Mary in reverential tones. 'This is the reason Anne Boleyn's bastard will never reign over England.'

Norfolk couldn't help looking at the area where 'this' reigned – albeit in embryonic form. There was no doubt that Mary's stomach was distended, and in a manner that suggested pregnancy rather than yet another increase in weight. It was, he thought, extremely puzzling.

Sensing his eyes on her, Mary looked up. In place of joy, her eyes were filled with angry resolution. 'Yet Elizabeth *must* still confess to her treachery.'

Norfolk remained mute.

Stephen Gardiner, however, did not. 'Your Majesty shall rest assured that . . . '

'Yes.' Mary leered up at the unctuous bishop. 'Your Grace will find some proof of it, I am certain.' Then, dismissing Gardiner and the laymen, she beckoned to the nun and the priest.

Norfolk was still in a rage when he left Mary's apartments. Apart from the strange and still scarcely believable news of Mary's pregnancy, there was little reason to rejoice. England had suffered another bad harvest; the Exchequer was still empty, Mary's persecution went on terrorizing her subjects – and Princess Elizabeth was still a prisoner in the Tower. Added to that, the confounded bells were continuing to clamour all over London.

Chapter 4

News of the Queen's 'most happy condition' reached Elizabeth in her own less than happy incarceration. As was intended by its harbinger, it was delivered as a thinly veiled threat rather than an expression of joy. Elizabeth's precarious position, Sir John implied with no small measure of glee, was now untenable. She, Henry's child, would be usurped in her claim to the throne by his grandchild. His Catholic grandchild. The irony wasn't lost on Elizabeth – and nor was the fact that the news had pushed her not merely away from the throne but deeper into the shadow of the gallows.

She knew full well that the 'wonderful, joyous and long-awaited' news Sir John imparted to her wasn't that of a forthcoming royal birth but of the imminence of her own trial. And as to the evidence against her, Elizabeth had no doubt that it would now be conclusive as well as spurious. She would be found guilty of treason and she would lose her head. And England would still have an heir.

Elizabeth conveyed nothing of her desperation to Sir John. She would be damned if she would give him the satisfaction of seeing her distress. Only after his departure did she allow herself to give vent to her true feelings. She threw herself on her bed and, abandoning herself to tears, raged against Mary, against her captors, against the world. And, ultimately, against herself. This was not, said a small voice of reason, the way Henry's daughter should behave – Henry's daughter would do something positive.

So Elizabeth pulled herself together and, willing her life-force to return, began to pace the room. A step, she reasoned, was a positive step, the precursor to positive thoughts and actions. Had anyone else been in the room, they would have realized that each step was taking her closer to the window and the view that would be her last. For directly below was Tower Green. And on Tower Green, traitors lost their heads.

But Elizabeth was saved from confronting her nemesis by the arrival of Kat Ashley. Soft, hurrying footsteps and the swift brush of a dress against the cold stone drew Elizabeth out of her reverie and stopped her in her tracks. To her astonishment, she noticed that Kat was smiling.

'Kat! What is it?'

Quick, madam. Follow me. We have very little time.' Beckoning with a finger, heedless to her shortness of breath and giving Elizabeth no chance to object, Kat turned on her heels and hurried back out of the room.

'Kat . . . !'

But the only response was the soft rustle of Kat's dress as she made her way down the dark stone passage.

Elizabeth shrugged, gathered the folds of her own dress around her, and rushed after Kat. For a mad moment she felt like laughing. A moment ago she had been lost in the contemplation of her demise. Now she was chasing her maid down a corridor.

'Kat!' she urged again when, at the end of the passage, she caught up with the other woman. 'What is it?' Whatever it was, she knew it called for a whisper. Both women were now well beyond the confines of their quarters. And walls – particularly these walls – had ears.

Kat's eyes were shining as she turned to face her mistress. 'Lord Robert Dudley,' she intoned, 'is also arrested. And kept here.'

'What?' The word rang out like a pistol shot, ricocheting against the stone walls, reverberating down the corridor with a mixture of shock, disbelief – and joy. Elizabeth had long feared that Robert's imprisonment would be true; had hoped it wouldn't be – and had prayed that, wherever he was, she would at least be able to see him one last time.

Kat, however, heard only misunderstanding in her mistress's exclamation. 'Lord Robert Dudley,' she whispered. 'He's . . . '

'Yes, I heard you.' Without realizing what she was doing, Elizabeth grabbed Kat's arms and held them in a vice-like grip. 'Where? Where is he, Kat?'

Kat smiled as she noted the light in her mistresses' eyes. 'Here, madam . . . in the White Tower.'

Elizabeth loosened her grip. 'The White . . . ?'

'It is not possible to see him . . . so I spoke in secret with one of the guards. I kissed him and . . .' modesty made Kat lower her eyes but mischief saw her raise them again '. . . and made him some . . . other promises. So,' she finished with a grin, 'I think he will allow it.'

'Kat!' The Royal princess in Elizabeth should have been shocked. Yet her exclamation was no admonishment. 'You are,' she said as she squeezed Kat's arm, 'truly most wonderful!'

Nothing short of a saint, thought Kat as she recalled the guard's rancid breath and lascivious leer. Yet Elizabeth's look of joyous anticipation more than compensated for her own small sacrifice. Yet . . . yet there was something else, something beyond joy in those eyes. Something that unsettled Kat.

It was only when she turned to descend the steep staircase that Kat realized what it was. Elizabeth was in love; not in the thrall of some youthful infatuation, but deeply, desperately in love. And Kat's heart bled for her.

The guard of whom Kat had spoken met them at the bottom of the stairs and led them, under cover of darkness, to a small door at the foot of the White Tower. His terror at being discovered, though tempered to no small degree by the rewards that Kat had promised, caused him to forget the identity of the taller, younger woman. He showed her little respect as, urging complete silence, he all but pushed her up the narrow staircase.

Elizabeth didn't care. All she could think about was Robert. In a matter of seconds . . .

'Robert.' Elizabeth had hardly been aware of the iron door creaking open, nor of being pushed into the confines of a small antechamber. But now, too suddenly, she was aware that she looking into a small cell – and facing Robert Dudley. And 'Robert' was all she could say.

She stood, momentarily embarrassed, and looked at him. His beard, she thought inconsequentially, needs trimming. And he looks old. Older then twenty-two. Gone were the fine brocades and velvets that constituted his normal attire: he was clad merely in breeches and a loose white shirt. Yet the simplicity of his garb served only to emphasise his masculinity: the shirt was open at the neck, revealing his chest hairs and barely concealing the taut muscles beneath them. And resting against his chest, rising and falling to the beat of his heart, was the medallion on the silver chain he had worn for as long as Elizabeth could remember. There was, thought Elizabeth, something raw about him; something feral. Something terribly disconcerting.

Equally awkward behind the bars of his cell, Robert inclined his tousled head. 'My lady.'

Then, staring straight into her eyes, he extended his arms through the bars, imploring her to come to him.

Half-laughing, half-crying, Elizabeth rushed forward, took his hands and pressed them to her face. For a few precious seconds she allowed herself the luxury of closing her eyes, of drawing strength from his nearness, of forgetting everything except the fact that they were together.

Robert too allowed himself the brief luxury of the embrace. Then, gently, he pulled away and looked once more into her soft green eyes. 'Have they hurt you?'

'No,' she whispered. 'But . . . but I'm frightened. I know they mean to kill me.'

'No!' Robert gripped her hands so tightly that she

winced. 'They *dare* not.'

His vehemence did little to convince Elizabeth. 'The Queen is with child', she said. 'Now I am nothing.'

'With child?'

Elizabeth nodded.

No elucidation was needed: the import of the words was all too horribly clear to Robert. With the birth of the child Elizabeth would indeed be nothing. Robert averted his eyes.

When he looked back into her eyes he was smiling. 'How long,' he asked, 'have we known each other?'

Elizabeth seemed taken aback by the question. 'All our lives . . . you know that. Why do you ask?'

'And what did we always promise each other?'

A half-smile hovered on Elizabeth's lips. 'That . . . that we would remain friends for the rest of our lives.'

'But what did we say about those lives?'

Now Elizabeth *was* smiling. But the smile didn't reach her eyes. 'That they would be long.'

'Exactly!' Robert reached out again and grasped Elizabeth's hands. She winced at the strength of his hold. And his voice, when he spoke again, was as urgent as his gesture. 'Never forget that you are still Henry's daughter. Show it in your face. Always. Show it in your eyes that you are not afraid of them.' Beseeching her, searching into her soul, he looked deep into those beloved eyes. 'Always remember who you are; that you are not afraid . . . do you promise?'

Not trusting herself to speak, Elizabeth merely nodded. Behind her, Kat Ashley was becoming increasingly nervous. Whilst greatly moved by the scene before her, her anxiety about the clandestine meeting was the greater emotion. The guard had promised 'a minute': already they had exceeded that brief time-span. 'Madam . . .' she began.

'Just a moment longer.' Elizabeth folded her hands around Robert's and continued to stare into his eyes.

Again, a smile began to play on Robert's lips. 'Come live with me,' he whispered, 'and be my love.'

'And we will,' she replied automatically, 'some new pleasures prove.' The oft-repeated refrain usually made her glow with pleasure. Now, it seemed hollow and meaningless – even childish. They were lines that belonged to another world; to the carefree, innocent world they had both once inhabited. And they seemed to mock the prisoners in the Tower. There would be no further pleasures here.

As if to illustrate that fact, the ensuing silence was broken by the sound of footsteps echoing at the bottom of the stairway. 'Madam!' urged Kat. 'We must leave. Now!'

But Elizabeth found movement impossible.

'You must go,' said Robert. Reluctantly, he pulled away from her. Seeing the look of panic in her eyes, he reached to his neck and unclasped the delicate silver chain. Dropping it into his right hand, he passed it through the bars to Elizabeth. 'Take this,' he whispered, 'and may God keep you, my lady.'

But Elizabeth didn't want God. Barely trusting herself to speak, she cupped the chain in her hands. 'And you, my lord.' As she spoke, she looked down at the medallion. She had seen it so many times before; the engraving of the Bear and Ragged Staff, the Dudley family emblem. She had even held it – but always it had been hanging round Robert's neck. Its exchange between the lovers precluded any further exchange of words: the medallion was something to remember Robert by.

As Elizabeth's fist closed over the chain, Kat stepped forwards and grabbed her arm. 'Madam!' she hissed. 'We cannot delay any further!'

Elizabeth seemed unable to move of her own volition; Kat was obliged to forcibly propel her out of the room. And she cast no backward glances, for the moment she turned away from Robert the tears began to flow.

She was still crying when they returned to the cramped apartment which for the last two months she had been obliged to call home. And it was there, finally, that she gave way to the despair and terror that she had tried so hard to suppress. The words 'Henry's daughter' no longer gave her any solace. Instead, they mocked her. She had used them earlier to bolster her flagging spirits. So had Robert. But now the words tasted bitter on her tongue. 'Henry's daughter,' she scoffed through her tears. 'What use being "Henry's daughter"?'

'Madam?'

'Being Henry's daughter, Kat, is not the key to my salvation.'

Kat knew that as well as she did, yet tried her best to disabuse Elizabeth of that notion. 'Madam, they would not dare execute the king's daughter . . . not on some trumped-up charge of treason. The people are behind you.'

'And there are many, more powerful people behind me – with daggers in their hands.' Then she held up her own, shaking hands to stall Kat's protest. 'Oh, we both know it's true, Kat. And as for being Henry's daughter – was my mother not Henry's wife? And what salvation did that give her? Did they not execute her on some trumped-up charge?'

Kat's protestation died on her lips. Again Elizabeth had mentioned her mother. And, for the first time, she gave indication that she knew Anne Boleyn's trial had been a farce. Kat wondered how much Elizabeth knew of the five charges of adultery, the accusations of witchcraft and of treason. She suspected her mistress knew every detail.

As Kat tried to find something – anything – to say, Elizabeth drew herself wearily to her feet and walked towards the narrow window. This time, with no positive thoughts to bolster her, she gave into the temptation to confront her fate.

'Kat?' she whispered as she stared out into the darkness.

'Yes, Madam?'

'You see that place? There. Before the church.'

Kat had to choice but to join her mistress. 'Yes, Madam.' As she looked down at the shadowy outlines of the buildings below, at the patch of well-tended grass directly beneath them, she quelled a shiver. She knew precisely what was coming.

'My mother was executed there.' The bald statement, the total lack of emotion was at odds with the import of the words. Kat looked closely at the other woman. Her tear-stained face was drawn, her lips pinched. She was, Kat realized, trying to fight back another flood of tears.

'She thought to look her best that day', continued Elizabeth. 'They say . . . they say she was still very beautiful.'

Silence descended in the small, dank tower room above the place of execution.

'On the morning . . . of it,' said Elizabeth with a new tremor in her voice, 'one of her gentlemen went to see her. She said she had heard she was not to die before noon, and was very sorry, for she had thought to be dead by then, and past her pain . . . '

Fighting back her own tears, Kat reached out to her mistress. Elizabeth shook her away. With unseeing eyes, she continued to stare out the window.

'He told her there would be no pain, that it was . . . that is was a subtle way to die. And then she . . . she said . . . "I have heard the Executioner is very good, and I have a little neck . . . "' Faltering again, choking back the tears, Elizabeth put her hands round her own neck. 'She put her hand about her neck . . . and then . . . and then she laughed!'

And then Elizabeth burst into floods of uncontrollable tears and collapsed into Kat Ashley's arms.

With silent tears coursing down her own cheeks, Kat cradled her mistress's head on her shoulder. For many minutes, she stroked the auburn head, uttering soothing noises as she did so. She sought only to alleviate Elizabeth's pain, yet a persistent question filled her subconscious mind: how had Elizabeth been able to reconcile her love for her father with what he had done to her mother? What on earth had her mother's

52

manner of death done to Elizabeth's ability to love, freely and openly? And how had her father's subsequent, desperate and disastrous forays into matrimony coloured Elizabeth's attitude to that happy state?

It was then, for the first time, that Kat found herself thinking of Elizabeth's death. Untimely it would be – but at least it would spare her further agonies of love and the terrible wrongs that parents visited on their children.

As if reading her mind, Elizabeth raised her head and looked Kat straight in the eye. 'It is fitting, in a way,' she said, 'that both Lord Robert and I are prisoners here.' Her voice, like her demeanour as she pulled away from Kat's embrace, was suddenly chillingly composed.

'Fitting, madam?'

'Yes. I am to die as my mother died. And Robert as his brother, father and grandfather before him.'

Kat lowered her eyes. Like everyone else, she knew of the link between the Dudleys and the Tudor dynasty: both had flourished together, yet where the Tudors went from strength to strength, the Dudleys were constantly thwarted by their own vaunting ambition. Edmund Dudley, Robert's grandfather and extortioner-in-chief to Henry VII – later beheaded on his orders. Robert's father John, who rose to become one of the most powerful men in the land – beheaded by Mary for treason. And his brother Guildford, also beheaded on Mary's succession.

'It is too fitting,' continued Elizabeth. 'It is perfect for Mary . . . '

'Madam, that was years ago . . . '

Elizabeth let out a bitter, brittle laugh. 'Mary will never forget. Did John's father and brother not lose their heads because they sought to prevent Mary succeeding to the throne of England?'

Kat could hardly deny that. They had spirited the unwilling Jane Grey to the throne – for all of nine days.

'So,' finished Elizabeth. 'My sister cannot afford to let another Dudley live. Nor can she allow another Lady Jane Grey the luxury of life.'

'Madam, you can hardly compare yourself . . . '

'Oh, but I can, Kat. And I do.' With a sweeping motion, Elizabeth indicated the room at large. 'Do you know who was the previous occupant of these quarters?'

Kat didn't need to be told.

'Exactly', said Elizabeth. 'The Lady Jane Grey. I feel it's no accident that Mary has assigned me to those quarters. She regards me in the same light as our hapless cousin. A threat to the Queen of England.'

What Elizabeth didn't know was the identity of another previous occupant of her room in the Lieutenant's Lodgings. Eighteen years previously, her own mother had spent the last miserable days of her life in that very room.

The Queen of England, in fact, regarded Elizabeth as a far more substantial threat than Jane Grey had ever presented. Elizabeth's claim to the throne was greater, her supporters were more numerous – and even less subtle than the Dudleys had ever been. Firmly believing – when it suited her – that the punishment should fit the crime, Mary ordered that Sir Thomas Wyatt's torture be as unsubtle as his efforts to usurp her throne in favour of Elizabeth. The royal command was greeted with great glee by the Constable of the Tower. Sir John Gage had a fondness for the more lurid of the 'instruments of persuasion' within the Tower, and had very little compunction about using any or all of them on his more recalcitrant victims.

Thomas Wyatt was proving to be the most recalcitrant of all. More than two months had passed since his capture and imprisonment. Wyatt's body was now bruised, bent and battered – but his spirit remained unbroken. Gage was of the opinion that his torture had not been sufficiently severe. He had undergone 'treatment' on the rack, his flesh had felt the iron pincers, several of his fingers had been crushed within the iron gauntlet – yet still he remained silent on one subject. Even when in agony, he refused to implicate Elizabeth in his rebellion against the Queen.

It was the Queen herself who decided upon the perverse course of bringing Elizabeth to witness Sir Thomas's torture. 'It has been said of my sister,' she told Gardiner, 'that she has a sensitive soul. Seeing Sir Thomas writhing in agony may prompt her to adopt any means to end his torment.'

'You think,' had been Gardiner's sceptical response, 'that seeing his . . . his discomfort may elicit a confession from her?'

'It may', said the Queen. 'I myself am a sensitive soul. I feel sure that I should adopt any means at my disposal to see an end to someone's suffering.'

Bishop Gardiner heard many an unlikely statement from his sovereign's lips, but none so blatantly untrue as this. He left Mary to her sensitive pursuits and went to inform John Gage of the 'treat' he was to prepare for Princess Elizabeth.

Elizabeth was convinced she was being brought to witness Robert Dudley's execution. That it was the middle of the night when the guards came for her only seemed to confirm her suspicions. Robert had had no trial: an execution in broad daylight would be too risky. A swift death within the confines of the White Tower, however, would arouse few suspicions. Robert would simply be sharing the fate of others who had taken the one-way journey to the Tower only to 'disappear' into its eternal embrace. No questions would be asked – no answers given.

But the sight that greeted Elizabeth when she was ushered into the ground floor of the Tower was more surprising and infinitely more horrific than any she had envisaged. Her relief that the individual in the centre of the room wasn't Robert was short-lived. In front of her, tied to a stone pillar, was Sir Thomas Wyatt: a shadow of the Sir Thomas she had met at court. His filthy hair was matted with blood; his tattered clothes were soiled with, she realized from the stench, his own filth, and his arms, legs and chest were raw with vivid lacerations.

'God's death!' Elizabeth's hands flew to her face. 'Sir Thomas. I . . . I . . . I had no idea . . . '

'Madam!' The cheerful, gleeful voice, quite at odds with the horrors on show, resonated from the far end of the room. Sir John Gage, holding a flaming torch aloft, stepped forward to greet his visitor. 'Madam ... here is your friend, Sir Thomas Wyatt.' As he spoke, he thrust the torch towards Wyatt's face. Unable to shield his eyes from the unaccustomed light, terrified of the sudden heat, Wyatt roared in anguish. Elizabeth let out an involuntary moan as she watched him writhe. Half his teeth, she noticed, had gone.

For Gage, however, the fun was only just beginning. 'Thus far,' he began, 'we have spared your friend our most effective instrument of persuasion. This,' he said as he walked over to a gruesome-looking instrument with a cast-iron hoop and all manner of clasps and spikes, 'is one of our newer acquisitions.' Acting for all the world as if he were demonstrating a particularly fine piece of riding equipment, he continued a chatty, conversational tine. It is called the Scavenger's Daughter. I myself would probably have chosen another name, but the name, like the instrument itself, was bequeathed to me by a previous Lieutenant of the Tower. Perhaps you knew him, Madam?' Gage turned to Elizabeth, relishing the sheer disbelief on her face. 'His name was Skeffington. He was Lieutenant during your father's reign.'

Even if Elizabeth had heard of Skeffington, she would have been unable to mention the fact. She was too horrified to speak.

'No?' Gage took her continuing silence as an admission of ignorance. 'Well, never mind. This,' he said, unfastening the hoop, 'is how it works. The head of the ... the interviewee is placed like this. Then his hands and feet . . . thus. Then, as the instrument bends, so does the body – but in rather an uncomfortable direction.' Sir John was only gesturing to Wyatt as he spoke, but the demonstration was enough to elicit another howl of terror from the hapless man.

Elizabeth somehow managed to block out Sir John's awful, incessant, ghoulishly bland explanations as he began to explain the merits of the iron gauntlets. 'Thomas . . . ' she whispered as she knelt in front of the groaning Wyatt.

But Wyatt tried to avert his battered head. 'You should not look upon me . . . No! No lady! Do not touch me.'

Elizabeth couldn't help but reach out to him. 'Poor Thomas . . . what have they done to you?'

'Ah!' It was John Gage who replied. 'The conspirators wish to converse. How touching. Perhaps I shall leave you to it. But rest assured, Madam,' he finished with a crowing leer, 'I shall be listening.'

Elizabeth ignored him. She leaned forward and saw the tears in Wyatt's eyes. With a tender hand, she brushed them away.

But the gesture was too much for Wyatt. More tears welled. 'Each day,' he sobbed, 'I pray to God they will kill me . . . but each day they do not. They only . . . hurt me more.' He looked up at Elizabeth and saw the tears in her own eyes. He tried to contort his bruised features into a smile, wincing in pain as he did so. 'All . . . all they ever ask is will I confess . . . to the guilt and complicity of . . . of the Lady Elizabeth.'

'Oh Thomas . . . '

'And,' he gasped, 'if I confess, they ... they promise to put an end to my ... to my agonies.'

In spite of the man's pain and wretchedness, a warning bell sounded in Elizabeth's mind. Would he admit to the untruth? Would he be tempted into a confession that promised to end his agonies?

She found the answer in Sir Thomas's eyes. He was almost as weary as he was in agony: weary of a life that he knew would not be spared under any circumstances. By staging his rebellion, Sir Thomas had signed his own death warrant. Implicating Elizabeth wouldn't save him.

Sir John Gage knew that as well. But still, he thought as he watched the tender scene through the iron grille in the door, anything was worth a try. He re-entered the room and, still smiling, began another demonstration of the Scavenger's Daughter. This time the victim was gathered in his embrace.

His efforts were in vain. Sir Thomas Wyatt lost consciousness before he uttered even a word. But to Gage's even greater annoyance, it was Elizabeth who fainted first.

Mary was most displeased that her ploy had failed. 'I told you,' she spat at Gardiner when he had imparted the news, 'that my sister was sensitive.'

'You did indeed, Madam.'

'So why did you subject her to such treatment?'

'But ... but ... !' Gardiner stared, open-mouthed, at the harridan on the bed. 'But Your Majesty ... !'

'But nothing!' screamed Mary. 'Elizabeth is a daughter of Henry VIII. She should not be subjected to such indignities.'

Gardiner couldn't even manage another 'but'. Even for Mary, this was extraordinary behaviour. Firstly, she cared not a whit how many indignities were heaped upon Elizabeth. Even more bizarrely, the 'daughter of Henry VIII' line was most unlikely. Mary had somehow managed to forgive her father for embracing the Protestant faith, but, until now, she had steadfastly refused to admit that Elizabeth was his daughter. As far as she was concerned, Elizabeth was the evil spawn of 'that whore Anne Boleyn.'

'Our sister,' continued Mary as she patted her stomach, 'is entitled to a fair trial. See to it that it happens.'

Sighing deeply, Gardiner nodded his assent and took his leave. At last, he thought, Mary hadn't insisted on being present at the trial. Her adamant refusal to countenance Elizabeth's execution without a trial begged that, on this occasion, the word 'fair' should be interpreted in the loosest possible way.

Witnessing Wyatt's torture – albeit briefly – had sent Elizabeth into the depths of depression. Nothing and no one could lift her out of it. In desperation, Kat tried to engineer another secret encounter with Lord Dudley – but to no avail. The guard whose 'acquaintance' she had made had moved on to pastures new; into the arms of a serving-girl who willingly provided him with her services without asking dangerous favours in return. The route to Robert's cell in the White Tower was firmly closed.

Elizabeth didn't even broach the subject. She talked little; her vitality seemed to have deserted her. Even her appetite disappeared. Accustomed from a tender age to the vicissitudes of power, to the oscillating fortunes of those around her and to her own precarious position, Elizabeth had nevertheless managed to maintain the illusion that she was her own woman. Now, within the confines of her dank prison, she began to accept that she never had been, and never would be the mistress of her own destiny.

If she needed any more proof of that fact, it came on the day of her 'trial'. The enthusiastic Gardiner, flanked by the Earls of Sussex and Arundel, conducted the travesty that passed more for an interrogation or, more aptly in the current climate, an Inquisition. To encourage Elizabeth – and much to Sussex's delight and Arundel's disgust – he arranged for the interrogation to take place next door to a torture chamber. Elizabeth wouldn't *see* anything, he explained. She would merely hear a few screams. There would be no fainting fit this time.

But what none of the men knew was that, even in the depths of despair, Elizabeth could be a formidable adversary. Outrage, injustice and anger always managed to rouse her. And today, she found herself the outraged, angry victim of a terrible injustice. Only the intermittent cries from the tortured man in the room next door frayed the edges of the nerves she had steeled for the occasion.

Alone on one side of the table, Elizabeth faced her three interrogators. Everything about the set-up seemed designed to intimidate her: they were provided with water and wine to drink. She was not. They were gorgeously attired in flamboyant clothes of

61

brilliant colours. She was wearing a simple cream dress. They had all the weight of the throne behind her. She had no one to defend her. Except herself.

'You deny,' began Gardiner, 'that you aided the traitor Wyatt, or were privy to his plans.'

'I do, my lords.' Elizabeth stared straight at Gardiner.

'Pah!' Gardiner gave a dismissive snort, sneered at Elizabeth and indicated the pile of letters in front of him. 'These are letters from Wyatt, addressed to you. In them, he pledges his allegiance to you.'

Elizabeth looked at the bundle. She was sure the letters were forgeries. The only epistle she had received from Wyatt had long since been destroyed. No one apart from Kat and a trusted messenger had seen it. True, it had made Elizabeth privy to his plans – but there was no way the men in front of her could know that.

'Wyatt may have sent me letters,' she stated with conviction, 'but I never received them.'

Gardiner banged his fist on the table. Arundel, however, leaned forward and smiled at Elizabeth. The smile had nothing of the John Gage about it; this one was kindly, genuinely concerned. 'Madam,' he said in his low, soft voice, 'you must have no fear of us. We mean no harm to come to you. But . . . if there is a small truth to these charges, however innocently and unknowingly you did proceed, then you had best confess it now, and throw yourself upon the Queen's mercy.'

Elizabeth wondered how much Arundel believed his own words. She gave him a shy, quizzical smile.

'But how could I confess to something I did not do – nor wish to have done?'

'You lie, Madam!' Gardiner slammed his fist on the table, harder than before. 'Sir Thomas,' he bellowed across the table, 'has already confessed that you knew of the conspiracy, and were party to it!'

Elizabeth turned puce. The words came as a slap in the face; she visibly recoiled from their impact. 'No!' she shouted. 'No! It cannot be!'

Gardiner leaned so far towards her that she could smell his putrid breath as he sneered at her. 'I see in your face,' he purred, 'that you are guilty.'

Panic welling in her breast, Elizabeth turned to Sussex. He raised his eyebrows and, in a gesture that made her flesh crawl, winked at her. Then he laughed. Beside him, Arundel had retreated behind a mask of impassivity. Elizabeth was convinced that he was here on sufferance. She also knew that mattered not a jot. He was doing the Queen's bidding. Were she his Queen, he would do the same for her.

But Gardiner and Sussex were cast in an entirely different mould. Aware that Elizabeth was on the verge of breaking down, knowing that the sudden renewed burst of screaming from the chamber next door was assaulting both her ears and her very being, the former continued his attack. 'You despise the Queen! And you despise the Catholic faith.'

'That is not true!' The outrage was genuine. Elizabeth had no quarrel with Catholics – only with the extreme implementation of their faith. 'You know I attend Mass,' she continued. 'I . . . '

'You pretend,' hissed Sussex. 'But in your heart you

are a heretic. In your heart you hate.'

Close to tears now, Elizabeth lowered her head.

'What's that? Speak up!'

As far as Elizabeth was aware, she hadn't said a word. 'I did not,' she intoned in a flat, defeated voice, 'say a word.'

'Yes you did!'

Very well, thought Elizabeth, regaining her fighting spirit. I did. Or at least I shall. 'I ask you,' she said with feeling, 'why we must tear ourselves apart over this small question of religion . . . '

'Small, Madam?' Gardiner was apoplectic with rage. 'You think it *small*?'

Two pink spots appeared on Elizabeth's cheeks. 'Aye,' she shouted. 'Even though it killed my mother! Catholic . . . Protestant . . . is it not enough that we may all believe in God?'

For once, Gardiner was lost for words. It was Arundel, ever gentle but this time with a touch of sadness, who replied in his stead. 'No, Madam – it suffices not. For one is true belief. The other is . . . heresy.'

The word hung in the air like a poison, tainting all in the room with its presence. Yet while the three men regarded it with distaste, Elizabeth reacted with despair. She had not confessed to treason – but she had branded herself as a non-believer.

Suddenly Gardiner began to smile, tilting his head as he did so. 'Hark!' he said. 'Does my Lady hear that sound?'

Elizabeth looked up, frowning. 'I hear nothing, Your Grace. I hear . . . oh!'

Gardiner leaped to his feet. 'Yes, you can hear it now, can't you? What is it?'

'A drum-roll,' said Elizabeth through pursed lips.

'Yes. Ominous, is it not?'

The slow, steady and ever more threatening sound sent a shiver down Elizabeth's spine. 'It is but a drum roll.'

'Ah!' Gardiner seemed delighted. 'There you are wrong, my Lady. It is the sound that accompanies heretics on their last journey to the flames of hell! Come', he finished, reaching out to her. 'Come and witness that journey.'

Even before she was propelled from the room, Elizabeth knew exactly what she was about to witness. The timing of her interrogation had been no accident. Gardiner was far too cunning for that.

And so proved to be the case. Elizabeth was escorted not to her own quarters but to the Bell Tower behind them. Once inside, she was ushered by the guards to the top floor and into a narrow chamber with two arrow-slits for windows. Her interrogators did not come with her. 'Your view befits your station', Gardiner had said with a high, hollow laugh. 'You will see events from on high. We, however, will have . . . what would they say? A ring-side seat.' With that, and with another, almost manic laugh, he left the terrified Elizabeth to her guards.

To Elizabeth's surprise, Kat was already in the Bell Tower. 'Madam!' she said, flying to her mistress's side. 'What is happening? Why did they take me here. Why . . . are you all right?' she asked, suddenly mindful of where Elizabeth had been.

'I am fine. Unfortunately ... unfortunately ... '
Elizabeth fought the bile that had risen in her throat.
'Sir Thomas Wyatt is not, Kat. I think they are to exe-
cute him.'

'Oh my Lady!' wailed Kat. Horrified as she was,
her quick brain filtered the news – and its implications. 'Does that mean he has ... '

'Implicated me?' Elizabeth smiled weakly. 'No. He
promised me that he wouldn't. And he doesn't share
the perfidies of those who would seek to have him
colour the truth with foul lies.'

But it wasn't for the want of trying on Sir John
Gage's part. As the two women watched from on
high, Sir John made his way through the throng surrounding the scaffold that had been erected on the
green. He was at the head of the column of marching
soldiers. Towards the rear was Thomas Wyatt, a pitiful, shuffling figure in a plain shift. Trailing behind
him was a figure of gargantuan proportions, clad
entirely in black – and carrying an axe.

Elizabeth and Kat were too far away to hear anything other than the muted buzz from the crowd
below.

'I had not imagined,' said Kat with a mixture of
awe and revulsion, 'that there would be so many
people. It is ... it's grotesque.'

Elizabeth didn't reply. She too was horrified by the
size of the crowd. People were jostling for space,
eager to secure the best vantage point from which to
witness Sir Thomas's execution. It was macabre, distasteful – and compelling. Part of her wanted to tear
herself away from the narrow window in the tower.

Another part saw her firmly rooted to the spot.

'Oh my God! He is on the scaffold!' Elizabeth watched as Sir Thomas, hands tied behind his back, hunched double and heavily bruised, was unceremoniously hauled on to the scaffold. It was then she noticed the spectators in the front row seats: Norfolk, Sussex, Arundel, Alvaro de la Quadra and, practically drooling with delighted anticipation, the repellent figure of Gardiner. Elizabeth shivered as she looked at them. Then John Gage stepped on to the scaffold and bent down to the half-conscious Wyatt. The crowd, noisy with anticipation, surged forward.

'What is he saying?' cried Kat.

Elizabeth didn't know – but she could guess. 'I believe,' she said in a voice that belied her inner panic, 'that he is being asked to make a last confession.'

But Wyatt was barely capable of movement, let alone speech. Evidently angry now, Gage bent down again and jabbed the wretched man in the ribs. 'Louder!' he screamed. The cry floated up to the tower. Elizabeth and Kat went rigid with fear.

Sir Thomas's reply, when it came, was also audible to them. Making a monumental effort, he tilted his face to the heavens and, contorted with pain, began his last speech. 'I confess before Almighty God,' he cried, 'that I . . . that I am guilty of treason and that . . . that the Lady Elizabeth . . . '

'Oh Kat!' In the Tower, Elizabeth clung to the older woman. Below, Alvaro de la Quadra and Bishop Gardiner exchanged a sly, smug smile.

'That the Lady Elizabeth,' screamed Wyatt, 'had no part in it! She is innocent!'

The mumblings of the crowd ceased: a profound silence enveloped the entire Tower precinct. It was broken by a lone, brave soul – he began to clap. For a moment the sound echoed quite alone. Then a slow groundswell rippled through the rest of the crowd as others joined in. To the impotent fury of John Gage, the noise rose to a deafening roar. And then, over the din, a voice cried out 'God save our Elizabeth!'

Elizabeth's knees almost gave way beneath her. 'Oh Kat!' she mumbled. 'Hold me!' Tears began to flow; of joy, relief, of the release of months of tension. Tears, too, of grief, for there would be no saving Sir Thomas now.

Below, his bulbous face beetroot with fury, Sir John bent down again to the prisoner. 'God damn you!' he screamed 'May you rot in hell!' As he spoke, he delivered a stinging blow to the helpless man.

But Sir Thomas's speech had exhausted the last reserves of his strength. He was now all but comatose. He hardly felt the blow, nor did he register Bishop Gardiner's sudden stream of invective from the front row. 'The prisoner is a traitor – and a liar! He condemns himself from his own mouth!'

The words fell on deaf ears. Beside him, Arundel turned to Norfolk. 'At last,' he sighed, 'the truth. Thanks be to God.'

Norfolk was less enthusiastic. He knew it would fall to him to inform the Queen that all their efforts had been in vain. 'A lie,' he bridled, 'would have served us better!'

On the scaffold, Gage had finally lost all patience. All he wanted now was to see an end to the wretched, futile business – and of the life had that caused him so much anguish and, ultimately, embarrassment. He signalled for the guards to drag Sir Thomas to the block.

To Elizabeth, the denouement of the whole grisly process seemed to happen in slow motion. Transfixed by the horrific tableau below, she was barely aware that she was gripping Robert Dudley's chain so tightly that she had drawn blood. Beside her, Kat let out a low moan as a priest shuffled forwards, cross held aloft, and recited a prayer in Latin.

Then the air was again filled with the ominous roll of the drums as the executioner knelt beside Wyatt to ask his forgiveness.

Evidently Wyatt had enough life to grant it: the executioner stood up and reached for his axe.

But Sir Thomas still had a breath left in his body. Suddenly, to the consternation of all present, he bellowed out to his killer. 'Executioner! Strike home!'

Elizabeth's hands flew to her mouth as she watched the axe swing in a giant arc and, with a sickening thud, made contact with both bone and block. A great jet of blood shot forth from Sir Thomas's neck – straight over the shoes of the stately Duke of Norfolk.

The rest of the crowd recoiled in horror. It wasn't the blood – it was the body from where it had emanated. Sir Thomas's head was only partially severed.

'Again, fool!' screamed Sir John Gage as, in the bloody throes of death, the victim's head twitched. His mouth opened and shut; his eyes, the windows to his departing soul, stared up at Sir John.

Above, Kat Ashley turned from the window and was violently sick. But Elizabeth remained rooted to the spot until the axe fell again; until, with another great fountain of blood, Sir Thomas's head was cleaved from his body and began to roll, drunkenly and grotesquely, across the platform.

A great roar of exultation welled up from the crowd. They had had their sport. The deed had finally been done.

But Elizabeth felt nothing. She was beyond even distress or disgust. She was even beyond fear for herself or for Robert Dudley. The only, incongruous thought that penetrated her numb brain was that, unlike her mother, poor Thomas Wyatt must have had a very big neck.

But that hadn't stopped the executioner. And nothing, she felt, would stop Mary in her hysterical vendetta to see Elizabeth suffer the same fate.

Three Years Later

Decadence. A state of decay. That was what the man in black saw before him. The others present saw something else: luxury, languor, richness and divine delight. Their creed was cupidity, their passion was pleasure – and they were indulging to the full.

The huge candelabras cast a soft, sensuous light on the beautiful people. Most were in a state of undress. Here, on a chaise, a languid, naked youth, taut of muscle and lean of waist. There a voluptuous siren with a cupid's bow mouth and tantalizing curves. Some were half-covered in rich drapes of silk and satin. Others were completely naked. All were drinking stupefying liquid from great goblets. And around them were the remnants of their giant tribute to Bacchus. Half-eaten peaches, bunches of grapes, huge sides of beef and discarded pastries lay on tables, were strewn on brocade cushions or simply lay abandoned on the floor. The feasting was over. Now the games would begin.

The man in black stepped forward from his place in the shadows. To the delight of the fairest, most beautiful man, he walked up to him and, with exquisite tenderness, began to caress his face. The young man smiled back, a silent anticipation of secret pleasures. Yet something in the older man's manner froze the smile on his face. And as he watched the intense, compelling face come closer to his own, he went rigid with fear.

The man in black began to laugh. 'N'ayez pas peur, mon petit!'

'What are you scared of? This?' Suddenly, a playing card appeared in the man's hand. 'Are you scared of this?'

Unable to speak, the young man looked, wide-eyed with fear, at the Jack of Hearts.

'Yes,' whispered the man. 'The poor knave. Young, brave, foolish. Impetuous. unworldly. 'But,' he added as he stroked the youth's golden hair, 'also beautiful, kind and loving.'

Then he laughed again. But there was no mirth in the sound – and no merriment in the dark eyes that feasted on the youth.

The sound of his laughter roused the others. One, a girl as dark as the boy was fair, reached out to the man in black. Her eyes were unfocused, her mouth agape.

The man in black moved to caress her. As soon as his cold, white hand made contact with her dusky skin, another card appeared. It was the Queen of Spades. The girl smiled.

'Alas!' said the man. 'See how easily the knave is trumped by the dark Queen!'

But the dark Queen would get no more attention. The man sank down to the cushions at her feet and reached out for another exquisite creature; this one a Greek Goddess.

She offered him a tentative smile. He offered the Queen of Hearts. Behind him, the black girl gasped in surprise.

'But she is powerless!' teased the man in black. 'She is unprotected. What can she do?'

No one uttered a word.

Then, with a wicked leer, he looked back at the youth. 'Ah! Wait.'

The boy, now accustomed to the game, smiled lasciviously and reclined deeper into the chaise. The man in black reached for his head, as if to tousle his hair.

And then, before he even touched the boy, another card appeared. The man placed it squarely on the Queen of Spades, obliterating her completely.

'Perhaps,' he whispered, 'the Queen of Hearts is not playing with such an empty hand . . .'

PART TWO

Chapter 5

'I am,' said Elizabeth with a deep curtsey, 'your Majesty's most humble sister and servant.' The curtsey was lower than was customary, and deliberately so. Elizabeth needed a moment to compose herself after the shock of Mary's appearance. The years had wrought significant, terrible changes. To Elizabeth's horror, Mary was now almost bent double. Her few remaining hairs were wispy and unkempt, her face cadaverous and pale as death. To the courtiers hovering in the shadows of Mary's eerie world of icons and monkeys, of shrines and burning candles, the contrast between the two women was startling. Elizabeth's long exile had kept her out of harm's way, but it had clearly done her a great deal of good.

Elizabeth felt genuinely sorry for her half-sister. While the last three years had hardly been pleasurable for her, they had at least been tolerable. For Mary, they had obviously been agony. Word had reached Elizabeth of each disaster that had befallen her. Her deteriorating health, her increasing unpopularity, her disintegrating marriage and, deeply damaging for the country as a whole, the alliance with Spain in that country's war against France. That exercise, borne of nothing more than Mary's futile attempt to save her marriage, had all but bankrupted the Treasury. And its personal cost to Mary had been infinitely greater.

Her judgement, previously sound on matters pertaining to finance, was no longer respected. The temptation was to regard her as a joke; the reality was different. For Mary had become increasingly dangerous, ever more intolerant, and her violent, vindictive onslaught against heretics continued apace.

And so did her persecution of Elizabeth. Under pressure from the more lenient faction at court, from the privy councillors who knew that another uprising would take place if Elizabeth remained in the Tower, Mary had been forced to send her, under house arrest, to the royal manor at Woodstock. And there she had remained while Mary ranted and raved against her, berating her councillors for their repeated failure to find evidence against her.

Yet still Elizabeth found it in herself to feel pity for the Queen. For the greatest event in Mary's life had turned out to be the most terrible of all. Her pregnancy had been a phantom one. After fourteen months, not even Mary had been able to sustain the fiction that she was with child. And then had come the cruellest blow of all: there *had* been a new life in her stomach. Mary was nursing a killer called cancer.

The agony was etched in her face as she glared at Elizabeth. But there was no pain in her eyes – only a frenzied madness and a violent hatred.

'Come here!' she snapped after a long, unnerving silence. For just as Elizabeth had noted the changes in her sister, so Mary had seen the poise, the grace and, infuriatingly, the regal calm that Elizabeth seemed to have developed. In her derangement, Mary had hoped to see a pitiful, pleading wreck. Instead, she was faced with a glorious creature in the prime of her life.

Elizabeth moved closer to the older woman. Not only was she repellent to look at, she also exuded an unpleasant, acrid smell. Elizabeth didn't know whether it emanated from Mary's clothes or whether it was the residue from the tinctures she was obliged to swallow, but it was repugnant in the extreme. The mustiness of the room, the aroma of incense and the feral smell of the monkey made it infinitely worse. Mary seemed oblivious to it. So did the female dwarf who lurked protectively by her side.

'Closer!' commanded Mary. 'So I might see your face!' There must, thought Mary, be some sadness there, some sort of despair. There must, she thought with a flash of anger, be some sort of distress. For Mary had seen to it that Elizabeth's exile had been a lonely one. Not only had she banished Kat Ashley and Elizabeth's other ladies from Woodstock, but she had exiled Robert Dudley as well, to the Continent. And for the rest of his life.

Elizabeth was far too astute to show anything but calm. There was no trace of grief or loneliness as she stood, towering over her crippled sister.

But Mary could find fault with any expression. 'When I look at you,' she sneered, 'I see nothing of the King in you – only that whore, your mother.'

'And yet . . . ' replied Elizabeth. 'And yet we are sisters.' There was forgiveness in her eyes; even an invitation to companionship.

But there was only fury in Mary's mad eyes. 'Why will you not confess your crimes against me?'

'Because I have committed none.'

At that Mary smiled; a ghastly, toothless, insane contortion. 'You speak with such sincerity', she all but whispered. 'I see that in your exile you have become a consummate actress.'

'I . . .'

Elizabeth's response was forestalled by a loud moan from Mary. Suddenly hunching even further, she clasped a hand to her stomach and, when the pain subsided, looked back at Elizabeth. The fury was still there, but with it was an intense sadness and a terrible bitterness. 'I have lost my child,' she said in a flat monotone. 'My barren womb bears nothing but a most malignant cancer. My husband is gone. I am abandoned by both God and men . . .' Too distressed to continue, she began to weep.

Instinctively, Elizabeth stepped forward to comfort her. As she did so, the dwarf sprang forward and, with a truly venomous look at Elizabeth, wrapped her arms lovingly round Mary's legs. The sobbing Queen reached out with a gnarled hand and began to stroke her hair.

Elizabeth, too, felt like weeping. The dwarf, a vicious, selfish creature, was another false child. A chimera in the litany of illusions with which Mary surrounded herself.

'Oh God,' she cried, 'is this all of my deserving? For what? . . . I did not burn those people to punish them!' She raised her head, crying out to the Almighty. 'I burned them in order to save them!'

The pain, the terrible genuine suffering of another human being was almost too much for Elizabeth to bear. Again, she reached out to touch Mary. The dwarf hissed and struck out at her with a stubby hand.

Elizabeth stepped back. 'Poor Mary', she whispered. 'Poor, poor Mary.' As she spoke, she thought not of the pitiful creature in front of her, but of the younger, cultivated creature who had been her friend. She saw the Mary she remembered from her childhood; quiet, reserved and sensible. A woman who had ascended the throne amidst great joy and celebration. She saw the woman who had tried to grasp at happiness with Philip of Spain, and who had been so cruelly let down. For Philip had left for Spain the previous year – never to return. Elizabeth saw, and her heart went out towards a woman who had not yet been consumed by fanaticism, jealousy and madness.

Mary looked up and saw the expression on Elizabeth's face. 'Do not pity me!' she shrieked. 'They say this cancer will make you Queen – but they are wrong! Look over there!' Mary gestured wildly to the nearby desk.

Elizabeth did as she was bid. The desk was bare, save for a crisp roll of parchment.

'That,' crowed Mary, 'is your death warrant. All I need do is sign it!'

Panic welled in Elizabeth's breast. Gripped by the cold fear of death, she looked again in horror at the paper. So this, she thought, is why I have been summoned. Mary has finally abandoned the pursuit of proof. She has capitulated to her Catholic councillors. Unbidden, an image suddenly floated before her eyes. It was of herself, standing by her bedroom window at Woodstock, scratching at the glass with a diamond.

'Much suspected, by me
Nothing proved can be,
Quoth Elizabeth, Prisoner'

Elizabeth's words had been the truth. Mary had no proof. Plainly, in her madness, anger and pain, she had at last decided that she didn't need any.

Elizabeth turned back to the raddled, wizened old crone who, tears now forgotten, was leering triumphantly at her. 'You would murder your own sister?' she whispered.

'Sister? I am not your sister!' But before Mary could continue with another string of invective against the whore who had begotten Elizabeth, she was seized by another searing pain. Again she bent double. Again the dwarf sought to console her.

But Mary ignored her small companion. When the pain had passed she brushed her aside and, with sudden purpose in her stride, she walked up to Elizabeth. 'You will promise me something', she said.

Surprised by the calm resolution in Mary's voice, Elizabeth merely stared.

'You will promise me that when I am gone, you will do everything in your power to uphold the Catholic faith. Do not,' she continued with a reverential look at the shrine in the corner of the room. 'take away from the people the consolations of the Blessed Virgin, their Holy Mother.'

Already surprised by Mary's complete change in attitude, Elizabeth was thrown into total consternation by her words.

'When I am Queen,' she said at length, 'may I not do as I like?' The calm reply had an alarming effect on

Mary. First she cast a sly, disbelieving look at Elizabeth. Then she shook her head in a curious sideways motion. Finally, she began to tremble all over. For the first time in her life, Mary had an indication that Elizabeth was a person in her own right, that she posed a threat not just by means of existence but also by her personality.

'Do not,' she spat, 'think to be Queen at all.' Her voice rising to a high-pitched scream, she brandished a shaking finger at the younger woman, 'For I am not going to die!'

Then, suddenly exhausted, she seemed to shrink in front of Elizabeth's eyes. 'You may now return to your house at Hatfield,' she sighed. 'But you will remain under arrest. Until,' she finished with calm certainty, 'I am recovered.'

'Your Majesty.' With another deep curtsey, Elizabeth stepped back and prepared to take her leave. She too was exhausted by the encounter. In the past few minutes she had been forced to contemplate her death, then her accession to the throne – and now her continued exile.

But for the first time since the dark day when she had been brought to the Tower, she felt a flicker of hope burn within her. For the first time in years she dared contemplate the notion that she may not, after all, lose her head. Instead, she may gain a kingdom.

But there were too many people with too much to lose to stand quietly by and watch Elizabeth ascend to the throne. There were powerful Catholics; there were those who had benefited from Mary's largesse; there were those who had encouraged the hounding to death of Protestants. And there were those who had spent so long seeking Elizabeth's death that they could not hope for any sort of a life under her rule.

Yet news of Mary's illness had spread abroad – and with it the assumption that Elizabeth would soon be Queen. Whitehall was awash with rumour about Protestants returning from France bringing their hated heresies and swearing vengeance against all Catholics.

Norfolk, however, dismissed those rumours. He could not conceive of a Protestant faction strong enough to unite and destroy the Catholic stranglehold on court. Further, he could not envisage losing his own power. That was one thing he would neither tolerate nor even contemplate.

Thus it was, on the same day as Elizabeth's audience with the dying Queen, he scoffed at the courtiers in the ante-room to Mary's chambers. 'What? You say they will return and massacre every Catholic in the land?' His tone implied this was plainly ridiculous.

'But it is true!' replied Lord Framingham. A credulous individual at the best of times, he had plainly swallowed the rumour whole.

'Pah! Then it would be butchery indeed,' said Norfolk with a dismissive smile. 'If such a plan were conceivable.'

'But it *is* true,' protested Framingham's companion. 'For we know who is behind it.'

'Oh?' Norfolk turned his attention to the Earl of Coglington. Framingham he took for a fool, but

Coglington was rumoured to possess something of a brain. And he was a brave man to boot; the last person to run away at the merest mention of a Protestant. 'And what is the name,' enquired Norfolk, 'of this . . . this madman?'

Coglington looked to his companion then, fearfully, back to Norfolk. 'Walsingham', he whispered.

His words had a most extraordinary effect. Norfolk bounded forward, grabbed the hapless lord by the lapel of his tunic and practically pulled him off his feet. '*Walsingham?* Walsingham, you say?'

'Yes, your Grace.'

'Walsingham,' said the Duke, suddenly letting go, 'is nothing. And,' he added as he pointed a furious, shaking finger in the direction of Mary's chambers, 'that child in there is just a little girl! And yet . . . and yet you still piss yourselves with fear! It's pathetic!' Then he turned on his heel and strode to the far end of the room.

The two men exchanged a glance. For all Norfolk's angry bluster, he had given himself away by the alacrity with which he had responded to the news. He may well have thought the two lords pathetic, but he certainly didn't regard Walsingham in the same light. He regarded Walsingham as the devil incarnate, a dark figure of mystery, danger and subterfuge. A player of lethal games. A dealer of deadly cards.

When he was well out of earshot of the two lords, Norfolk paused beside a man who, while affecting nonchalance, had been watching the proceedings with beady, attentive eyes.

'Is it true,' asked Norfolk in a low murmur, 'that

Walsingham is set to return from France?'

The other man nodded. 'I have heard it.'

'Then make sure that he does not!'

'Perhaps your Grace should consider another expediency?'

Norfolk whirled round, his face contorted with anger over the presence of an eavesdropper.

But it was only the Earl of Sussex.

'Oh. It's you.'

Sussex smiled and drew closer as the other man sloped off. Happy to eavesdrop himself, he made sure there was no one near enough to overhear his own words of wisdom. Particularly this little nugget. 'Go yourself to France', he urged in a whisper. 'Make alliance with Mary of Scots.' With excited, dancing eyes, he nodded towards Mary's chamber. 'By the means of an alliance, you can remove the bastard Elizabeth!'

Whatever reaction Sussex had anticipated, it certainly wasn't cold fury. To his utter astonishment, Norfolk beat him against the chest with both hands, shoving him backwards against the wall. 'Do you not know,' he growled, 'that the price of treason is death, and that the price of suggesting it, my lord, is also death?'

Sussex could only gawp in stunned disbelief. Were it not for the violence of Norfolk's reaction and the indignity of his own position, he would have laughed in the Duke's face. For Norfolk to take such a high-handed attitude was preposterous in the extreme. Yet the tightening of the other man's grip at his neck, the fury in his dark eyes told Sussex that Norfolk meant every word he said. What he didn't know was why.

As suddenly as Norfolk had launched his attack, he released the hapless Earl. Trying – and failing – to pretend that nothing untoward had happened, Sussex brushed at his lapels, cast a strange, puzzled look at the other man and, head held high, stalked off.

He didn't get very far. For directly in front of him stood the reason why Norfolk had released him, he belatedly realized.

A hush had descended throughout the room. Elizabeth was standing, pale and erect, tentative and apprehensive, at the door to the Queen's room. A terrible, palpable awkwardness enveloped the entire room. Several courtiers fell to their knees: most did not. Elizabeth herself looked as if she had just stepped into a lion's den. For the room, empty when she had been summoned to the Queen, was now full: full of people waiting for her to speak.

'I . . . I have . . . I have just,' she stammered, 'visited with the Queen, my . . . my sister.' She paused, surveying the faces before her. Some were anxious, others sceptical – several were openly hostile. It was the hostility that lent her the confidence to conquer her nervousness. She, Elizabeth, would be heard. 'We must all,' she continued in an altogether more confident tone, 'pray for her most complete recovery. And there is none amongst you, my lords,' she finished with a smile, 'who wish it more fervently than I!'

A few murmurs of assent greeted her speech. And then Elizabeth's confidence wavered once more. She had no escort, no ladies. Her only retinue was the team of guards waiting outside to escort her to her quarters. It was unseemly for a Princess to walk alone through the throng of men.

But this Princess didn't have any choice. With her head held high, staring straight ahead, she began to make her stately way to the door opposite her. Every pair of eyes in the room followed her progress.

Only when she reached the guard-chamber did she drop her composure. Letting her shoulders slump, she breathed a deep sigh of relief.

'Madam,' whispered a voice behind her. Then, as she made to turn round, a courtier brushed past her. 'Say nothing,' he implored in the same whisper. 'Do not look at me, but yourself walk one pace ahead of me.'

Puzzled but intrigued, Elizabeth did as she was bid. 'Sir William Cecil,' said the courtier, 'your father's old Councillor, is returned from abroad and must speak to you.' In one deft movement, he held out a hand, touching Elizabeth's own. 'Here is his seal, so you may believe me.'

Still uncertain, but realizing she didn't have any choice, Elizabeth allowed the man to slip a ring on to her finger. Then she pulled her hand from behind her and looked at the seal. It was, as promised, that of Sir William Cecil.

'But how,' whispered Elizabeth, 'am I to see him? I am still under arrest. They will not let me . . . '

'Hush, Madam. You are to remain here until your household at Hatfield is made ready. There will be an opportunity.' Then, as stealthily as he had ambushed her, he continued on his way.

So, after a moment, did Elizabeth. But her own

path, she realized, was now at its most precarious. And there was a crossroads straight ahead. One turning led to the throne: the other back to the Tower.

Norfolk was still in a rage. He had always taken Sussex for a fool: a loyal lackey, maybe, but still a fool. Now he realized that the man couldn't be quite that stupid. He had seen the opportunity in France. Worse, he had articulated his opinions about how Norfolk should use that opportunity. Had he never heard of caution? Didn't he know that walls had ears; that allegiances shifted; that everyone's position was precarious? Obviously not, thought Norfolk. Or else he wouldn't have been so stupid as to speak in public; to speak of a plan that Norfolk had already formulated – but as a last resort.

He *had* to see the Queen. It was imperative. Yet his way was barred by, of all people, her physicians. Her ladies, too, were adamant that she should receive no further visitors for the moment. The strain of the Princess's visit, they colluded, had taken its toll on Her Majesty.

But there was always a way – and that way was through Lettice. Not for nothing had Norfolk chosen a mistress who had the Queen's ear. And one who, by great good fortune, was extremely comely. Regretting – momentarily – that he had not shared Lettice's bed for some time, Norfolk determined to find her.

She was, by another stroke of fortune, in her own quarters.

'Your Grace! To what do I owe the honour?' Lettice's pleasure, he was glad to note, was even greater than her surprise. He was also delighted to see that she was in the middle of changing her attire; even more pleased when, a moment after his arrival, she dismissed her maid.

'Lettice,' he murmured, 'I feel I owe you an apology.'

'An apology, your Grace?' Lettice cast him a teasing, coquettish smile. 'Why would that be?'

Norfolk smiled and took her hands in his. Her near-nakedness, the thin white shift she was wearing, precluded pretence of desire on his part. And Lettice, as she pressed herself against him, was well aware of that fact.

'My Lord Norfolk', she purred. 'Perhaps . . . perhaps now is not the time. I am required to attend her Majesty.'

Precisely the words Norfolk wanted to hear.

'Oh.' The great duke affected disappointment. 'Then when? Tonight?'

Lettice didn't reply. He would take her when he wanted. The question, like his ham-fisted flirtation, was merely a ruse. Norfolk wanted something.

'Your Grace? Is something wrong?'

'You say you are about to see Her Majesty?'

'Indeed.'

'Then perhaps you would be so good as to tell her there is a plot against her.'

'A plot?'

'Yes. There are certain . . . certain people at court who would seek to form an alliance with the Queen of Scots, thereby usurping the Queen of England's throne.'

Lettice frowned. 'But the Queen of Scots is but a young girl. She is in no position to make any alliance.'

'No. But her mother is.'

'Mary of Guise?' Lettice knew the woman by formidable reputation only. Ruling Scotland as Regent until her daughter came of age, she was said to be exceptionally intelligent, often cruel and, where her family was concerned, overweeningly ambitious. And it was common knowledge that one of Mary's ambitions was to secure the throne of England for her daughter, also called Mary. It wasn't an impossible ambition. Betrothed since the age of five to the future king of France, her daughter would one day be Queen of both of England's greatest enemies. She could take England by force. Alternatively, she could claim to rule it already: like Elizabeth, she was a granddaughter of Henry VII. And her French father-in-law had lately, on her behalf, laid claim to the thrones of England and Ireland.

Lettice, like most people at court, knew of all the combined threats posed in the name of a girl who was not yet fifteen. And of how much greater those threats would be if Mary formed an alliance with someone in England. Affecting ignorance, Lettice looked at the duke through narrowed eyes. 'Are you saying, your Grace, that the Princess Elizabeth would make an alliance with the Queen of Scots? It is impossible.'

'Of course it's impossible!' Norfolk waved a dismissive hand.

'Then who is the conspirator?'

'That', said Norfolk, 'is something I think, upon reflection, I should tell Her Majesty myself.'

Lettice suppressed a smile. She was no fool. She was perfectly willing to admit that she *had* been foolish in the past, but now it was a wise head that sat upon her shoulders. Wise – and slightly desperate. She needed to rid herself of the Duke of Norfolk, of his terrible temper, of his cruelties and the beatings she was continuously subjected to. Now she thought she could see a way; an as yet faintly lit road that would lead her to freedom. It would take a long time to reach the end of the road, but it would be worth it. For Lettice was absolutely certain she knew the identity of the conspirator against the Queen.

Lettice *did* engineer a meeting between Norfolk and the ailing Queen – but the duke's entreaties were in vain. Showing no respect to the half-conscious woman on the bed, he brandished Elizabeth's death warrant in her face. 'Sign it!' he hissed.

Mary didn't respond.

'Sign it!'

Still Mary didn't speak. Yet as she turned to look at the duke, her expression told him that she had heard. And understood. But she made no attempt to sign.

'Would you leave your kingdom to a heretic?' Norfolk's face, livid with anger, loomed close to that of the Queen. Mary looked straight into his eyes and, slowly and painfully, she crossed herself.

'God's death!' shouted Norfolk. 'Will you not sign, woman?'

Mary's only response was to close her eyes.

Chapter 6

Elizabeth's opportunity to see Sir William Cecil came sooner than she had dared anticipate, and from a most unlikely quarter. The day after her audience with Mary, she was escorted to the Catholic church within the Palace. She didn't go of her on volition – she saw little point in any last-ditch attempt to play the devout Catholic. She went because the courtier who had passed her Sir William's seal suggested she may 'seek solace' in church. For one wild moment, Elizabeth let herself hope that solace would come from the one man she wanted to see above all others; that he, like Sir William, had returned from exile in France. But even as she walked into the church, she knew she was entertaining an impossible dream. Cecil had been a voluntary exile: Robert was not. He was banned from ever returning to his homeland.

Elizabeth hardly imagined that Sir William himself would be masquerading as a priest. Her surprise, when he pulled back the curtain in the confessional, was complete. And delighted.

'Sir William!' It had been years since she had seen him. His dark hair was peppered with grey, he had grown a beard and seemed to have shrunk in stature. But the intense, sparkling eyes were unmistakable.

But Cecil had no time to indulge in pleasantries. He stalled any further loud outbursts from Elizabeth with a warning finger at his lips. Then he leaned closer.

'My Lady, listen to me carefully. All things move in our favour. Many of our friends are even now returning from exile: Throckmorton . . . '

'Throckmorton?' Elizabeth's face lit up. 'I feared that he was . . . '

'No – exiled. Bacon has also returned. And Howard. And Walsingham . . . '

'Walsingham?' Doubt creased Elizabeth's features. 'I am not acquainted with Walsingham. But I have heard the name. They say he is dangerous.'

'Not to you', said Cecil with a smile. 'But these are still most uncertain days. Your life is in grave danger, and we must do all we can to guarantee the security of your throne.'

Your throne. It was the first time Elizabeth had heard those words. They sounded strange. Alien. Even, at the moment, distasteful. And they were not the words she wanted to hear from Cecil.

She leaned closer. 'Sir William. Can you tell me . . . ?'

'I beg you not to interrupt. We have so little . . . '

'*Please*. Can you tell me what has become of Lord Robert?'

Cecil exhaled deeply. He was well aware, and highly disapproving of Elizabeth's infatuation with Dudley. And as far as he was concerned, it was a relationship that would have to be curtailed as soon as possible. He simply couldn't have the Queen gadding about with one of her subjects. It hadn't even crossed Sir William Cecil's mind that he didn't, and may never, have any authority in the future court of Queen Elizabeth. His assumption that she would appoint him to her Privy Council was automatic, as was his current self-appointed role as her guardian and mentor.

He looked at the pleading, expectant face on the other side of the grille. The girl plainly had a lot to learn. 'I asked you to listen, child! You are most innocent in the ways of this world.' He glanced furtively behind him. 'There is someone else here, someone who wishes to speak with you on a matter of great importance.'

But there was nothing more important to Elizabeth than the fate of Robert Dudley. 'Please', she implored. 'I *must* know.'

Cecil waved a dismissive hand. 'They gave up trying to find proof. They revoked his exile . . . '

'Thank God!'

'So *now* will you speak with him?'

But Elizabeth was miles away. 'Who?' she asked without interest.

'The man who needs to speak to you . . . Monseigneur Alvaro de la Quadra, the Ambassador to Spain.'

'*What?*' Elizabeth's whole demeanour changed in an instant. She sat bolt upright; the colour drained from her face and, deep within her, the familiar and terrible knot of fear began to tighten. *De la Quadra?* Cecil must have taken leave of his senses.

'I will not,' she bridled, 'see that man! I regard it as an insult to my person that you can even suggest . . . '

'My lady,' said a voice that chilled her to the bone. 'How it pleases me to see you looking so well.'

Elizabeth gasped. She had been looking within

herself as she had spoken, back to the indelible image of de la Quadra on the day of Thomas Wyatt's execution. She had hoped never to see the man again in her life. Now, in Cecil's place, he was sitting opposite her.

Words failed her. She could believe neither her eyes nor her ears as she stared in disbelief at the politely enquiring eyes, the unctuous smile. Here was the man who had tried to hound her to death. Now, behaving for all the world like an old friend, he was complimenting her on her appearance.

Two high spots of colour appeared on her cheeks as the fear evaporated. In its place was a cold fury. 'Monseigneur,' she began, 'I . . . '

'I bring a message for you,' interrupted de la Quadra with another, this time conspiratorial, smile. 'The King of Spain is enraptured by you and offers you his hand in marriage.'

The words assailed Elizabeth with the strength of a physical blow. Shocked to the core, she recoiled in horror. Then, suddenly disorientated, she felt herself suspended above her physical being. She felt Elizabeth the woman disappear, to be replaced by Elizabeth the future Queen of England. It was as if she were no longer real. She was merely a symbol.

She stared through the grille. De la Quadra, it was clear, was addressing the symbol. As Elizabeth's position was changing, so were his allegiances. It was, she realized with a jolt, the way of the world. But the King of Spain? The request was not just unseemly, it was distasteful in the extreme.

At last she found her voice. No longer furious, no

longer disbelieving, she was instead diplomatic. 'I . . . I am most grateful to His Majesty for . . . for the expression of his affection, but . . . but my sister is not yet dead.' She heard her voice rise and become infused with revulsion as she addressed the Spaniard. 'Her bed is still warm.'

Without a trace of embarrassment, seemingly totally unaware of the gross impropriety of his mission, de la Quadra leaned closer. 'His Majesty, however, finds it already cold.'

Elizabeth shuddered. 'Tell His Majesty that . . . that I am unable to consider his offer at the moment. Tell him . . . tell him that I am flattered by his interest in . . . in my person and that I shall reply when circumstances . . . when it becomes appropriate.'

To her relief, the words seemed to satisfy the Spanish Ambassador. Without another word, he nodded and, as swiftly as he appeared, left the confessional.

Elizabeth sank back against the hard wooden wall of the cubicle. Her first lesson in diplomacy had exhausted her. It had also assaulted, repelled and revolted her. Was this, she wondered, what it would always be like?

'Well . . . shall you accept?'

Elizabeth sighed. Cecil's reappearance was answer enough to the question she had posed herself.

'Sir William . . . how can I possibly accept King Philip's proposal? My sister . . .'

Cecil waved away the objection. 'You sister is dying, madam. Are you aware that the country is all but bankrupt; that for the past three years the harvests have been poor, that the war against France has . . .'

'I . . .'

'. . . has all but exhausted the Treasury and that England is regarded on the Continent as small, insignificant and unstable?'

'I fail to see,' replied Elizabeth with an edge to her voce, 'what that has to do with an impertinent proposal from the King of Spain.'

'Madam!' Cecil was outraged. 'You may call it impertinence, but others would regard it as felicitous.' Again he sighed, ruing the inexperience and naivety of the girl before him. 'King Philip,' he continued, 'is not only the ruler of Spain and the Netherlands, but he possesses in addition a vast empire in the Americas. Furthermore, two-thirds of England's overseas commerce is transacted through Antwerp, part of Philip's domains. Nay, Madam,' he finished. 'Impertinence this is not.'

Elizabeth may have been inexperienced, but she was far from stupid. 'But is it wisdom?' she countered. 'Queen Mary lost the affection of the people of this realm because she married a foreigner.'

Cecil's expression, hitherto dismissive, was now appraising.

'And,' continued Elizabeth, 'King Philip is a Catholic.'

'That should be no bar to the continuance of your own religion.'

'Indeed?' Elizabeth raised her eyebrows. 'Then that objection is waived.' Then she played her trump card. 'The Pope, however, would not treat the matter so lightly. If my reading of the Bible is correct, the Book of Leviticus declares that such a marriage would be within the prohibited degrees. King Philip would not be able to marry the sister of his first wife.'

Cecil's appraisal turned to admiration. He didn't doubt that Elizabeth's reading of the Bible was correct. She was, he knew, extensively educated. And she was showing herself to be remarkably astute, and adept at diplomatic wrangling. He leaned forward and, with an avuncular smile, congratulated Elizabeth on her knowledge. 'But,' he added, 'the Pope would be sure to issue a dispensation to countenance such a union.'

'And if *I* still refuse to countenance that union?'

'There are other suitors.'

Their eyes met across the grille. Both knew what the other was thinking.

'But,' continued Cecil, damning Robert Dudley by omission, 'this country offers no suitable contenders for your hand in marriage.'

'Oh?'

'No. When you are Queen, you must seek a husband from abroad,'

'You seem so sure I shall be Queen.'

'I am positive. There are no further obstacles to your accession.'

'What about the Catholic faction at court?' Visions of Sussex and Norfolk floated before Elizabeth's eyes. She would forever associate them with plotting her demise.

'Pah! Sussex is small fry, and he swings like a pendulum. But more to the point, his loyalties lie with those in power – and he automatically likes anyone in whom it is invested.' Then Cecil smiled. 'Sussex is anyway the Hereditary Chief Steward of the monarch's household. You may rest assured that is a position he would not wish to jeopardize.'

'And Norfolk?'

Cecil grimaced. 'Norfolk can be . . . controlled.'

For some reason Elizabeth believed him. For the first time since she had entered the church that morning, her spirits began to lift. And, for the first time in her life, she allowed herself to contemplate – and relish – the prospect of becoming Queen of England. She felt confident of marrying the power within her with the power invested in her.

But as for that other kind of marrying . . .

'You seem equally sure,' she said with a cryptic smile, 'that when I am Queen I shall marry.'

Cecil's eyes nearly popped out of his head. 'I . . . I see no other . . . there *is* no other possibility.'

'Oh?' Elizabeth was amused – and not a little bemused – by Cecil's vehemence. 'If I *do* marry, I have it in mind to marry whoever I fancy to marry.'

'Fancy, Madam, has nothing to do with it,' thundered an almost apoplectic Cecil.

'Indeed? Then perhaps I shall not marry.'

'That, my Lady, is impossible.'

'Why?'

'No civilized country in the world,' said Cecil with no attempt to veil the threat in his voice, 'would even contemplate the idea of a Virgin Queen.'

Chapter 7

Two days later Elizabeth was taken to Hatfield. In theory still under arrest, she was, in practice, a free agent. No one had the spirit to perpetrate her farcical captivity. Elizabeth was Queen-in-waiting; she could do as she wished. Even the guards who watched over her were desultory in their duty. They followed her wherever she went – but always at a distance and never with a will to prevent her indulging in her every whim.

Sir William Cecil would have been livid had he known with which 'whim' she most amused herself. Robert Dudley had indeed returned from exile – and it took him but a day to discover that Elizabeth was at Hatfield, playing the peculiar waiting game of which the result was already a foregone conclusion.

Their reunion had been joyous. Elizabeth's greatest fear – that Robert had given up on her and fallen in love with another – proved to be unfounded. And he, worried that her ardour would have been dampened by her years of captivity and loneliness, was delighted that her feelings towards him had, if anything, grown stronger.

Yet such was the climate and the demands of decorum that the expression of their love had to remain muted. Physical proximity could only be countenanced whilst in the presence of others, and even then there was no real privacy. The steward of Elizabeth's household placed Robert in apartments in a different wing of the house; her ladies were with her at all times and even Kat Ashley, reunited at last with her mistress, wouldn't have dreamed of allowing her to sidestep protocol and meet Robert in private. There was far too much at stake.

Privations notwithstanding, Elizabeth and Robert still managed to spend most days in each other's company, and often at sufficient distance from their attendants for their words, glances and gestures to remain unheard and unobserved.

It was in the garden that they were able to achieve the greatest privacy. And it was there, as they walked in the shadow of the great oaks, that Robert realized a change had come over Elizabeth. She seemed to have grown, not in stature but in confidence. She held herself more erect, there was a new purpose in her stride and a different light in her eyes. Even her clothes had changed. Where before she had favoured simple dresses, she was now more often clad in richer, brighter and more luxurious attire. Velvets and silks, embroideries and lace – and most often in shades of yellow, green or gold. Her jewels, too, were more numerous and more elaborate. She was, thought Robert with a pang of regret, preparing for her role. And even if, as now, she regarded some aspects of that role with amusement, it seemed that it couldn't be long before she embraced it in its entirety – leaving him behind.

'They said,' she recounted with a mischievous glint in her eye, 'that the King would not expect to share my bed more than two or three times a year. His affairs would otherwise keep him in Spain!' The words had been Cecil's – a renewed attempt to persuade her to see the Spanish King in a different light.

'Then the King is a fool!' exclaimed Robert. 'What affairs could ever be important enough to keep him from *your* bed?' Robert delivered the words with a flourish and a dazzling smile – and with a seeming unawareness of the impropriety of his words.

Elizabeth blushed and lowered her eyes, yet couldn't help smiling as she did so. 'My Lord,' she demurred without much conviction, 'you should not say such things!'

'Then I shall only *think* them.'

Elizabeth looked up again, feigning outrage. 'Oh, but that is worse!' But as her eyes met his, the smile faded from her lips. There was a sudden sadness in his dark eyes, the playfulness of a moment ago had disappeared. In its place was a profound pensiveness.

'What . . . what is wrong?' she whispered.

Robert sighed and shrugged his broad shoulders. 'If you must know . . . it is the question on everyone's lips.'

'What question.'

Robert sighed again and looked away. 'Who you will marry', he said in a deadpan voice.

An uneasy silence prevailed. Robert still didn't look at Elizabeth. If he had, he would have noticed that she had flushed again, that his question had vexed her and almost roused her to anger.

'Why should I marry?'

Robert couldn't help grinning. She sounded as she

had when they had first met: a petulant little girl who was used to getting her own way. He half-expected her to stamp her foot as she spoke.

When at last he did look round at her, there was nothing of the little girl in her. There was a proud, haughty and rather agitated young woman. 'Because,' he said in a low whisper, 'of who you are.'

'But I am no different than I ever was!'

'Maybe not – but you *will* be. When you are Queen, all things will change.'

Now it was Elizabeth who was suddenly transported back to the royal nursery where they had played as children. Here was Robert, the sulky little boy, the gangly youngster with the pensive eyes and perpetual air of puzzlement. The little boy who recited the plaintive chorus of 'life is unfair!' when he didn't get his own way. Then she blinked and the little boy vanished. In his place was this splendid specimen of manhood for whose love she would lay down her life. And her throne.

'Do not say so, Robert,' she whispered, 'or I will have to think it.'

Robert kicked at the ground with the toe of his boot. 'I will be nothing to you when you are Queen.'

'Robert!' Elizabeth was profoundly shocked. Did he not know how she felt about him? And did he think her so venal that she would shrug him off as soon as she ascended the throne? 'That would be impossible!' she cried. 'Since you are everything to me, how could you ever be nothing? Does not love fill up every space, every vacancy? God knows!' she almost shouted. 'Let *everything* else change – but my love will not!'

She, as well as Robert, was shocked by the extraordinary outburst. Never before had she bared her soul in such an unequivocal manner, never had she declared her deep and abiding love for him. Never had she so blatantly transgressed the boundaries of the etiquette.

Robert was almost moved to tears by her words. He tried to find words to match them, but was thwarted by the lump in his throat. Instead, he reached out to touch her.

'Ahem!' One of the guards stepped forward. He made no further objection – he even tried to pretend he had been seized by a fit of coughing. But the message was clear.

A moment ago, overwhelmed by her outburst, Elizabeth too had been on the verge of tears. Now, suddenly, she burst out laughing. Relief; joy; the unburdening of emotions she had kept in check for years; even laughter over the ludicrous constraints of their position – all conspired to produce great gales of laughter that lit up her eyes, her face – and her life.

'So,' said Robert, also beginning to laugh, 'it is true?'

'What is true?' A fleeting panic assailed Elizabeth. She looked in sudden trepidation at her lover.

'It's true that you can still laugh!'

Several paces behind them, Kat Ashley and Isabel Knollys looked up in surprise as the sound of the unbridled laughter regaled their ears. A fond smile spread across Kat's features. 'Is it not wonderful?' she sighed. 'Two people so in love.'

Isabel wasn't so sure 'Wonderful, yes – but it is also dangerous.'

'Dangerous?'

'Do you really think,' she asked the other lady-in-waiting, 'that they will let her marry him?'

'But they are so in love!'

'Since when did love have anything to do with it?'

Even Kat had to admit that Isabel had a point. Dynastic considerations, the shifting balance of power, the strengthening of alliances – those were the driving forces behind the nuptial unions of the great and the good. Love had absolutely nothing to do with it.

'Well,' said Kat, 'if she doesn't take a foreign prince for a husband, Robert Dudley is as fine and noble a man as any other in England.'

'In looks, maybe,' said Isabel. Like most of Elizabeth's ladies, she considered Dudley the handsomest man in England. Tall and exceptionally good-looking, he had a habitually brooding expression and unusually dark skin – attributes that had earned him the nickname of 'the gypsy'. He had seemingly inexhaustible energy, extraordinarily long and well-shaped legs and was reckoned to be the finest horseman in England. He was also a fine huntsman, a gifted mimic, a superb dancer, a learned scholar: in short, he shared all Elizabeth's passions. And like Elizabeth, he had a propensity to flirt.

'But,' said Isabel, 'he is a Dudley.'

Kat sighed. There was no escaping the fact that Robert's antecedents stood as impediments in his suit for Elizabeth. There were too many people still active at court who remembered both his father and his grandfather. Both had professed undying allegiance to the monarch; both had been hoist on the petard of their own self-aggrandizement.

Yet Kat felt obliged to come to Robert's defence. 'There is no reason to suppose,' she protested, 'that Lord Robert possesses the same arrogance as his forebears. Indeed it is said that he is kind, modest and gentle. I myself can vouchsafe for those qualities.'

Isabel cast a sidelong glance at Kat. She was, as usual, exaggerating. 'And there are those – some of the most powerful in the land – who would vouch for Lord Robert's haughtiness, his temper, his wilfulness and his duplicity.'

'No!' Kat had heard enough. Isabel, poor thing, was often bitter when it came to the subject of marriage. But there was no reason why she should listen to more gratuitous insults. Casting a particularly withering and, she hoped, pitying glance at her friend, she hitched up her skirts and walked on.

Behind her, Isabel remained still. Her expression, too, was still – and sad. Perhaps it was just as well she hadn't continued. Kat didn't need to hear any more. And she certainly didn't want to hear of the one, extremely good reason why Elizabeth would not be allowed to marry Robert . . .

Two weeks later Elizabeth was again under the oaks in the garden at Hatfield. Robert had departed to his Norfolk estate the previous week, leaving her with heartfelt promises of a speedy return and, more tangibly, with a small jewel that had belonged to his mother. Its intrinsic value was minimal, but as far as

Elizabeth was concerned it was the most valuable object she possessed. Apart, of course, from Robert's silver chain and medallion now safely secured in the box containing her private papers.

As were the letters she had received from Sir William Cecil. Every day he penned her an epistle, detailing the state of play at court and, more importantly, the state of the Queen's health. Both were precarious in the extreme. Mary's court had never been the most gay or vibrant of places; in recent years it had become positively sombre. Even such luminaries as the Countess of Lennox, swimming against the ever-stronger tide of repression, had lost their sparkle and all but retired from Whitehall. Yet now, with Mary hovering on the brink of death, the court was already funereal in atmosphere. Elizabeth's accession was now commonly regarded as inevitable. The majority of courtiers, echoing the sentiments of the country at large, were ready to welcome her with open arms – by default if for no other reason. No one could be exactly sure what Elizabeth's reign would herald. The only certainty was that it would end the religious terror of the past few years.

Elizabeth already knew that Sir William Cecil was erudite, astute and seasoned in the ways of the world. His letters convinced her that he would also be indispensable to her. Like her, he was a confirmed believer in the established social order and the means by which it was maintained. Like her, he was a committed Protestant at heart, with none of the hatred of Catholics that so many converts had developed. Yet of all his qualities, Elizabeth was learning to prize one above the others. And that quality shone out from every sentence he wrote: Cecil was completely trustworthy.

That morning she had written to him, promising to appoint him as her Principal Secretary of State. Far from being borne out of any girlish naivety or a rash need to give thanks where it was due, the gesture was the product of some long and hard thinking. Elizabeth was short of people she could trust at court. She had no doubt that most – even the Duke of Norfolk – would swear their allegiance and loyalty, but trustworthiness was an entirely different matter.

'This,' she had written in her elegant hand, 'is the judgement I have of you: that you will not be corrupted with any manner of gifts, that you will be faithful to the State; and that, without respect of my private will, you will give me that counsel which you think best.'

The last clause had been the one that had caused her most trouble to write, and the one upon which, sitting under the shade of a giant oak, she was now reflecting.

For she knew herself only too well. She knew she could be hot-headed. Her poor brother Edward had called her 'sweet sister temperance'- a name that still brought a rueful smile to her lips. For Elizabeth was well aware that she was highly strung, prone to bouts of near-hysteria and had a temper that could send grown men running for cover. Worse, she knew that despite her extraordinarily broad education, her intuitive grasp of politics and her perceptiveness she could also be extremely indecisive. And she knew, therefore, that where the greater good of the country was concerned it was of the utmost importance to grant someone like Sir William leave to advise her against her will. Or against, she thought wryly, what men like Cecil would call her 'capricious nature.'

Yet that didn't stop Elizabeth from wondering, after the letter had been dispatched, if she had gone too far. She wondered if she shouldn't, perhaps, have been a little less effusive. Then she thought that maybe she had been a little too stilted. Then, catching herself in mid-indecision, she began to laugh.

A few yards away, two of the guards cast disapproving, slightly disappointed glances in her direction. Over the past few weeks, and greatly to their surprise, they had grown to respect Princess Elizabeth. She was always polite to them, treated them with a courtesy rare to those in her position, let alone prisoners in her position. She had even laughed with them on several occasions.

But now she was laughing on her own – a clear indication that she was no different to others of her gender. For both guards – in common with most of their own gender – were of the opinion that while women had their uses (one in particular) they also had their place. And that place, as far as they were concerned, was most definitely not on the throne of England. Their suspicions about Mary had been confirmed. She had proved herself to be inconstant, variable, cruel and lacking in any spirit of counsel or regiment. And Elizabeth, about whom they had lately begun to entertain higher hopes, was clearly going soft in the head. 'Laughing to herself', said the first guard, nudging his companion in the ribs. 'Always a bad sign.'

'Aye', said the second. 'Weak, frail, feeble and foolish – what did I tell you?' He had, in fact, told his companion nothing of the sort. 'And,' he added darkly, 'ruled by lust.'

The other guard nodded. 'She'll be missing Lord Dudley.'

'King Robert.'

'Never! She'll not be allowed to marry that man.'

'Does she look,' said the other man, 'like the sort to pay heed to advisers? Headstrong', he added with conviction. 'Just like her father.'

'Maybe – but she's a woman.'

The two men pondered this unpalatable and incontrovertible fact in silence. Then the younger, taller one who considered Elizabeth 'ruled by lust', started to recite one of the favourite refrains of the day. 'Light of credit,' he began, 'lusty of stomach, impatient, full of words, apt to lie, flatter and weep . . . '

' . . . all in extremes,' continued his grinning friend, 'either loving dearly or hating deadly, consumed by unruly motions of tickling lust . . . '

' . . . desiring rather to rule than be ruled. Despising,' they finished in unison, 'everything that is offered to them.'

Feeling rather pleased with themselves, they looked again at the beautiful young woman under the tree. She was no longer laughing, but, in sharp contrast to her earlier merriment, looked as if she were about to burst into tears. 'Aye,' declared the older guard, nodding sagely. 'Inconstant. You never can tell with

111

them. One minute they seem as if they're in heaven. Next thing you know, they're looking as if someone's just walked over their grave.'

'Eh? What does that mean?'

The other man shuffled uncomfortably. He didn't, in all honesty, know exactly what the expression meant. Still, it sounded good; dark and uncomfortable. As if something deadly had happened. 'It means,' he declared with authority, 'as if something deadly's just happened.'

Something had. A minute previously, at the exact moment when Elizabeth's mood had changed from merry to morose, Queen Mary of England had breathed her last.

Chapter 8

The supreme irony was that the Earl of Sussex had been despatched to Hatfield to impart the news. Elizabeth could still remember the expression on his face: his eyes were strangely pleading; his brow furrowed and his tone, when at last he spoke, was utterly devoid of emotion.

'The Queen,' he had intoned, 'is dead.'

Then he had sank to his knees and held out a hand. 'Long live your Majesty!'

Elizabeth had felt somehow dissociated from her real self. She remembered looking, almost disinterestedly, at the coronation ring in the palm of Sussex's hand. She vaguely recalled holding out her own hand for him to slip it on her finger. She dimly remembered that her ladies, fanning out around Sussex, had lowered their heads and, like him, fallen to their knees. And she knew that she had raised her own eyes to the heavens and had whispered words that, she was now assured, had been reported far and wide. 'This is the Lord's doing – and it is marvellous in our eyes!'

And she truly believed those words: divine intervention had elevated her to the throne. It was God who wanted her to rule England. The fact that she was young, inexperienced – and a woman – were of no consequence. Then a short, awed silence had descended on the leafy grounds at Hatfield – followed by a frenzied bout of activity.

And now, today, that activity was reaching its climax. Memories of this would not be dimmed by the passage of time. Elizabeth herself had seen to that. For she had not been idle since that momentous day at Hatfield. In private with Robert Dudley and in public with William Cecil, she had planned her coronation down to the last detail.

At first Cecil had counselled that she should exercise restraint. 'Your Majesty,' he told her, 'has inherited a most parlous and degenerate State. Prices have risen faster than wages. One bad harvest has followed another. Your Majesty's subjects are impoverished and disillusioned. I would urge that your coronation, while reflecting the glory of the occasion, should reflect the state . . . '

'And I would contradict you, Sir William. Is my coronation not a signal of a new age? Of a new dawn?'

'Yes, but . . . '

'So it shall reflect that the new age shall be a golden one. A rich, prosperous and joyous one.'

And, initially to Cecil's consternation, Elizabeth began to set in motion plans for the most lavish coronation yet seen in the country. For she knew one thing he had yet to learn: she already had the love of the people. She knew that they would expect her to herald her reign with scenes of unparalleled magnificence.

Cecil's doubts were assuaged when, ten days after Mary's death, Elizabeth rode to London to take formal possession of the Tower. Wearing a dress of deep purple that emphasized the paleness of her skin and the fairness of her hair, she rode in an open carriage as far as Cripplegate. Then, surrounded by Sergeants-at-Arms, she rode through streets specially gravelled in her honour to Tower Hill. Huge crowds greeted her on every thoroughfare and at every turn, showering her with flowers, support, love and praise.

Riding some distance behind her, Cecil found that he was genuinely moved by the performance – even more so when Elizabeth alighted from her carriage and, before mounting her horse, walked over to greet the crowds. Never had he known of a monarch to do such a thing; never had he seen such expressions of unaffected joy on Elizabeth's face and on those of her adoring public.

At that moment he resolved to join Elizabeth in trying to make the coronation itself the most glorious event in living memory. His motivation, it was true, was more subtle and indeed cynical than Elizabeth's. He envisaged a brilliant exercise in propaganda, an ostentatious inauguration of a new and fabulous era in England's history. He saw a total redressing of the balance of Mary's reign. Where her rule had started with dour sobriety and rigid formality, so Elizabeth's would begin with laughter, spontaneity and a celebration of the good things to come.

Yet Cecil's innate conservatism nearly got the better of him. Unfairly, he blamed Robert Dudley for the extravagances of the coronation day. He was well aware of the fact that Elizabeth had consulted with him over every detail. He knew that even the day itself had been chosen by Robert, Elizabeth and an astronomer called John Dee. 'John Dee!' he had spat when informed of the secret consultation. 'A notorious necromancer. An invocator of devils. He will have to go when all this is over.'

Later, Cecil would be successful in ridding the court of some of Elizabeth's more dubious favourites – but not John Dee. Elizabeth's faith in astronomy was unshakeable.

As was her faith in Robert Dudley. He hardly left her side in the days leading up to the coronation. And now, as she walked down the great aisle of Westminster Abbey, he was only a few paces behind her.

But Elizabeth felt herself to be alone. The feeling of unreality that had overtaken her on the day that Mary had died returned. Again she found herself dissociated from events, as if part of her had left her body and was looking down from on high.

It was a magnificent sight to behold. She saw herself walking towards her anointment along the specially laid blue carpet beneath hundreds of burning tapers and lamps. She heard the near-deafening sound of the church pipes, the drum rolls, the music of the organ and the exultant voices of the choir. She saw every notable person in her realm filling the Abbey to capacity, vivid and gorgeous in their coronation robes, glittering in their jewels. She congratulated herself on allowing her ladies two rolls of velvet and two yards of cloth of gold; for they, she determined, would not be outshone by her richer subjects.

But no one outshone Elizabeth herself. Her own tunic of gold cloth was the richest of all, her jewels the finest, her crimson velvet robe the longest and most magnificent. And its train, several feet behind Elizabeth, was carried by the Duchess of Norfolk. Elizabeth had been appalled when Cecil had informed her of the Duchess's role. 'But she can't!' Elizabeth had all but wailed. 'It would be as if I were slapping her in the face. It would be seen as a subjugation of the Howards to have the Duchess hobbling behind me, weighed down by my train.'

'Madam,' Cecil had bristled with disapproval, 'it would be seen as the correct thing to do. By hereditary right, the Duchess of Norfolk carries the monarch's train.' Then he had added, with a wicked little smile. 'It won't do her son any harm to be reminded that his family belong behind and not in front of Your Majesty's person. And, remember, it is an *honour* to carry the monarch's train.'

That, Elizabeth reminded herself, was a concept she would have to get used to. Physical proximity to her person was now highly valued. Numerous unctuous courtiers had already jostled with each other for places near her, next to her – even in view of her. But there was only one person she wished to be physically close to.

That was her only sadness during the coronation. As she drew nearer to the throne, she felt increasingly distanced from Robert. And as, to a great fanfare of trumpets and drums, she turned and sat down, she felt herself utterly alone, completely removed from the scene of magnificent medieval pageantry before her. Yet her face was an inscrutable mask.

Not for a second did her expression waver as the Bishop of Carlisle placed the heavy, jewel-encrusted

crown of St Edward on her head. Four times he pro-
claimed her Queen: four times the congregation
roared their approval. Then she heard herself swearing to uphold the laws of the country, to defend the
Church and to use justice, discretion and mercy in her
judgements. Then, in a departure from tradition, the
gospel and epistle were read – in English as well as
Latin.

'You know,' whispered a furious Norfolk from his
place near the throne, 'what that means.'

Sussex turned to face the other noble. His whole
countenance spoke of disapproval. 'Yes', he said. 'It
means that she intends to uphold both the Protestant
and the Catholic faiths.'

'Ridiculous!' spat Norfolk. 'She can't do both.'

But Elizabeth knew that. She had planned this part
of the ceremony with great deliberation. Had Norfolk
looked more closely, he would have seen that she did
not elevate the Host and that her oath was adminis-
tered from an English Bible. The message was clear:
she would be the liberator of the Protestant conscience and practitioner of the Protestant faith. But
she would tolerate Catholicism.

Then came the climax of the ceremony. Another
trumpet fanfare reached its deafening crescendo and
the Bishop stepped forward again. Taking Elizabeth's
right hand, he slipped the coronation ring on to her
fourth finger. Had he not himself been shaking with
nerves, he would have noticed that Elizabeth was also
trembling, that her eyes were moist and that her hand
was as cold as ice.

For the ring confirmed Elizabeth's exalted and

lonely status. It bound her to her people, not to the one person with whom she wished to be united. She withdrew her hand and looked down at the ring. Then she allowed herself a small smile. The ring may confirm her public persona, but the private one was still the same. Around her neck, hidden beneath the jewel-encrusted collar and gold lace ruff she was wearing her most precious and private jewel – Robert Dudley's silver chain.

Then the bells high above Elizabeth began to ring and, once more hiding her feelings behind an impassive mask, Elizabeth rose from the throne and began the long, stately journey back down the aisle. A veritable cacophony accompanied her: the organist played like a man demented; the pipers and trumpeters seemed to wage a battle against him and the drummers, determined not to be outdone, beat their instruments with deafening force. The choir didn't stand a chance. Only those standing near the choristers could hear their thin, defeated voices.

The Venetian Ambassador turned to his companion. 'It sounds like the end of the world!'

'Nay!' shouted the other man above the din. 'It is the beginning of a new one!'

Then they both turned to their left as Elizabeth made her slow, stately progress down the aisle. Neither man had the slightest idea that she was trying her utmost to suppress a giggle.

For Robert Dudley, two rows in front of them, had just winked at her as she passed.

Three hours later, in the Great Hall of Whitehall

Palace, a faint smile was playing at the corners of her mouth. The smile wasn't occasioned by Dudley. Nor was it on account of the gaiety of the scene before her; it was more to do with the memory of her last appearance at court. She had, to her shame, been instructed by Mary to yield her precedence to the Duchesses of Suffolk and Lennox. A personal snub, the demotion had also been a public humiliation – a courtly corollary of Mary's hysterical subjugation of heretics. Elizabeth had not returned to repeat the experience.

Now she was back in a different guise. And now, for the first time, she realized there had been something more fundamental about her late sister's court that had unsettled her. Every gathering had been sombre; a strange oppressive atmosphere had clouded every festivity. Henry's court – synonymous with intrigue, social manoeuvring and sexual license – had, under his elder daughter, become a dark and joyless place.

And now the light had returned.

'How they love you, my lady', said Kat with a warm, affectionate smile.

Elizabeth smiled as well – this time in appreciation of the moment. One would, she reflected, have to have a heart of stone not to take delight in the scene before them. The Great Hall was packed; not just with people but with activity; with dancing, feasting, music and conversation. Taking their cue from the lute players, the revellers plucked a new, living tune from the dead, hollow wood of Mary's reign and filled the great room with laughter.

And Elizabeth felt part of it. The isolation she had

felt in the Abbey had disappeared. Robert's winking at her had been the start of the descent from her pedestal. For outside the Abbey, the jubilant crowds had thronged around her as she began her walk to Whitehall. To the horror of some courtiers, Elizabeth had stopped to accept nosegays, to exchange pleasantries – even to laugh with them. And now her more exalted subjects were laughing as well. But while Elizabeth knew she had the love of the people, she was not so certain about her court. Their gaiety was on account of the pageantry – not the personage behind it.

'I think,' said Elizabeth, 'the moot point is how they hated Mary – not how much they love me.'

Kat demurred – but Elizabeth knew she was right. She was far too astute to believe that the people before her were celebrating her accession to the throne. How could they? They didn't know her. The majority of the people in the room were rejoicing in the lifting of the veil of Mary's brooding Catholicism. The Protestants, many returned from exile, were dancing to the vindication of their beliefs. And the young and the beautiful were celebrating the passing of the old and the ugly.

But Elizabeth was under no illusions. She knew that this was but a hiatus; everyone – herself included – was floating on the cloud of her coronation. Tonight marked the ending of the unspoken amnesty occasioned by her accession to the throne. Tomorrow would be a different story.

Behind Elizabeth, Sir William Cecil was entertaining similar thoughts. Yet where Elizabeth was procrastinating, he was contemplating the morrow. Elizabeth would have to address herself to matters of state. She would have to accept, and act upon, the unpalatable truth about her tarnished crown. Her country was bankrupt, her throne precarious, her courtiers divided – and her life was in danger. Further, her weakness as well as her potential strength lay in the fact that she was cast in the same mould as her father. Highly educated, clever and wilful, she had the makings of a great ruler. Yet she was also young, naive, highly strung – and unmarried. Where Henry's plurality of marriages had marred his reign, Elizabeth's seeming indifference to that desirable state was equally dangerous. A queen without a husband was like a ship without a rudder. Everything, as de la Quadra had pointedly remarked, depended on whom she married. It was no small consolation to Cecil that she most certainly wouldn't marry Philip of Spain. De la Quadra's less than delicate approach had horrified Elizabeth. Yet her peremptory refusal of Philip's hand had already sown the seeds of an insidious rumour: de la Quadra was now passing abroad the information that Elizabeth was unhealthy and incapable of bearing children.

Sir William Cecil had his own way of quashing rumours.

'Who is that?' Elizabeth's whisper, intended for Kat alone, reached Cecil's ears.

'John Harrington,' came the reply. 'They say he's a great scholar.'

'Hmm. Too skinny!' Elizabeth laughed behind her fan. 'I think he reads too many books. What about him? The one on his left.'

Cecil looked at the golden youth who, aware that he was the centre of the Queen's attention, offered her an exquisite – and exquisitely theatrical – bow. Cecil frowned at him. A peacock; the perpetrator of some vicious rumours – and the salacious subject of others.

'Too beautiful!' he heard Elizabeth giggle to Kat.

Cecil couldn't agree more. Philip Sydney was glorious to look at – and that, in Cecil's view, should be both the start and the finish of his appeal to his sovereign.

Increasingly irritated by Elizabeth's skittishness, anxious to be about his business, Cecil moved a step closer to his sovereign.

Elizabeth was well aware of Cecil's presence – and also of his intent. Yet for the moment she ignored him. Her metamorphosis was not complete: tomorrow she would be a sovereign. Today she was celebrating. And she was, she had to admit to herself, deriving an innocent and delightful satisfaction from the novelty of her position.

'And that one? Who's he?' she whispered to Kat.

'That's Thoms Elyot. A poet.'

'And with nice legs to boot!' Elizabeth smiled at Elyot and then, behind her fan, giggled again.

But her merriment ceased abruptly as she noticed, out of the corner of her eye, a black-clad individual lurking on the fringes of the group surrounding Elyot. He was staring at her; a gaze that sought to expose her soul while revealing nothing of itself. A blank. Elizabeth shuddered and felt the mantle of her reign descend on her shoulders. It was, like this man, uncomfortable. An unknown entity.

Then the man in black moved out of her sight. He could still see her out of the corner of his eye, but he had no intention of letting her see him. He had witnessed her admiration of Thoms Elyot, an admiration that would surely turn to suspicion if she saw him leave the room with the man in black.

Cecil seized on Elizabeth's sudden stillness to capture her attention. And with it his business. 'Majesty!'

Elizabeth turned and, with a half-smile, acknowledged the statesman. The smile wavered when she noticed the man at Cecil's side.

'May I introduce his Excellency, Monsieur de Foix, the French Ambassador.'

The mantle tightened its grip on Elizabeth. A fleeting sensation of panic overcame her. Not understanding its source, she ignored it and extended her hand to the dapper, exquisitely dressed de Foix.

If the Frenchman was surprised by Elizabeth's sudden *froideur*, he disguised it well. He took her hand, kissed it with a curious yet inoffensive intimacy and them smiled up at her. 'Madam, they told me you were beautiful – but I find it is not so. You are more than beautiful. You are,' he finished with aplomb, 'incomparable.' De Foix was used to making such compliments – and, until now, a stranger to delivering them with sincerity.

Elizabeth noted, and acknowledged, his admiration.

Encouraged by her smile, yet not noticing that it failed to reach her eyes, de Foix drew closer. So, on her other side, did Cecil. It was then that Elizabeth's panic returned. Again it was momentary, but this time she understood it. She, Elizabeth, was being subsumed by her other persona, the one that had threatened to overcome her as she had sat on the throne. Inwardly, she was the same as she had always been, but it was the outer manifestation that others saw. In the eyes of men like Cecil and de Foix, she was no longer a person. She was the Queen of England.

'King Henry of Anjou,' said de Foix, 'sends you his brotherly love. He trusts that, with your accession, the relationship between our countries may be much improved.'

And now that Queen, thought Elizabeth, is being moved on her chessboard. 'That,' she said, fighting a hollow despair, 'is also my hope.'

Both Cecil and de Foix heard the resignation in her voice. But neither man noticed the look in her eye as she spoke. For her attention had been diverted away from them, towards the dancefloor. There, resplendent in his finery and exuberant in his step, was Lord Robert Dudley. Laughing, carefree and oblivious to Elizabeth, he was lost in the movement of the dance. A dance that had him partnered with Isabel Knollys and saw him moving, with every joyous step, further away from Elizabeth.

De Foix, however, moved even closer. 'With such consideration,' he continued, 'the King expects that you will consider the suit of his brother, the Duke of Anjou.'

It was as if Elizabeth hadn't heard. She continued to stare in the direction of the dance.

'The Duke is a young man of the greatest virtue.'

Still Elizabeth didn't respond.

'He is also,' prompted de Foix with an edge to his voice, 'very handsome.'

As disconcerted as de Foix by Elizabeth's seeming indifference, Cecil stepped into the breach. 'Her Majesty,' he assured the Frenchman, 'will naturally consider the proposal most carefully.'

But Her Majesty was considering something altogether closer to her heart than the doubtful appeal of the Duke of Anjou. She was struggling to answer a question that had posed itself, uninvited and unwelcome, in her head; struggling to reconcile a divided self.

Neither man had any idea of what she was thinking. Yet her continued silence served to fuel their worst fears. Elizabeth was not interested in governing. Not for her the minutiae of diplomacy nor the strains of sovereignty. She was going to reject the sceptred orb of State for a life of galloping frivolity. She had eyes only for the gilded creatures around her: her ears were attuned to music and laughter and not to the heavier rhythms of her heritage. She hadn't heard their words.

But when Elizabeth rounded on de Foix it became clear that she had heard every word, every nuance and every unspoken assumption of a wilful ignorance on her part. She had also listened to – and quelled – her inner disquiet. She had solved the problem of how to reconcile her two selves by ... not reconciling them. They would remain separate. She would not confuse Elizabeth the person with Elizabeth the Queen. When the latter was called on, as now, she would forget the former. She would simply play the game. And she would play to win.

Elizabeth turned, eyes ablaze, on the hapless Frenchman. 'How fortunate for the Duke that he is considered handsome,' she snapped, 'but how unfortunate that his mother, Mary of Guise, chooses to garrison Scotland with French troops!'

Both the vehemence and the nature of her response took de Foix by stunned surprise. He stared open-mouthed at the woman in front of him.

So did Cecil. Having all but dismissed her as flighty and capricious, he was now obliged to consider her as dangerously sharp – and sharp-tongued.

De Foix was the first to recover his wits. 'Your Majesty,' he began with an unctuous bow, 'what is Scotland to you? A rough, barbarous realm which our troops are only there to pacify?' Yet even as he spoke, de Foix rued his words. Elizabeth would know better than that. And if he needed confirmation, it came through her stony glare. 'You would not deny, Madam,' he said, deftly shifting tack, 'that your cousin, Mary of Scots, is the rightful Sovereign of that poor country?'

'No. I . . . '

'Her Majesty,' said Cecil quickly, 'does not deny it.'

'Then, as she *is* your cousin, she can mean no harm to you. The Queen Mother is only safeguarding it in her absence.' De Foix offered an innocent shrug. 'No more than that.'

Elizabeth suspected a great deal more than that. She knew of the fierce reputation and vaulting ambition of Mary of Guise. She knew that Mary had taken it upon herself to secure the throne of England for her daughter and the man to whom she was betrothed: Francis II of France.

Reading her mind, fearing that she would articulate those thoughts, Cecil again intervened. 'Her Majesty,' he repeated to de Foix, 'will naturally consider most carefully the suit of the Duke of Anjou.'

De Foix was obliged to be content with that. For Her Majesty's demeanour had changed yet again. With one last, enigmatic smile at the French Ambassador, she moved away and, followed by her ladies, joined the throng.

Her Majesty had, in fact, retired for the evening. Elizabeth had not. She was going to dance. And Robert, suddenly, was beckoning her.

De Foix, too, melted into the crowd. Cecil did not. His momentary relief in preventing Elizabeth from making a diplomatic *faux pas* had passed. Now he was left with a deep sense of foreboding about his sovereign. In one brief encounter, she had shown herself to be at once flighty, haughty and disingenuous. And she seemed suddenly all but indifferent to Cecil's counsel. Had she merely been amusing herself in the days before Mary's death and prior to her coronation? Had she just been playing at diplomacy? Cecil was now forced to contemplate the disquieting notion that Elizabeth's promise to appoint him Secretary of State had been merely the simplest way of divesting herself of the burden of ruling.

But he couldn't rule for her. It was imperative that Elizabeth make her own, preferably indelible, mark on the nation. And it was imperative that she recognize her allies at court. And her enemies.

Cecil shook his head. Something would have to be done. Elizabeth would have to be watched as others were watching her. And Cecil could hardly do the job alone: the tableau unfolding before him was already straining his eyes.

At the far end of the room, incongruous beside a pair of minstrels, the Duke of Norfolk and the Earl of Sussex were engaged in grave conversation. And every few seconds, they turned their attention to the couple in the centre of the hall: to Elizabeth and Robert Dudley, dancing to the ever-louder, ever-faster tempo of the volta. Neither looked as if they ever wanted the music to stop.

But it would. And soon.

'I wondered . . . if you were different?'

'Different? How should I be different?'

'Now that you are Queen.'

Elizabeth felt herself stiffen in Robert's arms. She pulled away from his embrace and, beside him on the bed, looked deep into his eyes. 'I may be Queen,' she said, 'but am I not still the same person?'

'Are you?' A playful smile hovered on Robert's lips. 'Show me.'

Elizabeth breathed a sigh of relief. He was teasing. Two could play at that game. She took a lock of her hair, now freed of its elaborate dressing and burden of jewels, and brushed it against her face. Do I not have the same face?'

Robert grinned.

'The same body?' Elizabeth let the hair fall against

her nightgown, allowed it to gently caress her breast.

Robert's smile broadened.

'And do I not have the same feelings?'

'I don't know.' Robert fell back against the pillows.

'Hmm. I wonder how I can prove it to you?'

Robert reached out and pulled gently at her hair. 'Like this?' he whispered.

'Or,' suggested Elizabeth as she bent towards him, 'like this.'

It was a suggestion that met with his unbridled approval.

Later, their love consummated, their appetite for each other at last sated, Elizabeth lay entwined in Robert's arms. For the first time in her life, she felt absolutely safe; completely secure. She had never dared imagine she could feel like this, had never entertained the possibility that physical love could be even more powerful than spiritual love. She had explored the extent of her passionate nature – and she did not find it wanting. Nor, in any way, did she find Robert lacking. Now, even more than before, he was her everything.

'Robert?' she murmured.

'Mmm?' Robert opened one lazy eyelid, reached out and caressed her breasts with a long, languid hand.

'Do you love me?'

'Yes.'

'Forever?'

'Forever.'

For a moment they lay in blissful, contented silence. Then Robert pushed her gently from him, raised himself on one elbow and looked deep into her eyes. 'Elizabeth?'

'Mmm?'

'Say you are mine.'

Elizabeth reached up and traced the sensuous outline of his mouth with a delicate finger. 'I am yours', she whispered.

'Forever?' The eyes were dancing now, filled with the joy that had been there for all to see when they had danced at the coronation banquet. Then, as now, they had eyes only for each other. Laughing with unabashed delight, he had thrown her high into the air and, to audible, even shocked gasps from the onlookers, caught her in a strong embrace. But then there had been ears to hear their words. Now there was no one.

'I am yours,' said Elizabeth with sudden seriousness, 'forever.'

'And I am yours,' replied Robert, 'forever.'

Again they lapsed into silence. Then, teasing again, Elizabeth looked up to him. 'I thought to have lost you.'

'Lost me?' A brief flicker of alarm crossed Robert's face.

'Yes. When you were dancing with Isabel.'

Relieved, Robert nudged her playfully in the ribs. 'Am I not allowed to dance with one of your ladies? You yourself were engaged at the time.'

'Yes.' Elizabeth made a *moue* of distaste. 'With the French Ambassador.'

'What did he want?'

'Oh', said Elizabeth with a weary sigh. 'That I

marry the French King's brother.'

Robert was aghast. 'And will you?'

'Well,' said Elizabeth with a lazy smile, 'the Ambassador said he is a young man of the greatest virtue.'

'And you like young men of virtue?'

Elizabeth ignored the question and continued her tease. 'And he is by all accounts extremely handsome.'

'And you like handsome men?'

'I know so few.'

'But the ones you do know?'

'Oh . . . I like them well enough. In fact, there is one who has caught my eye?'

'Really?'

'Yes. I even have it in mind to ask him to be my eyes. To look out for me, to tell me who is against me, who is with me.' Suddenly impassioned, Elizabeth felt her heart begin to race. I want him to be my all. My protector, my guide, my counsel, my spirit. My lover. Robert,' she finished after a momentary silence, 'will you be my eyes?'

Robert reached for her hand and began to smother it with delicate, tickling kisses. 'Yes, my love. I shall look out for you. I shall be your eyes.'

Neither of them knew it, but there were other eyes upon them. Elizabeth's ladies had known it would be only a matter of time before their mistress took Lord Dudley as her lover. They had known it from the moment she had allocated him the suite of apartments next to her own. Kat Ashley had known it for years. Only she was aware of the fierce, burning love between Elizabeth and Robert. Only she knew how long and with what difficulty they had waited to seal their love. She hadn't even told Isabel Knollys that Elizabeth's love for Robert was neither whim nor infatuation, that her commitment to him was long-standing and total.

And Isabel still hadn't told Kat what she knew about Robert.

Loyalty to Elizabeth apart, neither Kat nor Isabel could restrain themselves from joining the other ladies at the door of Elizabeth's bedchamber. They shouldn't, they knew, stand so close. They shouldn't be within earshot of the whispered mutterings from within. They just couldn't help it. And they *really* shouldn't, they knew, take it in turns to peek through the keyhole. Half-awed and half-embarrassed by the sight of the couple in the bed, they blushed and only just manage to suppress their giggles.

It was by pure chance that they had moved away from the door when Sir William Cecil strode in from the anteroom. Isabel and the younger ladies blushed crimson and turned away. Only Kat stood her ground, challenging Cecil with a protective stance and an almost threatening eye.

'Does Her Majesty sleep?'

'Not . . . not yet, Sir William. But she is . . . she is overwrought.'

Cecil spent half his life being overwrought. As far as he was concerned, that state was precious little excuse for retiring to bed.

'Er . . .' Kat moved swiftly to block his way as he advanced towards Elizabeth's door. 'She really ought

133

not to be disturbed.'

Cecil frowned. Surely? No. It was impossible. Inconceivable. And yet . . . Suddenly he stopped and spun round to glare first at Kat and then at the rest of the ladies. 'You must show me Her Majesty's sheets every morning.'

'What?' Kat was aghast. The other ladies, too, could hardly believe their ears. But worse was to come.

'You must tell me when she bleeds', insisted Cecil. 'And you must show me her stool. I must know *all* her proper functions.'

The other ladies were too stunned to speak. Kat managed a stunned, high-pitched squeak. 'Her . . . her proper functions, Sir William?'

'Indeed. Her Majesty's body and person are no longer her own property.'

'Er . . . whose are they, sir?'

'No one's,' barked Cecil as he turned to stalk out of the room. 'They belong to the State.'

Chapter 9

'Your Majesty should know that she has inherited a most parlous and degenerate State.' Cecil didn't mean to sound so brusque; he was just irritated by the beatific smile Elizabeth had been wearing all morning. She was on the throne of England – not on cloud nine. And the sooner she realized she had nothing to smile about then the better for all concerned.

'I am well aware,' said Elizabeth in a still, small voice, 'that there is room for improvement in the state of the country.' But none, she thought, in the person of Robert Dudley.

'That, Madam, is an understatement', said the other man in the room.

A flash of anger crossed Elizabeth's features. She ignored him and addressed Cecil. 'And who is this, pray, who dares tell her Majesty what type of statement she is making?'

'Waad, your Majesty', answered the man for himself. 'From the Treasury.'

'It was the Treasury,' said Elizabeth, 'that countenanced the cost of the coronation. With,' she added with a sly look at Cecil, 'the agreement of Sir William. I hope, therefore, you haven't come to tell me that the Treasury is empty?'

'It has been depleted by the sum of sixteen thousand pounds, Your Majesty – excluding the cost of the banquet.'

Elizabeth blanched.

Noting her ashen face, Cecil suddenly felt sorry for her. Waad was being a complete idiot. The cost of the coronation was neither here nor there, and was in any event money well spent. 'Waad,' he spat. 'Get to the point.'

Waad bowed and tried again. 'Madam, the Treasury is . . . is *nearly* empty. The navy is run down. There is no standing army and we are bare of munitions. And,' he added in his peevish voice, 'there is not a fortress left in England which could withstand a single shot.'

Elizabeth stared at the short, fat harbinger of doom. Then she turned back to Cecil. 'Is this really true?'

'Yes. And nor is that the end of it. There are those, both here and abroad, who wish Your Majesty ill . . .'

'. . . we are well aware of that, Sir William . . . '

'. . . but it is worse than I . . . than perhaps you were at first led to believe.'

'Oh? How so?'

'As you know, Mary of Scots already lays claim to your throne. And Mary of Guise isn't just garrisoning French troops north of the border. She is now preparing them for action.'

'What? She plans to invade?'

Cecil nodded. 'And Norfolk covets your throne for himself.'

'I thought,' said Elizabeth with a distinctly unfriendly look, 'you said he could be controlled.'

'As indeed he can be. But not,' finished Cecil with

utter certainty, 'until you marry and produce an heir.' And not, he felt like adding, if you marry Robert Dudley.

Elizabeth didn't reply. She knew well what Cecil was thinking. And Waad. She knew they were echoing the thoughts of those who had watched her and Robert dance to the frenzied strains of the volta the previous evening. She knew they thought she was going to renounce all potential suitors in favour of Robert.

And that was what she intended to do. But not yet. 'Sir William,' she said at last, 'your wise counsel of a few days ago informed me that the time is not yet ripe for change. That I would succeed only through a discreet beginning. Marriage,' she added with haughty disdain, 'is not a discreet step to take. We shall wait.' Then, to Cecil's intense annoyance, she stood up and clapped her hands. Now to the business that brought us here. Bring forth the gifts!'

A moment later the door opened and a fleet of servants entered. Kat and Isabel followed. All of them were carrying gifts.

Elizabeth was delighted. She revelled in presents – both in the giving and receiving of them.

Waad, too, began to cheer up. It was his job to examine each coronation gift and value it. Those that Elizabeth declined for her personal use would be sold and the proceeds added to his sorely depleted Treasury. With any luck, he thought, he could recoup the cost of the coronation itself.

But not if the present from the King of Sweden was anything to go by. 'Horse blankets!' he stammered as he peered into the first box. 'Horse blankets from

137

King Eric of Sweden! Pah!' Rigid with disapproval, he extracted a pen and a scroll from his valise. 'Can't be worth more than . . . more than forty pounds.'

Behind him, Elizabeth and Kat did their best to stifle a giggle. 'Oh look', said Elizabeth with delight as she looked into a more promising box. 'Jewels.'

'And silverware, Madam. Brocades, too. Oh, how beautiful!'

'And this, Kat! See?' Elizabeth pulled out a jewel-encrusted crucifix from another box. Then her face fell as she studied it in detail. 'Perhaps . . . no. It's a little . . . a little too Catholic for my tastes.' She winked at Kat. 'We'll give it to Waad.'

Cecil, meanwhile, stood by and watched. There was no doubt about it: Elizabeth was something of a riddle. One minute business-like, the next abandoned to frivolity. One minute biting the head off the French Ambassador, the next flirting with Robert Dudley. It hadn't yet occurred to Cecil – indeed it never would – that Elizabeth was perfectly normal. He couldn't understand how someone with such an enormous capacity for hard work and learning could also have a huge appetite for dancing, laughing, hunting and generally making merry.

Waad, who only had an appetite for money-making, pounced with glee on an inlaid rosewood chest that had just been brought in. 'Something of value!' he enthused. 'Gold filigree too . . . one hundred pounds – at least!' Then, writing the sum in his neat round hand, he moved on to the next item. 'This,' he announced, 'is a gift from Lord Robert.'

Elizabeth rushed to his side.

'It's a box', said Waad in great disappointment. 'But what's inside it?'

'Another box.' Puzzled and not a little suspicious, Waad opened to second box. 'Yet another box inside! This is insane! And another . . . and so it continues!' As box opened into box, he shook his head in disgust. 'What manner of gift is this?'

Beside him, Elizabeth reached for the tiny box he now held in his hand. Smiling to herself, she opened it. It was quite empty.

Waad snorted in contempt. 'There is nothing in it!'

'Nothing that the eyes can see, Mr Waad. And yet,' she added with a heavenly smile, 'it is very full.'

Waad looked at her as if she were mad. Women, he thought. Each as feeble-minded as the next. Boxes indeed! What use had anyone for a whole lot of little boxes? Positively quivering with indignation, he moved on to the next item. He didn't even bother to try and gauge the value of Lord Dudley's present.

But to Elizabeth the boxes were priceless. Each, she knew, contained his love. And had it been possible, he would have sent her an infinite number of boxes.

'Oh Madam!' shrieked Isabel as she delved into a large chest. 'Come look!'

Laughing at her childish enthusiasm, and with the smallest box still in her hand, Elizabeth joined her lady-in waiting. 'God's death!' she exclaimed as she saw the ravishing silk gowns, 'these are very fine indeed. And silk stockings!' she gasped. 'The finest, sheerest silk I ever saw.'

'From the King of France', said Waad with a meaningful look.

But Elizabeth wasn't interested in who they came from. The moment she had learned she was going to be queen, she resolved to dress accordingly. No more simple gowns, she had decided. From now on her dress would reflect her position. Never again would she appear in public without the finest jewels, the biggest pearls and the most luxurious, elaborate dresses. And, truly, these were luxurious indeed. Wreathed in smiles, she reached for a particularly splendid gown of green silk and held it against her. No sooner had she done so than it was snatched away from her.

'You must not do that, Madam!'

Elizabeth stared, open-mouthed with outrage, at the man who had torn the dress from her and thrown it, like an old rag, to the floor. He seemed to have materialized from nowhere. And he seemed vaguely, somehow frighteningly familiar. Yet she couldn't place him. 'Who, 'she snapped as her anger overcame the frisson of fear, 'are *you*, sir, that you dare to take such liberties with our person?'

It was Cecil, moving to her side, who replied. 'Madam, this rude gentleman is ... Sir Francis Walsingham.'

The man in black. With a start of recognition, Elizabeth was transported back to the coronation banquet, to the man whose eyes seemed to see behind her own. The man who, if rumours were to be believed, was feared throughout Europe. And if Cecil were to be believed, Walsingham presented no threat to her.

As if to prove the point, Walsingham bowed and

gestured towards the dress. 'The scents upon such clothing may be poisoned. Your Majesty must beware of *anything* which might touch your bare body.'

Again, Walsingham's dark eyes seemed to bore straight into Elizabeth's green ones, to search behind them for the secrets of her soul. Elizabeth felt herself flush. It was as if he knew. And the barely perceptible nod he gave her as she stood transfixed to the spot served as confirmation of his knowledge. Elizabeth felt an involuntary shudder run through her. There would be no keeping secrets from Sir Francis. There would be no point.

But Walsingham didn't know about Robert Dudley. He *suspected* – but suspicions did not suffice for Sir Francis. Knowledge was his creed. 'Intelligence,' he was fond of saying, 'is never too dear.'

And he often paid generously for the receipt of intelligence. His recent business in France had not come cheaply – but it had reaped great rewards. And the latest intelligence from the Continent, equally expensive, was much worse than any news from France.

He wondered how Elizabeth would react. As he stared at her he sought not to expose her soul but to judge her character. He saw intelligence in her eyes, curiosity in her brows, strength in her bone structure and capability in her hands. He also saw a hesitancy, a certain trepidation in her manner. That he put down to her inexperience. She would do. She would react well to the news.

Suddenly he smiled, wrong-footing Elizabeth. Like

the decadent creatures he had wooed in France, Elizabeth was surprised to see that he had an extraordinarily seductive smile. And it seemed quite genuine – as indeed it was. The beautiful blond boy in France had also thought it genuine. Only when Walsingham had taken him into a private room for further pleasures had it revealed itself to be artificial. And by then it had been too late for the boy, for the young French spy who had thought Walsingham putty in his hands.

Walsingham had slit his throat.

To Elizabeth, the smile appeared heavenly – but the eyes were still an enigma.

Then Walsingham gestured at the dress. 'I had no wish to alarm you, your Majesty. You may rest assured that whatever else you have heard about me, I have only your best interests at heart.'

Elizabeth glared back. 'I have heard nothing whatsoever about you, Sir Francis. And as I am your Queen it is a natural assumption that my best interests are uppermost in your mind.' And, with that magnificent rejoinder, she turned her back from him and stalked towards the door.

Behind her, Cecil was unable to suppress a grin. Walsingham, too, was impressed. She would definitely do, he thought. As well as fire in her eyes and passion in her heart, there was a brain in her head. And a very quick one too.

'Madam!' Cecil rushed up to Elizabeth as she reached the door. 'I had hoped you had not forgotten. The council meeting . . . '

'. . . is to happen within the hour.'

'No, I had not forgotten.' Her face still stony, Elizabeth turned to him. 'Women may be weak and feeble, Sir Cecil, but I have yet to hear that forgetfulness is a womanly vice. And it is most certainly not a queenly one. No,' she repeated, 'I had not forgotten. Nor had I forgotten that it is my duty to present myself at my best for my Councillors. I was going to change.' Abruptly, she turned towards the pile of gifts. 'I have it in mind to wear something new. Kat!' she commanded, pointing to the dress on the floor, 'bring that dress to my chamber. It will suit our person. And our purpose.' Then, without so much as a glance at Walsingham, she turned again and strode out of the room.

It was Kat who was the most surprised by the astonishing performance. Never before had she seen her mistress act with such imperious hauteur. And never before had Elizabeth asked her to do anything that might endanger her life.

Walsingham saw the doubt on her face as she looked down at the offending dress. 'You may pick it up', he said. 'It has already been examined for poison.' The expression on his face left Kat in no doubt as to who had ordered the examination. Relieved but also suspicious, she looked over to him.

'I was merely making the point,' he said, 'that your mistress should exercise some caution. And so should you. Her Majesty has many enemies.'

'Yes. Yes . . . Sir Francis. Thank you.' Kat picked up the dress and followed Elizabeth out of the room. A chill of foreboding accompanied her. For so long she had entertained the notion that once Elizabeth ascended to the throne she would be safe. Now she realized just how wrong she had been. The dangers had, if anything, increased. And where Elizabeth's life was threatened, so was Kat's.

An hour later Elizabeth approached the door of the Council Chamber. Her outward appearance, she knew, was dazzling. The sheen of the green silk enhanced that of her auburn hair. Its cut accentuated her slim waist; its jewelled cuffs complimented her hands and her own precious stones; the pearls in her hair, the rings on her fingers and the brooches at her breast lent her a magnificence that truly accorded with her title.

Inwardly it was a different matter. Elizabeth was quaking. The poise and chilly self-control she had shown in Walsingham's presence had been real enough. But they had been borne of anger over Walsingham insulting her person. Now she was gripped by fear on account of her first major act as Queen. She was about to walk into her first meeting with the men she had chosen to guide and advise her through her reign. Some of them, she knew, loved her and would serve her loyally. Others respected the throne of England and would serve its incumbent as a matter of duty. One adored her – and another despised her.

And one, it seemed, was her shadow. 'Remember what I told you!' he whispered as they approached the doors to the Council Chamber. Then, as the Chamberlain preceding them indicated for the guards to open the doors, Cecil lowered his tone even further. 'This is what I meant by the time not being yet ripe for change. You will only succeed through a most discreet beginning.'

Elizabeth nodded. He would find out soon enough that she had heeded his advice – with one notable and highly controversial exception.

Then, suddenly, they were in the hall and the Chamberlain was announcing her presence. 'The Queen!' he boomed in stentorian tones.

The forty or so men in the room bowed low – but not before they noted the glittering apparition before them. Elizabeth's appearance was in splendid, sumptuous contrast to that of her predecessor. Every man in the room murmured his appreciation. And most hoped fervently that the contrast would end at the question of apparel. Members of Mary's Privy Council, they expected to retain their positions under Elizabeth's rule.

Only one man in the room noticed that Elizabeth was paler than usual. Only he knew, as she took her seat on the throne, that she was shaking with nerves.

'My lords,' she began. 'The Council . . . the Council is the Sovereign's eyes and ears, and I . . . I make you this promise that I mean . . . mean to direct all my actions by your good advice and counsel.' Still devoid of expression, she surveyed the room. More murmurs of appreciation greeted her opening remarks. She breathed an imperceptible sigh of relief and, with a new confidence, addressed her audience once more. 'I hereby appoint the following positions.'

Noting that approval had turned to apprehension, she turned to address Cecil. 'Sir William Cecil, I hereby appoint you Principal Secretary of State.' No one was surprised by the first appointment, least of all Cecil himself. He stepped forward and bowed to the throne. 'You once served my father', said Elizabeth with a smile. 'Now you will serve me. I have this opinion of you.' Then, with the merest suggestion of a twinkle in her eye, she repeated the very words that she had written to Cecil from Hatfield. Over the past few days his devotion had been proved, but she had been understated in her praise. Now was the first time the words had been articulated – and they resonated with a conviction that, to several of those present, sounded positively threatening: '. . . that you will not be corrupted by any manner of gifts, that you will be faithful to the State and that, without respect of my private will, you will give me the counsel which you think best.'

Even the normally inscrutable Cecil was visibly moved. Reading the words had been pleasurable enough: hearing them was a joy, and a vindication of the unofficial role he had assumed as Elizabeth's protector. He stepped forward and kissed her hand. As he did so, he looked her in the eye and whispered, 'Norfolk now. You must.'

Elizabeth knew that. She had always known that Norfolk was too powerful to alienate. Much as it rankled with her, she had agreed to Cecil's insistence that she must retain the Duke. 'I also keep in Council,' she declared, 'his Grace the Duke of Norfolk.'

Another man in the same position may have looked smug. Not the Duke of Norfolk. He was far too arrogant. It hadn't even occurred to him that Elizabeth would consider dropping him from the Privy Council.

He was a Howard of Norfolk.

'I am,' he said as he sank to his knees and took her proffered hand, 'Your Majesty's servant.'

'I trust with all my heart,' replied Elizabeth in a cold whisper, 'that it may be so.' But as Norfolk looked up and caught her eye she knew it wouldn't be so. She knew he was still as dangerous as ever. Having failed to prevent her from succeeding to the throne, he would now direct his energies to toppling her from that throne.

Only be marrying and producing an heir will your throne be safe. Cecil's oft-repeated refrain rang in her mind as she locked eyes with Norfolk. But not even that would stop the man. For Norfolk hated the man she wanted to marry even more than he hated her. Elizabeth shuddered as Norfolk stepped back.

'I also retain the services,' she called out as he retreated to the body of the room, 'the services of the Earls of Derby, Sussex and Arundel.'

There was no exchange of knowing looks with Derby. Kindly, gentle and loyal, he was that rarest of individuals: a politician with no motives other than to serve his country. He stepped forward, bowed, kissed her hand and moved on.

The Earl of Sussex followed, echoing Norfolk's promise to be Her Majesty's servant. The echo was weaker – and equally hollow. Sussex was transparently the servant of Norfolk, and of his own greed and ambition. The look he gave Elizabeth as he pledged his allegiance was the same as the one he had given her when he had stalked into the chapel at Hatfield to arrest her: at once haughty, supercilious, sly and superior.

But past events clearly troubled the more sensitive Earl of Arundel. As he approached Elizabeth, she saw the memory of their last meeting etched on his face. Elizabeth smiled at him. Of all the men in the barge that terrible day when she had been taken to the Tower, he was the only one who had shown any kindness to her. And yet he still looked ashamed. 'I do not forget,' whispered Elizabeth as he kissed her hand, 'kindnesses of the past.' The Earl backed away into the room, happy of countenance and pink around the ears.

And so it went on. Under Cecil's guidance, Elizabeth had determined to decrease the size of her Privy Council. Mary's Council of forty had proved an unwieldy apparatus of State, more given to internal strife than external good. By decreasing it, Elizabeth had a greater chance of keeping control. Yet she had been obliged to tread carefully. Only the lesser members were dismissed; those with ambiguous roles and, more importantly, little power.

But Elizabeth did appoint new members of her own. Sir Nicholas Throckmorton became her Chief Butler and Chamberlain of the Exchequer. Sir Francis Knollys she appointed as the Vice-chairman of her Household. The extremely fat and highly capable Nicholas Bacon became Lord Keeper of the Privy Seal. Lord Admiral Clinton also joined the Council.

It was only Knollys' appointment that gave rise to a faint ripple of dissent. An ardent Protestant, he had fled to Germany for the duration of Mary's rule in order to practise his faith. The Catholics on the

Council saw his return and his appointment as the thin end of a wedge that Elizabeth would surely drive home as time went on: an outlawing of the Catholic faith.

Norfolk saw it as something more: Knollys was the husband of Elizabeth's cousin Katherine. The Queen was obviously seeking to surround herself with her own family. Fat lot of good that'll do her, he thought. Hadn't she had direct experience of the Tudor's propensity for cutting each other's heads off?

The ripple of dissent over Knollys didn't reach Elizabeth's ears. But the shock and outrage that greeted her next and last appointment was unmistakable. 'I appoint to Council,' she declared in a voice that was already defensive, 'Lord Robert Dudley – and make him Master of the Horse. And,' she continued as the groundswell of disapproval reached her ears, 'I create him the Earl of Leicester.'

Robert had no need to ask the others present to move in order that he may approach Elizabeth. Almost to a man, they were already distancing themselves from him, both literally and metaphorically. To most present, Dudley was already a pariah. Now he was an important one. Several cast suspicious looks at him; some were overtly hostile. The Duke of Norfolk muttered obscenities under his breath.

Robert didn't notice. He, too, was as amazed as they. Not by his being appointed to the Council as Master of the Horse – Elizabeth had already informed him of her intention – but by his elevation to an Earldom. That was a complete surprise. A gift from his lover.

'Your Majesty,' he whispered as he knelt before her. 'I . . . I offer you my . . .' Then he looked up and into her eyes. '. . . my heart.'

Elizabeth nearly giggled at the incongruity of the situation. He was kneeling before her, offering her his heart as she offered her hand. They had eyes only for each other – yet they were in the middle of the Council Chamber, surrounded by the most powerful men in the land. It made their moment of privacy, snatched from the midst of the public world, all the more intense.

Only Cecil saw the expression on Dudley's face as he gazed up at Elizabeth. His own expression registered consternation, disapproval, and a fleeting sadness. For Cecil was not without the more delicate sensibilities of the human condition. Behind the almost obsessive devotion to his country he possessed a surprisingly romantic nature; a nature attuned to what was happening before his eyes. Yet in his position he had found it incumbent on him to suppress that side of his character. Elizabeth, he thought, would be well advised to do the same.

Then Dudley moved away, signalling for the return of the public world.

'My lords!' Elizabeth's voice was more forceful now. Robert's closeness had been like an injection of confidence. No longer on the defensive, Elizabeth was now in full command. And she was determined both to quell the unrest in the room and address the issue that had divided and nearly destroyed England for so many years. 'My lords,' she repeated. 'Lately our kingdom has suffered much from the diverse opinions upon matters of religion. I have no desire to make windows into men's souls. This Council is both Protestant – and Catholic.' Very pointedly, she looked at the Duke of Norfolk. 'For I care not what a man believes. I care only that he be loyal.'

This time her words were greeted with a chorus of approval – and no small amount of relief. The last thing anyone in the room wanted was an era of reprisals against Catholics. The reign of Bloody Mary had demonstrated all too clearly the tragic internal attrition that resulted from religious persecution. But the more seasoned statesmen in the room wondered at Elizabeth's naivety. She could not just pretend that five years of terror had not happened. And she could not ignore the fact that she, a Protestant, was sitting on the throne of England. To others – and especially to other countries – it signalled the end of Catholic ascendancy in the country.

As usual, Cecil was behind Elizabeth when she walked out of the room. But, uncharacteristically, he could barely control himself. 'Madam!' he hissed as soon as they were out of earshot of the others. 'For God's sake, Madam! Lord Robert's father was executed as a traitor! And his grandfather . . . his brother also! He is not regarded as . . . he has no friends at court!'

Elizabeth turned on him. 'He has *one* friend!' Then she took a deep, calming breath and looked dreamily into the mid-distance. 'I have known him since we were children. I trust in him, don't you understand that, Sir William?'

Sir William did not; in his book, a loyal Dudley was

151

a contradiction in terms.

Elizabeth saw the answer to her question in his eyes and her anger flared again. 'If I wish to favour him,' she snapped, 'then that is all of *my* concern – and none of yours!'

It was with an even greater sadness that Cecil watched Elizabeth stalk off down the corridor. Yet behind that emotion was a genuine, and growing concern. There was much he had underestimated in Elizabeth – her volatility and unpredictability most of all. She had heeded his advice on the creation of her Council: then she had thrown caution and good sense to the wind by elevating Dudley. A fine seat on a horse and a twinkle in his eye, thought Cecil in disbelief, and she makes him Master of the Horse and an Earl to boot. He foresaw great trouble ahead. And not just on account of Dudley. Elizabeth had not heeded his advice on the subject of religion.

Deeply troubled, he went to seek out Walsingham.

Sir Francis was in his apartments, quaffing wine and pouring over a map of Europe. He was, as usual, clad entirely in black.

'Ah! William! To what do I owe the pleasure!'

'I fear that I bring few pleasures', said Cecil. He sat down opposite his friend and, looking a good decade older than his thirty-eight years, drew a weary hand across his brow. 'Her Majesty has just appointed her Privy Council.'

'So I heard. Wine?' Walsingham raised the claret jug.

'Please. And she has made Dudley . . . '

'. . . Master of the Horse and Earl of Leicester. Yes. A bad business indeed.'

'How . . . ?'

'William.' The other man shook his head. But he was smiling. 'You know I make it my business to know. And never to tell.'

Cecil smiled as well. Francis never ceased to amaze him. And, sometimes, to annoy him. As Principal Secretary of State, with the diverse and powerful duties the position entailed, it was Cecil's job to know everything. It was he who would draw up the agenda for all future Council meetings, he who would draft all Royal correspondence to foreign princes and ambassadors. It was he who should know everything first. Suddenly a mischievous gleam came into his eye. He would wager there was something he knew that Francis didn't. 'Do you know,' he asked, 'what Her Majesty has chosen to call you?'

'No.' Walsingham looked annoyed. 'What?'

'The Moor.'

'The *Moor*? Why on earth would she want to call me that?'

'Oh come on, Francis. Dark? Mysterious? A riddle wrapped in an enigma?'

'Well . . .' Walsingham was, unusually, lost for words. And strangely pleased. 'At least I made some sort of impression on Her Majesty. But . . . how much does she know about me?'

'Not much. Not nearly as much as I do.'

Nobody knew as much about Walsingham as Cecil did. Very few people knew that he was the son of a lawyer from an old Protestant Norfolk family, that, amazingly for one of his intelligence, he had come down from Cambridge without a degree – and then trained himself as a lawyer. Some people knew that he had spent all of Mary's reign on the Continent, yet few knew what he had been doing.

Cecil knew exactly what he had been doing. He had been spying. For Cecil – and on behalf of the English Protestants. And now he was back in England, officially as the Member of Parliament for Lyme Regis. Unofficially, he was the head of the England's secret service, supervising the activities of over seventy agents and spies in European courts.

Elizabeth hadn't a clue. And, for the moment, Cecil wanted to keep things that way. Especially as she had appointed a Dudley, a traitor in their midst, a viper to her bosom.

'This . . . this Dudley', said Walsingham, as if reading Cecil's mind. 'I don't see it was a problem.'

'No?'

'No. Is he not there simply to share Her Majesty's . . . private pleasures?'

The prudish Cecil went slightly red. 'If that is the case then her ladies have been remarkably discreet.'

Walsingham knew exactly what that meant. He knew all about the sheets.

'But,' continued Cecil. 'The Queen *must* marry – and she must *not* marry Lord Robert.'

'She will not marry Robert Dudley.'

'Oh? What makes you so sure?'

'I cannot yet be sure – but I will be.'

'Oh for Heaven's sake, Francis! You can tell me, can't you?'

But Walsingham shook his head. 'No. What is the point of rumours? We deal in facts, don't we?'

An exasperated Cecil knew he would have to be content with that. The trouble with spies, he thought with sudden venom, was that they were so *secretive*.

'And while we are on the subject of facts,' continued Walsingham, gesturing to the map on his desk, 'there are some very unsavoury ones to contend with.'

'Yes.' Suddenly Cecil was weary again. 'I know. But Her Majesty doesn't. She will persist with this notion that we can all, Protestants and Catholics alike, live happily together. She said in the meeting that ...' He trailed off into silence, realizing that Walsingham would already know exactly what Elizabeth had said.

'She doesn't know, then, about the bishops?'

Cecil shook his head. He hadn't had the heart to tell her that Elizabeth's own archbishops and bishops had refused to crown her, that their consciences prevented them from sharing the people's adulation of her. The Bishop of Carlisle had been a last resort; had agreed to crown her only under duress – and at a price.

'You must tell her, William.'

'Yes', sighed Cecil. 'I suppose I must.'

Walsingham jabbed at the map. 'And you must tell her soon. For there are dangers from two sides.' His finger rested on France and then, in a long arc, traced a path to Scotland. 'That is one threat – and it is increasing. The other,' he finished, 'is more insidious. It comes from there.'

Cecil looked down at the map. Walsingham's finger was resting on Rome.

'There are some of our own countrymen,' said Walsingham after a heavy silence, 'who are Papist spies against us.'

'And who do you have against *them*?'

Walsingham met Cecil's enquiry with an even look of his own. 'Elyot,' he said.

With the finely tuned antennae of the very young, the children knew that the old man's heart was not in his job. Yet those same antennae, combined with well-remembered voices from the adult world, told them to stay still, to look upon him with reverence and to listen in awe as they were blessed. For they were in the presence of God's representative on earth.

Each child tried not to flinch as the gnarled old hands were placed on their heads. Some were scared of the old man himself. Most were simply awed by their surroundings; by the Cardinal in attendance, the several priests looking on; the incense in the air and the vast number of flickering candles.

Soon the strangely dispassionate service was over and they were ushered by the priests into a brighter world. The memory of the Pontiff's blessing would remain with the children forever – but so would a strange sensation that there was conflict in the house of God.

Back inside the chapel, the Pope sighed and made to leave the room. He loved welcoming children into the church. What he disliked, and what had been preying on his mind, was the dissent of the adults who refused to join that church. He rued the historic schism between East and West, the departure from Rome of other countries. And he rued the day Elizabeth I had ascended the throne of England.

'Father', whispered the Cardinal in attendance. 'He is come.'

'What? Who?'

'The English priest.'

'Ah!' The Pope smiled. 'This is good news indeed. Where is he.'

'Here, Father.' Taking the Pope's arm, the Cardinal guided him to the priest who had been standing at some distance from the others, watching the blessing with cold, clinical detachment.

But as the Pope shuffled towards him a brightness entered his eyes and he bowed to kiss the ring on the old man's proffered hand.

'Tell me: what news of our brothers and sisters in England? Do they accept the sovereignty of that . . . of that illegitimate whore?'

The English priest looked with reverence at the angry old man. His eyes were no longer merely bright, they were shining with a zealous lust. 'No, father,' he said. 'They pray ceaselessly that England may be recovered from heresy.'

The Pope adopted a pensive, pious expression. 'Perhaps, my son,' he said at length, 'prayer is not sufficient. We are men of God – but we must also act in this world, so to serve him.' Then he looked upwards and closed his eyes. 'I will ask for guidance in this matter.'

When he looked back at the English priest he was

157

smiling. *'Do not despair, my son.'* Then he patted the other man on the shoulder. Coming from such a frail, stooped figure, the gesture was surprisingly strong. *'It is truly said,'* he finished, *'that the righteous shall inherit the earth.'*

Chapter 10

'You will not stay the night with me?'

'I cannot. It would be too dangerous.'

Elizabeth grimaced, an ugly gesture at odds with the beauty of the rest of her. She lay supine against the pillows, her loose hair cascading over the crisp linen; her pale skin naked; her arms around Robert.

'Elizabeth?'

'Mmm?'

'You know that what you have done is already dangerous?'

'How do you mean?'

Robert sighed. 'The position you gave me ... Master of the Horse. There are those who think it importune of you to have elevated me to your Council.'

'Why? You are easily the finest horseman in England. You are ...' But then Elizabeth saw the look in Robert's eye and gave up the pretence. 'Yes', she said with a weary sigh. 'I know what they think. They think you will follow in your father's footsteps. They think you are consumed by ambition, that you will topple me off my throne and make it your own. Isn't that what they think, my Earl of Leicester?' There was now a twinkle in her eye as she gazed at Robert.

'The Earl of Leicester.' Robert sampled the words

on his tongue, weighing their effect. 'Yes. I like it. It suits me well, don't you think?'

'Admirably. But are you going to topple me from my throne?'

'No.' Robert pulled away from her embrace and gave her a playful push. 'But if I had a mind to it, I could topple you out of your bed.'

'You wouldn't dare!'

'I would. See? I can push you . . . like this . . . and like this . . .'

'No!' Consumed by a fit of giggles, Elizabeth tried to wriggle away. 'No!' she screamed again.

'Shh!' Robert put a finger to her lips. 'Walls have ears.'

'No they don't. My ladies have ears – but they would never tell. Nor would they dare enter.'

'No. True.' But the talk of eavesdroppers had spoiled the moment. Robert drew back and angrily pushed back the hair that had fallen over his eyes. 'But others would enter. That is why I can't stay.'

'Who would enter?'

'Your Cecil.'

Elizabeth shot a curious look at Robert. The petulance in his voice was unmistakable. Her lover, she was amazed to discover, was jealous of Sir William.

'And,' he added before she could challenge him, 'Norfolk would also dare to barge past your ladies.'

The thought sent a shiver down Elizabeth's spine. She knew Robert spoke the truth. Norfolk was the one who sought to topple her from her throne. And what better excuse could he hope for than to find the Queen in bed with the son of a traitor?

'Robert', she said after a long silence. 'It's late. You'd better go.'

'Yes.' The response was flat. No impassioned protest. No regret. He swung his legs over the side of the bed. 'I had better . . . go.'

Elizabeth lay, listening to the soft tread of his footsteps as he crossed the room to the secret door that led to his own apartments. He left without another word; without a backward glance.

Elizabeth knew why. It was for the same reason that she herself felt dispirited. There was now an unacknowledged gulf between them; a subject that was suddenly taboo. So simple in its concept, so complex in its ramifications. Marriage.

Two hours later Elizabeth drifted into an uneasy sleep. Some time later she started to dream the dream that had been her nocturnal companion for as long as she could remember. She and Robert were laughing together in the grounds of a great country house. She was dressed in the simpler clothes she had favoured before life became so complex. He looked exactly the same. Elizabeth's subconscious mind followed herself and Robert as they entered a maze; saw him reach for her hand and heard him promise that he would never leave her, would never lose her. A beatific smile formed on the face of the sleeping Elizabeth as she closed in on the couple in her dreams.

Then she woke up screaming as the dream turned into a nightmare. For while Robert was exactly the same as ever, she was different. The girl with the tumbling mane of hair and the dancing eyes wasn't Elizabeth.

Many hours after that, as a cold dawn settled over London, as the first rays of sun penetrated the leaded windows of Elizabeth's chamber, she woke from the restless, traumatic sleep that had followed the nightmare. At first she thought the nightmare had returned in a different guise: she fancied she heard the Duke of Norfolk shout from outside her room. She imagined she heard his heavy tread as he stormed towards her bed. Then she screamed as she imagined the curtains being pulled back to reveal the triumphant face of the Duke himself.

It was several seconds before she realized she wasn't dreaming. She was sitting up in bed, with the sheets drawn protectively to her breast – staring in horror at the Duke.

'Your Grace! Whatever . . . ?'

'Madam!' Norfolk made no attempt to apologise. Instead, he glared at her as if she had committed some terrible transgression by being asleep, at dawn, alone in her own bed. 'Madam!' he repeated in the commanding tone he used with his dogs. 'You had best get up. There is some grave news.'

'Grave news? What . . . '

'Your Councillors, Madam, shall await you in the Council chamber.' And with that Norfolk turned on his heel and marched out of the room.

Elizabeth stayed where she was, sitting bolt upright in bed. Robert, she thought. Something had happened to Robert. But she dismissed that notion almost as soon as it entered her head. Any accident that may have befallen him would be good, not grave news to Norfolk. 'Kat!' she screamed. 'Kat!'

'Madam?' Already woken by the stampeding Duke, a dishevelled Kat scurried into the room.

'Something terrible has happened.'

'Madam?'

'Yes. Something has happened that threatens the country.' Elizabeth leaped out of bed. 'Quick! Get me some clothes.'

Kat did as she was bid. And as she helped her tousled mistress shrug into a simple dress, she couldn't help thinking that something else was wrong. Something really quite simple. Elizabeth, she reflected, should not have to cope alone. Elizabeth needed a husband. Then she looked to the door that led to Robert Dudley's apartments. But she didn't need *that* husband.

'My lords – what is it?' Without the Chamberlain and the attendant ceremony of sovereignty, Elizabeth rushed alone into the Council Chamber. Less than half her privy councillors were present. All looked as if they had dressed in a hurry. And they all looked extremely agitated.

'Sir William?' Elizabeth addressed her shadow.

For once, Cecil looked as if her were about to lose control. 'Madam, we have reports that Mary of Guise has increased the French garrison in Scotland by four thousand men – perhaps more. I cannot doubt that the French mean to attack while we are still weak, and your Majesty's reign still uncertain.'

Elizabeth's stared, open-mouthed, at her Principal Secretary of State. The news itself was dramatic enough – and so was Cecil's choice of words. 'Weak' and 'uncertain' were not words he would use lightly in front of other people. Elizabeth sat on the edge of the precarious throne in question and asked Cecil how he would advise her.

'Madam,' he replied without hesitation, 'we must with all haste raise an army to march upon Edinburgh.'

War. The dread word formed like a lump of bile in Elizabeth's throat. She had lived through Mary's misguided war against France and the misery and penury it had brought. She had vowed that if her reign were to be remembered for anything apart from the religious tolerance she was still bent on, it would be for lasting peace. She cast desperately about the room, hoping for a dissenter. There was none.

'Can we not instead send emissaries,' she suggested, 'to discover the truth of it?'

It was the Earl of Derby, in the same frame of mind as Cecil, who replied with vehemence. 'There is no time for that! If we delay, the French may receive yet more reinforcements.'

'What say you, Norfolk?' The moment Elizabeth asked the question, she regretted it. Norfolk was the last person on earth she would expect to agree with her.

As proved to be the case. Still bent on her destruction, he saw a war with France as the perfect means to that end. 'I say there has never been a better time or occasion to abate the French pride!' he shouted.

Elizabeth felt her heart heavy in her chest. 'You *all* agree to war?' she asked, willing someone to protest.

It was Robert Dudley who replied. 'Aye.' Clearly

embarrassed, he hung his head and stared fixedly at the stone floor.

Elizabeth feared she was not far short of hysteria. This was worse than she ever could have imagined. The very beginning of her reign, the golden reign of peace and prosperity she had envisaged, and already the councillors she had appointed were rising as one against her to promote a war with France.

Then Elizabeth noticed Walsingham in the far corner of the room. He shouldn't, she dimly perceived, be there at all. Yet her inscrutable 'Moor' was a law unto himself – and probably the only man who would dare contradict her Council. 'What say you, Walsingham?'

Walsingham stepped forward out of the shadows. Silhouetted in a glancing ray of sunlight falling through the mullioned window, he looked eerily gaunt; a black creature from another world. When he spoke, his voice carried no trace of outrage or wounded pride on behalf of England, merely a quiet certainty. 'I say that a prince should rather be slow to take action, and should watch that he does not come to be afraid of his own shadow.'

Strangely, it was Cecil who articulated the other men's thoughts. He rounded on his protégé. 'You are not in the majority!' he raged. 'And you are not on Council!' And damn you, he thought, eyes flashing with fury. Spies were all very well – in their place. But they cannot prevent amassed troops crossing borders.

Walsingham didn't even make an attempt to respond. He faded back into the shadows.

And Elizabeth sat alone on her throne, the solitary

voice of caution. 'I do not like wars', she said after a long silence. 'Wars have uncertain outcomes.'

'Your Majesty has no choice,' barked Cecil, 'as you value your throne!'

Elizabeth's reply, after a seemingly interminable silence, was barely audible. 'Then let there be war.'

'I do not like this business, Kat. I fear I am hazarding not only money and men, but the state of the crown, the realm and all that depend thereupon.'

'But, Madam . . . your reputation . . . '

'My reputation is already in tatters. The storm clouds are gathering, Kat.'

'Outside, maybe', said Kat as the thunder rolled in the distance. 'But all will go well in Scotland.'

Elizabeth didn't bother to contradict her. She knew in her heart of hearts that all would go very badly in Scotland. How could it be otherwise? England was without money, men, armour, fortresses – even good captains. And it was without a strong leader. For not only had her own councillors dragged her into war against her will, but . . .

'God's death!' shouted Elizabeth as a flash of lightning crashed overhead. 'What it happening? This, I tell you, is an omen.'

'It is but a storm, madam. It will pass.' But even as she spoke, Kat could tell that the storm was also raging within her mistress's soul and that it would not pass quickly. 'If you would just stay still, Madam, we could undress you more speedily.'

But Elizabeth couldn't stay still, and her ladies were obliged to follow her as she paced the room, lending the scene a faintly comical air. One lady was trying to remove the jewels from her hair, another the rings from her hand. Kat was endeavouring to divest Elizabeth of her dress while the others prepared the bedchamber for her night's rest. Unnoticed by Elizabeth, Isabel Knollys was preparing the bowl of warm water for her to warm her hands. As she did so, she kept looking, with a decidedly strange expression on her face, at the door leading to Robert Dudley's apartments.

Then the rain came. Great lashing pellets of water against the mullioned windows. Elizabeth shivered. The room itself was warm, but her heart was dark and cold.

'Madam,' said one of her maids of honour, 'if it would please you to sit before the mirror . . .'

'Oh very well.' Elizabeth strode across the room and sat on the stool in front of the jewel-encrusted mirror. The face that looked out at her did not please her. Old, she thought. And there were the beginnings of lines around the eyes. It was only as the maid removed the diamond combs from her hair, as it tumbled around her shoulders that the face began to soften. And only when the maid began to comb the auburn tresses did Elizabeth begin to relax. Each rhythmic, therapeutic stroke eased the tension in her shoulders and calmed her breathing.

But deep within she remained troubled. The call to arms had been bad enough – Sir William's choice of moment to impart further troubling news had been infinitely worse. That very evening he had told her about the bishops.

As the heavens erupted above and the torrential rain battered against the windows, Elizabeth stared at her reflection and wondered at her fate. The storm seemed to mock her belief in astronomy; the clouds had obliterated the stars, wiping her guiding principles from her sight. She was lost.

Then her ladies began to withdraw. Only two remained in attendance; one to fold down the covers on her bed, the other to wipe her fingers after she dipped them into the scented water Isabel had prepared. That ritual completed, Elizabeth climbed into bed.

'Goodnight, Madam,' said her youngest maid as she pulled the covers over her and made to withdraw. Then she pulled the curtains around the bed, curtsied low, and left the room.

Elizabeth had never felt quite so alone in her life. And she knew that she would remain so. Robert would not come to her that night. He wouldn't dare.

Chapter 11

It was a different storm that raged over Scotland. Longer in duration, greater in cost and more ferocious in violence. And it had nothing to do with the elements.

Rain came later, when the attack on Leith Castle was over. The black night gave way to a bleak dawn as the heavy clouds drifted from the Pentland hills, enveloping the Forth Estuary in a dismal shroud of grey. But when the rain fell the river below turned red as the blood of the dead was washed to the sea. The only other colours on the raw, brutal landscape were the white and gold of the Fleur de Lys fluttering in the breeze above the castle ramparts.

The dawn mocked the dying who had survived the bitter night. Darkness had spared them the sight of the carnage around them; now they could see the extent of the massacre.

But not for long. With dawn the French soldiers came again. Haste was no longer necessary; nor was full battledress. They appeared from the castle and walked slowly towards the battlefield. Every few moments one of them paused, raised a sword and drove it deep into the writhing body at his feet. Occasionally there was a faint moan, sometimes a loud cry – always a grunt of satisfaction from the French. For there would be no prisoners; no survivors

169

to tell tales. Only more bodies and more blood and a river that ran scarlet beneath the deluge.

When the soldiers returned to the castle and the rain abated, the other scavengers appeared. The wolves came from the forest; the carrion from the skies. And the rotting, fetid bodies of the English boy-soldiers were their prey. Some, even now, were still alive. But none survived their last, brutal indignity as the animals tore at their flesh and the birds plucked out their eyes.

High on the castle battlements, a lone woman surveyed the scene. Impervious to the chill of the morning air, oblivious to the rain, she smiled at the field of the dead. Her dark eyes gleamed as she saw the broken scaling ladders, and she laughed at the flags of England, trampled in the mud. And then she tilted her head to the heavens and thanked God for the victory he had delivered. Then Mary of Guise turned to the fluttering Fleur de Lys. '*Vive le Roi Français!*' she shouted.

The words were snatched by the wind, buffeted from the battlements and floated south to England.

'Where are my councillors today?'

The Palace Chamberlain averted his eyes.

'Where *are* they?'

'I . . . I know not, Madam. Perhaps . . . '

'*Perhaps?* You think I am interested in conjecture?'

'No, Madam . . . I . . . ' But the hapless Chamberlain faltered and lapsed into silence. Still he didn't dare look at Elizabeth. One glimpse had been enough. Instead he studied the flagstones at his feet.

'Where is Lord Robert?'

'Er . . . '

'. . . Look at me when I speak, damn you!'

The Chamberlain looked, and was shocked. In front of him stood a fury, a maenad, a blazing inferno of anger. A terrifying, magnificent incarnation of rage.

'Lord Robert,' he mumbled, 'is gone hunting.'

Elizabeth recoiled as if from a blow. '*Hunting?*' The utterance of the word appeared to deflate her and a momentary disbelief overcame her anger. Disbelief – and hurt.

'Yes, Madam. He is gone hunting.'

Elizabeth didn't reply. She hitched up her skirts, brushed past him and stormed off down the corridor. The ladies behind her followed in her wake. Their actions were instinctive, yet their demeanour reluctant. The Chamberlain breathed a sigh of relief as the distinctly unregal procession disappeared at breakneck speed down the corridor.

At the end Elizabeth turned left, towards the old, disused part of the Palace.

A breathless and puzzled Kat turned towards the lady on her right. 'What would she be going in there for?'

'Ours is not to reason why', panted the other, significantly more portly lady. Despite the almost unbearable cold of the stone passageway, a sheen of perspiration had broken out on her forehead. She carried on, puffing her way towards the guards at the entrance to the old Palace.

But then Elizabeth turned to her retinue. 'Leave me!' she shouted.

All except Kat held back. She, more than any of the others, knew there was something other than the débâcle in Scotland preying on Elizabeth's mind; something the unwitting Chamberlain must have told her. 'But . . . Madam . . . ' she beseeched.

'Leave me!'

Even Kat could see that Elizabeth had worked herself into such a state that no calming blandishments from her old nurse could soothe her. 'Yes, Madam', she said with a low curtsey.

Elizabeth ignored the guards as she swept into the dim hallway of the Old Palace. Barely aware of where she was let alone what she was doing, she rushed straight into the first of the *enfilade* of rooms. She didn't notice the dust, the eerie desolation of the long-abandoned chamber. All she knew was that she wanted to be alone.

Like a demon possessed, she ran into the second room as the tears began to flow. They were tears of multifarious emotions; anger, disbelief, sorrow – but most of all of humiliation. On this, the worst day of her young life, her lover had chosen to go hunting. He who had promised her safety, succour and salvation had abandoned her. The man who had urged her to embark on a futile, fruitless and fatal campaign – and who knew of the terrible consequences – had absented himself from Whitehall.

Sobbing openly now, crying out like a wounded animal, Elizabeth struck out at the objects around her. Indiscriminate in her urge for destruction, she swept Venetian glasses to the floor. They spilled on to the cold stone, splintering into a thousand fragments.

Far from a catharsis, the action spurred Elizabeth to further excesses of rage. She saw an old globe in the corner, picked it up and threw it as far as she could. Like the glassware, it shattered with a deafening crash.

And still Elizabeth carried on with her orgy of destruction. Stumbling now, on the verge of exhaustion yet fuelled by the adrenaline of hysteria, she threw herself against another table and, with great sweeping motions, thrashed out at anything within her reach. More glasses went flying off the table; a marble bust crashed to the floor; an inkpot soared into the air, trailing an arc of bright red ink in its wake.

And then, abruptly, Elizabeth stopped. Her head was still bent low over the table, but her eye was caught by an object just above it. Her glance never wavering, she drew herself upright until she could see it in its entirety. It was inanimate, yet it seemed to glow with life and pulsate with power. It was Holbein's magisterial portrait of her father.

The great man stared out at her. In likeness as in life, he looked indomitable; the very incarnation of the glory of sovereignty; the embodiment of kingly virtues, supreme confidence and absolute power.

Elizabeth herself felt suddenly ridiculous, small, humble and unworthy. Choking back her sobs, she extracted a handkerchief from her flowing sleeve and blew her nose – very loudly. The noise echoed around the room and, as it reverberated, brought a smile to Elizabeth's face. The small, very human action seemed to signal an end to her madness. She felt calm, composed – and full of resolution. She felt like Henry's daughter again. He was watching over her; guiding her and protecting her, willing her to pull herself together and act like the monarch she was.

Then the sensation of being watched began to unsettle her. She looked once more at the portrait, at the beady eyes set deep in the fleshy folds of the face. Then she moved to one side. The eyes followed her. She moved to the other side. Still the eyes remained on her. Telling herself she was being stupid, that eyes in portraits often appeared to move, she turned round.

Yet still she had the unshakeable conviction that she was being observed. A cold stab of fear ran through her. Someone else was in the room.

'Who . . . who goes there?' she called out in a quavering voice. A man stepped forward from the shadows to her left. He was clad entirely in black. Walsingham.

The lick of fear turned to a burst of anger. 'How *dare* you come into my presence?' screamed Elizabeth.

Walsingham took another step forward and bowed to her. 'Because, Madam, it is my business to protect Your Majesty – against *all* things.'

Again the elliptical emphasis, the enigmatic smile. How much, thought Elizabeth in sudden panic, does he know about me? How long has he been watching?

Everything. Forever. Walsingham's unwavering gaze seemed to answer for her.

Aware that she could unleash all her fury, all her majesty and all her might against this man and that she would be wasting her time if she thought he would flinch, Elizabeth gestured, somewhat help-lessly, to the room at large. 'Where is Sir William?' she asked in a small voice.

'He is gone to Scotland – to salvage what he may.'

Elizabeth bit her lip. She was on the verge of tears again – and Walsingham knew it. His expression softened and, to Elizabeth's amazement, he appeared - suddenly avuncular and compassionate. And approach-able.

'Why did they only send such children to Scot-land?' she whispered. 'Why did they not send proper reinforcements?'

Walsingham knew Elizabeth wanted some sort of reassurance; an easy explanation. An answer that would absolve everyone of blame for the catastrophe. There wasn't one.

'Why?' he said in the same soft, resigned tone as Elizabeth had used. 'I can tell you why, your Majesty.' Then his voice rose. 'The bishops, Madam. Your bishops would not let them. They spoke against it in the pulpits.'

'They ... they spoke against saving lives?' Elizabeth was appalled. And then, again, the anger flashed forth. 'Which means ... they also spoke against *me!*'

Walsingham looked straight into her eyes. 'What did Your Majesty expect? They are against you – and they have no fear of you.'

Elizabeth stared at him for a moment. Then, dis-concertingly, she smiled. 'No one appears to fear me, Sir Francis. I think it's time to change that, don't you?'

Walsingham gave her a cool, appraising look. Followed by a dazzling smile. 'Yes, Your Majesty. I do.'

'Good.' Elizabeth gathered up her skirts and turned towards the door. 'It is a fine day, is it not, Sir Francis?'

Completely nonplussed by the question, Walsingham couldn't find a reply. 'Er . . . well . . . '

'A fine day for hunting.'

'Hunting?'

'Yes. I have a mind to go hunting.' And with that, and a new purpose in her step, Elizabeth took her leave.

'Kat! Fetch my hunting clothes.'

'Your hunting clothes, Madam?'

'Why must everyone repeat my words? Can they not find ones of their own?'

'I only meant, Madam, that . . . '

'. . . well never mind what you meant. Just do it.'

Kat cast a sidelong glance at her mistress, trying to gauge her mood. The words were strong enough, but her tone was different from that of earlier in the day. She seemed more amused than irritated. Kat frowned. No, the expression was not of amusement. More of calm resolution.

'Lord Robert, Madam . . .'

'Yes. I know. Lord Robert has gone hunting. I have a mind to join him. Oh!' Elizabeth waved an impatient hand. 'You might as well know – you know everything else. I am not best pleased with Lord Robert.'

Good, thought Kat. That man is going the same

way as his father and brother. First the total devotion. Then the arrogance. After that would come the lust for glory. Then the treason. 'Indeed, Madam?' she said, affecting indifference.

'No. I am not pleased. Do you know,' she said, reaching for a scroll of paper on her desk, 'who sent me this?'

'No, Madam,' lied Kat.

'The poet Thomas Elyot. He has taken to writing me poems. Do you not think that very fine?'

'Yes, Madam.'

'And he has as good a pair of legs as Lord Robert. No, better.'

'But, Madam . . . '

'But I cannot marry a poet, is that what you're thinking? Indeed I cannot. Nor would I wish to. I could,' she added, more to herself than to Kat, 'marry Lord Robert, however.'

'No, Madam.' Surprising herself with her temerity, Kat walked towards the desk and stood over Elizabeth. 'You cannot marry . . . you cannot marry Lord Robert . . . *now*.'

'Ah!' Elizabeth looked at Kat in a new light. 'So you know?'

'Yes.'

'You surprise me. But then again,' sighed Elizabeth, 'I suppose everyone knows.'

'Not *everyone* . . . '

'But enough people are aware of the situation to believe that I am not in control of my own destiny.' Elizabeth leaped to her feet and walked towards the window. 'But I *am* in control, Kat. Or I can be. If I

177

had kept my own counsel I would have never have got into this position.'

Kat frowned. 'I'm afraid I don't quite understand . . . '

'I should never have sent troops to Scotland in the first place. We are not yet strong enough to fight the French. I should never have listened to the Council – Robert amongst them. And,' Elizabeth waved a finger at Kat, 'I should have tackled the bishops before now.'

'The bishops?' Kat was completely lost now.

'Yes. Must you always repeat me? I should have imposed my will before now. For the bishops are the key to everything.' Again Elizabeth seemed to be speaking more to herself than to her puzzled companion. 'If I can break the power of the bishops then I can exert my own will. And if I bring them into line then that incessant chorus will cease.'

'Er . . . what chorus?'

'The wretched refrain of "who shall she marry – and when?". *I* shall decide whom I shall marry. *I* shall decide when. And,' she finished with a flourish, 'I shall decide *if*.'

'Yes, Madam.' Kat looked at the polished floorboards. A gulf had arisen between her and Elizabeth. Not just the terrible gulf of misunderstanding over Robert Dudley, but a greater one; one that was widening all the time. For despite Kat's knowledge of Elizabeth, she was removed from her. She was standing on one side of a great divide. With her stood the rest of the populace of England. And on the other side, quite alone, stood Elizabeth.

'My Lord . . . ' The manservant, taken completely by surprise, was in a blind panic. 'My Lord . . . the Queen!'

But his Lord didn't hear. He had just dismounted from his horse and was standing several feet away, crossbow at his feet, contemplating the wounded stag. As the quivering creature looked up with soulful eyes, he reached to his belt and withdrew his hunting knife. Never let it be said, he thought with a grim smile, that I let an animal suffer unduly.

But this time he had no option. The sound of the thundering hooves reached his ears and he turned, open-mouthed in astonishment, to see the Royal party galloping towards him. At its head, magnificent astride a white horse, was Elizabeth. Her head-dress was billowing out behind her, her shapely thighs were visible beneath her skirts, and her expression was one of sheer abandonment.

Robert's own expression turned to one of unease. The look of exultation, of pure happiness, brought back painful memories. It was a look he had seen on her face when she was in the throes of passion. And there had been no passion between them for the past two weeks.

Elizabeth reined in beside Robert and, with athletic alacrity, dismounted from the sweating beast.

'Your Majesty.' Robert sank to one knee.

Elizabeth ignored him and looked instead at the wounded beast. Its flank was rising and falling with its last, painful breaths. And its breath, like that of her exhausted horse, rose as steam in the crisp, autumnal air.

'It is a fine beast, my Lord.' Elizabeth's eyes were positively gleaming now. 'Let me kill it!'

Feeling distinctly uneasy, Robert rose to his feet. There was something more than exultation in Elizabeth's manner. Something he couldn't identify. Something that frightened him.

'Elizabeth', he whispered.

'Hand me the knife!' The voice was a command – and loud enough for all around to hear.

Robert handed her the knife.

Taking its handle in both of her hands, Elizabeth knelt beside him. Then, tight-lipped and with total concentration, she raised it high above her head and then lunged downwards at the stag's neck. The knife carved a clear arc through the air and sliced straight into the animal's jugular.

Robert recoiled as a great jet of blood spewed forth. Elizabeth remained where she was, bent over the animal, until its tortured heart beat its last. Then she pulled out the knife and handed it back to Robert.

'Fine sport, my Lord. But 'tis a pity I could not have had more of it. Still,' she said with a forced laugh, 'I should not complain that affairs of State keep me from my beasts!'

Robert felt as if he, not the stag, had had a dagger plunged into him. He knew what her words meant. He knew, as his retainers and her courtiers laughed with her, that she was deliberately goading him, that she was at once annoyed, upset and hurt. But the look in her eyes told him she was something else as well. Something that he could now identify. She was all-powerful.

As if to illustrate that fact, she rose to her feet and called to her courtiers, 'Follow us at a distance! I wish to ride alone with the Earl of Leicester. We shall convene at the lodge for supper.'

Doubt settled on the faces of all around. Her Majesty alone with Robert Dudley? This was the first time she had been so blatant about her favourite. The first time she had overtly declared she wished his company above – and exclusive of – that of any other.

Robert too was taken aback by her peremptory statement. 'Elizabeth . . . ' he cautioned.

'My Lord', interrupted Elizabeth as she returned to her horse. 'Will you mount me?' Her eyes were almost mocking, yet behind the merriment Robert could see the hurt as he walked over to help her into the saddle.

'If there is something you wish to discuss . . . ' he whispered as he helped her into the saddle.

'Then we shall discuss it in the hunting lodge.' Astride her white horse now, Elizabeth looked down at him. The smile was again that of pure exhilaration, of the fearless sportswoman, of the indomitable woman.

Her courtiers and Robert's attendants, making a desultory departure in their wake, looked on in curiosity. The beautiful, captivating creature on the white stallion was a continual source of puzzlement to them. She was their Queen, yet she seemed by turns capricious, coy, hesitant and headstrong. Wilful one moment; full of woe the next.

'You would not think,' said one in rigid disapproval, 'that she had just lost an army in Scotland.'

'No', said his companion. 'And you would have

thought that she'd had her fill of dangerous games.'

'Aye', answered the other as he watched Elizabeth gallop off into the distance with Robert in hot pursuit. 'But she hasn't. Now she's playing the most dangerous of all.'

They didn't stop until, a full hour later, they reached the hunting lodge. Dusk was falling as the little building came into view, and with it came a chill that settled on Elizabeth's heart. She knew she had been playing games with Robert. Reluctant to tackle him about his absence in her hour of need, she had procrastinated, urging him on to the chase, tacitly challenging him to prove his love again.

It had been a stupid game, she thought as she dismounted. She was the Queen of England. If she requested that a member of her court accompany her on a ride it was, in whatever terms she couched it, an imperious command. Robert had been unable to refuse to ride with her. Robert would have to agree to whatever she requested. Robert . . .

'Walk with me, Elizabeth, while they prepare the supper.'

Robert's hands were on her shoulders. His head was at her neck and his lips were at her ears. 'Elizabeth', he whispered. 'I love you. I have always loved you and I always will.'

Oh God, thought Elizabeth. Her head arched backwards, her eyes fluttered and closed and the tension in her shoulders melted away as she leaned backwards into him. She felt the taut, sinewy muscles of his body support her. Her rock, her anchor. Her refuge against the cruel tides of an unfair world. She dimly perceived that this wasn't what it was meant to be like. She was annoyed with him. She had been leading him a merry dance through the forest. She had intended his reward to be the venom of her spleen, not the fruits of her love for him.

Then, as the courtiers arrived in their wake, they drew apart.

'Come', he murmured. 'Walk with me.'

'No. We shall help them . . . help them light the fire. And lay out the food.'

'Help them?' Robert looked at her through amused eyes. 'You? The Queen of England?'

'And why not? It is said that I have the common touch.'

'Touch. Yes.' Robert was suddenly pensive. 'Your touch.'

Elizabeth's common touch left her an hour after that. Again she requested that their attendants leave them as they settled on the cushions in front of the fire. Sated with wine, they didn't demur. Nor, this time, did Robert. Elizabeth's mood had mellowed.

He still smells of horse, thought Elizabeth as they sank on to the cushions. The warm, slightly feral and intoxicating smell of an animal in the wild. So, she supposed, did she. She wondered if it was having the same effect on him.

He turned to face her and unhooked her cloak. Then he shrugged off his own. 'Warm', he said with a smile. 'Too warm.'

Then he rested his hands again on her shoulders and pulled her gently towards him.

'Robert . . . '

183

'Shh.' Robert put a hand to her lips. 'Don't speak.' An image of Elizabeth on her horse came unbidden to Robert's mind. She had been magnificent, utterly imperious. Then he saw Elizabeth at the throat of the stag; the huntress, the victor. The killer. And then he remembered the look she had given him.

Her expression was different now. There was a strange look of wonder in her eyes, a hint of doubt. A suggestion of vulnerability.

Robert leaned forward to kiss her. At first she didn't respond. Then, as if reacting to him for the first time, she responded with a delicate, tentative kiss of her own.

'I know you have been teasing me', he murmured after a moment. 'Tease me if you want. Do with me what you will. I will always be here for you.'

The caressing words hit Elizabeth like a slap in the face. 'Always be here?' she gasped as she pulled away. 'Always?'

Not understanding, Robert gazed in astonishment at his lover. They were only a foot apart, yet suddenly an abyss had opened up between them. 'Yes. Always.'

'You were not there today.' The words cracked through the air like a whip.

Robert averted his eyes. 'I . . . I . . . '

'For God's sake!' shouted Elizabeth, leaping to her feet. 'I had need of you . . . but you were *not there!*' She glared down at him and then turned to the table behind her. She reached for the jug of wine and poured some into a goblet. For one mad moment Robert thought she was going to throw it at him. Instead she put in to her lips and gulped it down.

184

She never did that, thought Robert as he stared up at her. Elizabeth rarely touched wine. And when she did, she sipped.

For a moment they just looked at each other. Then, like a supplicant, Robert reached out. 'I did not think . . . ' he began.

'No! You did not think!' Elizabeth was shaking now. The wine had had an immediate effect. It seemed to poison her soul and rise back like bile in her throat. She felt sick – and desperate for reassurance.

Robert knew that look. 'I did not *know*', he beseeched. 'If I had known . . . '

'Stop! Say no more.'

'Elizabeth. *Please*.'

Elizabeth looked down at the kneeling man. There was no mistaking the pleading expression, the yearning to placate her and, behind that, the lack of comprehension. He looked as if he had transgressed some rule he didn't know existed. Elizabeth sighed and sank back down on to the cushions. 'It doesn't matter now.'

'It *does*.' Robert reached out and stroked her cheek. 'The last thing I would ever do is hurt you. I didn't know. I should have known – but I didn't.'

'Why,' asked Elizabeth in a small voice, 'did you side with the others about sending troops to Scotland? Were you afraid to cross them, to speak your own mind?'

'No.' Robert shook his head. 'I *was* speaking my mind. I truly believed that it was the best action to take.'

'They died, you know. All of them.'

185

'I know.'

Elizabeth took more wine. This time a pensive sip. 'You men,' she sniffed, 'think too much of war.'

'Perhaps.' Robert stared into the flickering flames. 'But we dwell upon the opposite polarity also.'

'Peace? I don't think so. Your hearts are never peaceful.'

'No.' Robert's lips searched for hers. 'I meant love.'

This time Elizabeth gave no resistance. With a low moan, she sank against him, eager of his kisses, hungry for his caresses. A moment later they were lying as one, side by side, with their bodies pressed tightly together. Then Robert's hands moved away from her breasts.

'No!' Despite her yearning, Elizabeth stiffened. 'No . . . I cannot.'

'Why? They will not disturb us.' Robert's face was so close that she felt his breath on her lips. And she saw the surprise, the sudden hurt in his eyes as he stared longingly at her.

Elizabeth looked away. 'It . . . it's past my time of bleeding. I cannot.'

And that, thought Robert, was the crux of the matter. There was the flaw in their relationship, the constant source of contention. The invisible barrier that lay between them. Unless . . .

'Elizabeth?'

'Mmm?' Still she averted her gaze – but her heart began to pound.

'Will you . . . will you . . . I mean . . .' suddenly Robert's tone changed as the question died on his lips. Then he sat up and gazed into the fire. 'I mean, what will you do?'

A solitary tear welled and trickled down Elizabeth's right cheek. Her hands loosened their grip on the cushions beside her and her heart became still. She thought for a moment it had stopped. When she replied it was in a flat, disinterested monotone. 'Do about what?

'About the situation.'

'What situation?'

'Scotland.'

So now, thought Elizabeth, they were hundreds of miles away. The gulf was widening.

'I don't know,' she mumbled. Then Robert reached behind him for her hand and gripped it tightly. He uttered no words, but the gesture was enough. 'I am blamed for our disaster in Scotland,' she said, 'but my enemy was not only Mary of Guise.'

'No?' Robert looked away from the fire. Slowly Elizabeth turned as well and looked him in the eye.

'No. My own bishops are against me. I think I must confront them. In fact, I *know* I must confront them.' Filled with a sudden resolution, with a new fire in her eye, she raised herself until she was crouching on the cushions.

But Robert was horrified. 'No! You *must* not. They are too powerful. Let them be.'

'Oh!' Now there was scorn in her voice. 'Then I am not Queen!' Her expression, however, was regal enough. But her question concerned Elizabeth the woman. 'Would you not support it – for *my* sake?'

'It is for your sake that I tell you not to do it! If you should fail . . . '

But the consequences of failure were too dire for him to contemplate.

Not for Elizabeth. 'What then . . . would you go hunting again, my Lord?'

The barb cut into Robert like a knife. He winced and, in the heavy silence that ensued, sprang to his feet. Like Elizabeth before him, he reached for some wine. She watched as he poured some into a goblet, stared over the rim on to the mid-distance and took a deep draught of the amber liquid. His knuckles, she noted, were white against the silver of the goblet.

'Elizabeth', he said with a forlorn sigh. 'This is getting us nowhere. All we are doing is going round in circles.'

Indeed we are, thought Elizabeth. But if you wanted to square the circle you would ask me to marry you.

'Why do you not send me poems any more?'

'What?' Robert nearly dropped the goblet.

'You heard. Why don't you send me poems any more? Other men send me poems.'

To her surprise, Robert threw back his head and laughed. 'That is only because you are Queen!' He dismissed all poets with an impatient wave of his hand. 'They mean *nothing*.'

But it was the arrogance, not the impatience, that Elizabeth heard, 'How do you *know*? They say,' she added with hauteur, 'that I am everything to them!'

Robert laughed again. Then he saw the expression on her face. The hauteur had been a guise. She looked frightened, almost wounded.

'Oh Elizabeth!' Robert rushed forward, knelt

beside her and gathered her into his arms. 'You are *everything* to me. And I to you! Nothing else is!' He gripped her fiercely, as if imbuing the passion of his words into her heart. 'Yes!' he urged, all but shaking her. 'You cannot deny it!'

But his vehemence, his frightening possessiveness was cloying to Elizabeth. 'No!' shuddering with distaste, she drew back and pushed him away. 'No', she shouted again. 'I love you – but my love is not so locked up in you that no one else may ever partake of it!'

The words surprised her as much as they hurt Robert. It hadn't meant to be this way, she thought. She had sought to breach the divide between them – all she had done was widen it into a yawning chasm. She had meant to test Robert's love for her, and had recoiled from the manifestation of that love. Now she didn't know what to do. She stared, wild-eyed and haunted, at the man in front of her. And he, on the other side of that chasm, stared back in shock. Then, half-blinded by the tears that had started to flow, Elizabeth fled from the room and rushed out into the night.

She knew not where she was going. All she wanted to do was put distance between herself and . . . herself. The ghastly realization stopped her in her tracks after barely a few yards. Horrified, she put her head in her hands and abandoned herself to grief. It was as if she were back in the chambers of the Old Palace; a demented creature overwhelmed with an all-consuming sorrow for which there was no panacea. Yet back in the Palace solace *had* come to her. Her father had stared down at her with an inalienable divinity. Isolated, unconquerable and inviolate. Yet she felt only one of those things. Total isolation.

She wanted Robert to come running after her. No, she thought, she didn't. She *wanted* to be alone. One of the courtiers would have seen her exit from the lodge. They would come. Soon she wouldn't be alone. Queens were *never* alone. They didn't like being alone.

But it was neither Robert nor one of her retainers who rescued her from her agony of isolation and indecision. It was Sir Francis Walsingham. Like a spirit from the forest, he seemed to transmute himself from the dark of the trees into the equally dark presence that used to frighten her so. Now she was surprised to realize that she almost welcomed him – as if her subconscious mind had expected him to be there.

'Your Majesty is hurt?' he enquired.

'Er . . . no. I . . . I . . . ' Overcome by a sudden shyness, Elizabeth looked down at her dress. The shyness turned to shame as she saw how crumpled it was. Instinctively, she put a hand to her hair. As she feared, it was dishevelled and beginning to tumble loose from its dressing of combs and jewels.

'Nobody saw you.' Walsingham's mellifluous tones drifted over to her, carrying with them a hint of amusement.

'Saw what?' she snapped. 'What did you suppose I was doing?'

Walsingham shrugged. 'I suppose nothing.' Any trace of a smile vanished. His face was totally devoid of expression. Yet they both knew exactly what he had supposed. And that he had been right.

If either of them needed any proof, it came in the shape of Robert. Silhouetted against the light from the open door, he appeared, looking equally as guilty as Elizabeth, at the threshold of the lodge.

Walsingham stepped forward. 'Madam', he whispered. 'Believe me. I do not judge you. You may do as you please.'

Elizabeth *did* believe him. The look she bestowed on him was grateful, relieved, friendly – and unabashed in its openness. Their tacit understanding was sealed.

Then, as Robert emerged from the hunting lodge, the quiet of the night was disturbed by the pounding of hooves on the forest avenue.

'God's death!' exclaimed Elizabeth with her old vigour. 'To what do we owe this invasion? Sir Francis? Are you aware of who comes by?'

'I am afraid not, your Majesty'

'A state of affairs,' said Elizabeth drily, 'that must disquiet you.'

Walsingham grinned. It didn't take much, he mused, to see her on form again.

As Robert stood, suddenly hesitant, two paces behind her, she seized the moment of waiting to rearrange her hair and unfold the creases in her dress.

'Ah!' said Walsingham as the shadowy figures of horses and men emerged from the night. 'I think we have Sir William.'

It was a very breathless Sir William Cecil who emerged from the midst of the band of horsemen and rode towards them. 'Madam', he panted. 'I bring some news.'

'You don't say!' Elizabeth was gay now; back in control. 'I presumed that you would not have come to join our little party. But I must insist you come in from the cold, Sir William. You too, Sir Francis', she said as she turned back into the lodge. 'We shall see that there is a goblet of wine for you both.'

Robert looked at her in amazed, if confused admiration. She changed direction faster than the wind, he thought. Inconstant, impossible to predict, and affecting everyone in her wake. It made her even more irresistible.

Inside, Elizabeth herself poured the goblets of wine for her guests. But she was far too astute to waste time with talk of her skills at housewifery or her common touch. 'So,' she said as she proffered the wine, 'what brings you here Sir William? I am hoping that you bring an apology from my bishops.'

'Alas, Madam, I do not.' Cecil took a welcome gulp of wine. 'But the news I bring does concern Scotland.'

'Indeed?'

'Yes. Mary of Guise promises to make no further threat against Your Majesty – but upon one condition.'

Elizabeth greeted the news with wary scepticism. 'Oh? And what would be the nature of this . . . this condition?'

'That . . . that Your Majesty considers the proposal of her nephew, the Duke of Anjou.'

Elizabeth didn't miss a beat. 'Ah. That would be the young man of greatest virtue – who is also very

192

handsome. I recall Monsieur de Foix extolling his Grace's virtues at my coronation banquet. I also seemed to recall that I wasn't very impressed.'

'Madam!' This time it was Cecil who wasn't very impressed – with Elizabeth. 'I recall that you repelled Monsieur de Foix with . . . hasty talk of the Duke's aunt.'

'Hasty?' Elizabeth's eyes had narrowed. 'I may have mentioned Mary of Guise and her now proven intentions against me, but I don't recall being hasty.'

Cecil sighed. 'The Duke of Anjou, Your Majesty, would be a very good match. And a marriage would see an end, once and for all, to the situation in Scotland.'

Elizabeth all but flinched at the word 'marriage'. Cecil noted her reaction – and the look that passed between her and Robert Dudley. No, he said to himself. This can never be. Never. He lost his temper.

'For the love of God, Madam, let not the care of your diseased estate hang any longer in the balance!' Pointedly turning one shoulder away from Dudley, he stepped closer to Elizabeth. 'In marriage, and in the production of an heir lies your *only* surety!'

Elizabeth looked at Dudley again. Then a slow smile spread across her face. 'Very well. Invite the Duke of Anjou. We will see him in the flesh.'

Surprised by how easily she had capitulated, Walsingham and Cecil smiled delightedly. Robert Dudley did not. He looked like thunder.

Chapter 12

'I do think Your Majesty would be well advised not to take this course of action.'

'I know what you think, Sir William. You have made your thoughts on this matter abundantly clear.'

Cecil let out a long, exasperated sigh. Elizabeth, too, was making herself abundantly clear. She was bored of his objections. And obdurate in her resolve. 'Perhaps,' he persisted, 'now is not the time.'

'Now is *never* the time for you!' Eyes flashing, Elizabeth turned to him as they reached the top of the steps.

'With the Duke of Anjou arriving . . . '

'His Grace honours us with his visit next week. This matter will be resolved by then.'

Cecil gave up. 'As you wish, your Majesty.' In his heart of hearts, he knew it was already too late. Today the House of Parliament was voting on the most important and most contentious issue yet raised in Elizabeth's reign. And it had been raised by Elizabeth herself.

After that momentous day at the hunting lodge, Elizabeth had been true to her word in tackling her hostile, recalcitrant bishops. She had proposed what she called a Bill of Uniformity, a device whereby Protestants and Catholics would be free to worship alongside each other, each without threat of persecution from the other.

Even Cecil had had to admire the completeness of her understanding of the religious disharmony that still divided her country, and the cunning way she set herself to ending it. The Bill proposed the 1552 prayer book be used in all church services, but that it be modified so as not to offend traditionalists. Even more importantly, the wording of the communion service was to be altered, allowing for the interpretation that Christ was present in spirit – and for the interpretation that he was not.

''Tis a hybrid formula, Your Majesty', Cecil had remarked.

'Aye. And one that shall work. For I know that many people share my non-doctrinaire approach.'

'Maybe. But how many of them sit in Parliament?'

And therein lay the greatest problem; the problem that Elizabeth, walking beside Cecil up the steps to the Houses of Parliament, was hoping to solve today. She was about to present herself to the House, pleading the case for her Bill. In front of and to the Catholic bishops.

'The bishops,' said Cecil as they passed into the courtyard and towards the Great Hall, 'will never vote for a Bill that would see their power decline.'

'Their power shall not decline. Merely their ability to fine and terrorize people. And if that is their view then I would suggest that power has been vested in the wrong people.' With that, Elizabeth stalked ahead towards the monumental doors of the Great Hall. Cecil and the rest of her retinue quickened their pace to keep up.

Nicholas Bacon, wheezing with the effort of manoeuvring his great bulk at speed, craned forward to Cecil. 'You *must* dissuade her', he whispered. 'This is madness – and she will make a fool of herself. They will *never* agree.'

'I know it and you know it.' Cecil shook his head and looked at Elizabeth. Now she was at the door, surrounded by her ladies. They were making last-minute adjustments to her attire. 'But she is convinced she has the power to persuade them.'

'Dressed like that?' Bacon was looking at the sweeping red gown. 'Emphasizing her Protestantism with that colour?'

'It's for the people', sighed Cecil. 'She knew they would throng the route to see her. She says it is her duty to look dazzling.'

And she was dazzling indeed. Jewel had been heaped upon jewel; on her dress, on her bodice, on her sleeves and in her hair.

But Cecil was feeling uncharitable. 'Finery may endear her to the people, but it won't make a whit of difference in the House.'

'Well, go on', urged Bacon. 'Tell her.'

'What? That they won't be impressed by her clothes?'

'*No!*' Bacon rolled his eyes. 'That she must stop this foolishness.'

'Oh very well. But it won't work.'

It didn't.

'How,' asked Elizabeth as Cecil made his last efforts at dissuasion, 'am I to rule this country if my own bishops will not serve me, and speak against me?'

'But they are in a majority! Parliament is over-whelmingly on their side! They will never pass a measure that severs them from Rome!'

Elizabeth wavered for a second. This was Cecil's most impassioned plea yet, and it unnerved her. For the first time since she had known him he looked almost frightened. She wondered if he knew how she felt. Terrified – but utterly resolute.

'Shall we enter?' was her only reply.

The whole panoply of State entered with them. Elizabeth barely noticed. So accustomed was she to the pomp and ceremony that surrounded her whenever she was in public, she hardly registered even this, the most arcane of ceremonies. For here, at the seat of government, her retinue was augmented by men she had once referred to as 'strangers in strange garb'. Her Majesty's Waterman, the Silver Stick in Waiting, the Swanmaster to the Queen and others whose title, let alone existence, she was only dimly aware of.

But more apposite and more worrying was the fact that she was only here on sufferance. She had come as a supplicant, and all present knew it. If the point needed emphasis Elizabeth found it in the clothes of those in the chamber. Most of the two hundred men present were wearing black. All of them bowed as she entered; nearly all looked grim. All of them fell silent.

Elizabeth appeared unperturbed. In contrast to the speed with which she had approached the Great Hall, she appeared to glide with exquisite slowness to the chair of State on the dais at the end of the room. Then she bid her courtiers to take their places beside her and looked round the chamber. There was hardly a friendly face to be seen. And she didn't dare look up to the Strangers' Gallery. She knew that her most powerful enemies would be there. Sussex and Norfolk would be willing her humiliation. She didn't care to dwell on the whereabouts of Robert Dudley.

Then Elizabeth cleared her throat and began the most important address of her young life. 'Members of Parliament. My lords. My lord bishops.' At each stilted phrase she inclined her head to a different part of the chamber, willing everyone present to recognise her humility. Hundreds of blank faces stared back at her. 'I come here today as a humble petitioner, and what I ask is not for myself, but for my people ... who are my care.'

'Oh her *people*', said Norfolk from the gallery. 'Who cares about her people? We are the only *people* that matter.' Beside him, exquisite in a plethora of gold, lace and jewels, Sussex smirked his agreement.

'By this Act of Uniformity,' continued Elizabeth, 'I mean to settle the differences which still tear this country apart ... '

'Oh!' Norfolk turned to his neighbour. 'So it is an *Act* already? I thought it was merely a Bill until it had been passed.'

'Her Majesty,' grinned Suffolk, 'does not understand these things.'

But her Majesty understood perfectly well. By calling it an Act she was instilling into the minds of those present that the passing of her Bill was a *fait accompli*.

'I mean to settle the differences that make one man enemy unto another, even though both be English and more proud of it than anything else!'

Elizabeth paused and looked around to gauge the effect of her words. If anything, the scepticism of her audience had increased.

Undaunted, she pressed on. 'If there is no uniformity of religious worship here, then there can only be fragmentation, dispute and quarrel. My father was made head of a Church of England!' she cried. 'Many did not like it then – and some still find objection, even though he claimed no spiritual authority over the people.'

'Church of England', sneered Norfolk in a whisper. 'And we all know why he became head of *that!*'

'Aye – to marry that whore Anne Boleyn!' grinned Sussex.

'But the Church of England was a broad church for *all* the people, with a common prayer book and a common purpose . . .'

But this was too much for some of the bishops present. A groundswell of dissent rippled through the chamber.

'She has absolutely no chance', said Norfolk. 'Listen to them! She is like a lamb to the slaughter.'

But the lamb was unbowed. 'I ask you to search in your hearts,' finished Elizabeth with passion, 'and tell me if it would not be better now, as English men and women, to find that common purpose again.'

Beside her, Cecil stared out with unseeing eyes as Elizabeth's folly threatened to topple her from her precarious throne. Soon the members and the bishops would begin the voice their objections. It would take only someone like Bishop Gardiner to rouse the entire chamber into a seething mass of discontent and violent opposition.

But Gardiner wasn't there. Walsingham had seen to that. His intelligence had informed him that Gardiner, along with two other bishops, was the most dangerous and powerful of Elizabeth's enemies in the House. It had informed him, as Cecil knew, that she stood no chance against their objections. So he had forestalled those objections with the simple expedient of locking them in the cellars in the bowels of the building.

Gardiner was too pompous to have suspected anything when Walsingham had approached him and asked him if there was somewhere private where they could have a word. He assumed his advice was being sought on how best to dissuade Her Majesty from proposing her ridiculous Bill. Still seething from his failure to divest Elizabeth of her head all those years ago, Gardiner's preferred method of dissuasion was to send her back to the Tower. Yet he knew he couldn't do that. Not yet anyway.

He hadn't the faintest idea that as soon as he and his fellow Bishops were out of sight of their fellow Members of Parliament they would be seized upon by men whom he later referred to as 'Walsingham's brigands' and hustled down to the cellars. Walsingham followed them.

Gardiner soon realized that the last thing Walsingham wanted was his advice.

'I would like to know,' he screeched as the cellar door slammed behind them, 'under what authority you have taken us here? How dare you lock us up when we are wanted on important business else-where?'

'Your Grace must forgive me,' said Walsingham with a smile, 'but it is only for a little while.'

'You have no business to do this. I demand to be released. Guards! Guards! Open this door at once!' Frightened now, Gardiner stormed towards the door and slammed his fist against it.

'The guards,' said Walsingham, 'have departed. You can shout as loud as you wish, but no one will hear you.'

Gardiner began to sweat. Fear was an unfamiliar sensation to him and, like all bullies, he was ill-equipped to deal with it. His fellow bishops stood quietly in the corner. They were content to let Gardiner do the talking. They always were.

'I do not believe,' he lied, 'that you intend to keep us here while the House is voting on the Bill.'

'It is a matter of complete indifference to me what you do or do not believe.' As if to illustrate the point, Walsingham extracted a pack of cards from his cloak and began to shuffle them.

Gardiner jabbed an angry little hand towards the ceiling. 'It will not serve *her* in any case! She has no chance of passing her Bill.'

'No?' Walsingham grinned. 'I could not really answer as to that matter, your Grace, although it is true that I have shortened the odds a little.'

Gardiner began to tremble. Whether from rage or fear Walsingham neither knew or cared. He wagged a finger at Walsingham. 'But there's one thing I *can* tell you. We are not the only members of the House who would oppose her Majesty. As I speak to you now so her detractors will be haranguing her in the Chamber!'

Gardiner was not mistaken on that count. The bishops were voicing strong and concerted opposition and Bishop Smithson, a more respected, balanced and less vituperative individual than Gardiner, was now addressing Elizabeth.

'By this act, Madam, you *force* us to relinquish our allegiance to the Holy Father.'

'I do not *force* you!' countered Elizabeth, 'I ask you!' Then she turned to the room at large and repeated her impassioned plea. 'Can any man, in truth, serve two masters, and be faithful to both?'

Unable to contain himself, Bishop Langley leaped to his feet. 'This is heresy!' he yelled. 'Blasphemy!'

'Hear! Hear!' cried the chorus of dissenters.

'No!' Elizabeth shouted above the din. 'No. Your Grace, it is common sense – which is a most English virtue.'

Some members of Parliament began to laugh. Common sense was not a quality normally associated with Bishop Langley. Even some of his fellow clerics joined in the merriment. Elizabeth sighed with relief. The tide was turning. Hilarity would serve her purposes to greater effect than hostility.

Then a third bishop stood up and looked Elizabeth straight in the eye. 'Your Majesty would improve all these matters,' he said, 'if you would agree to marry.'

Every eye in the room turned to Elizabeth. Even those bored by the religious debate looked at her with keen interest.

Elizabeth only paused for a moment. 'Aye', she said with spirit. 'But marry *who*, your Grace? Will you give me some suggestions?'

Again, a ripple of laughter filled the room. Looking thunderous, the Bishop sat down.

'For some say France,' continued Elizabeth, 'and others Spain, and some cannot abide foreigners at all, so I am not sure how best to please you – unless I marry them all!'

The chamber erupted into gales of laughter. Even Sir William Cecil allowed himself a wry smile. Elizabeth was really playing to her audience now. Playing well – but still losing.

But as there were numerous detractors on the issue of the Bill of Uniformity so there were those who took umbrage at the levity of Elizabeth's remarks about marriage.

Lord Harewood was one of them. Bristling with indignation, he leaped to his feet. 'Now your Majesty makes fun of the sanctity of marriage.'

Elizabeth reacted like lightning. 'I do not think you should lecture me on that, my Lord – since you yourself have been twice divorced, and are now on your third wife!'

Applause as well as more laughter greeted that rejoinder and Lord Harewood, red as a beetroot, sank back into his seat. 'How was I to know,' he later asked his third (and soon to be ex) wife, 'that her Majesty would be so well-informed?' Like others before him – and countless after – Harewood had made the fatal mistake of underestimating his sovereign.

The gales of laughter filtered down into the cellar

beneath the chamber. Walsingham affected not to notice; Gardiner and his fellow bishops looked at each other in alarm. 'Why do they laugh?' gibbered Gardiner. 'What can make them so amused?'

Walsingham, too, was amused. Not so much by the activities in the Great Hall but by his own pursuits. Sitting quietly in the corner of the cellar, he was dealing out the cards. And the card he had just turned over gave him great pleasure. It was the Hanged Man – and it was pointing at Gardiner.

Elizabeth knew she had made enormous progress in striking up a rapport with her audience. But cheers and laughter would not ensure the smooth progress of the Bill through the House. 'Each of you,' she cried out when the laughter had subsided, 'must vote as your conscience dictates. But remember this: in your hands, upon this moment, lies the future happiness of my people, and the peace of this realm.' Then she rose to her feet. 'Let that be upon your conscience also, as I trust in God it will be!'

The bows that accompanied her departure were significantly more deferential than those that had signalled her arrival. Elizabeth felt she was floating on air as she walked out of the room. She had entered the lion's den and emerged unscathed; she had encountered hostility and turned it into respect. She had, she was sure, a good chance of success.

But Cecil took the wind out of her sails. 'Madam,' he whispered as they reached the courtyard. 'What a waste of fine words!'

Elizabeth turned and looked at him through narrowed eyes. It wasn't so much the words that annoyed her, but the manner of his saying them. 'Sir,' she snapped 'do I detect a certain smugness in your tone?'

'Indeed not, Madam. Merely sorrow.'

Elizabeth didn't believe him. 'So you think the Act shall not be passed, you think that my efforts have been in vain?'

'I admire you,' said the master of evasion, 'for your handling of the House.'

'And I used to admire you, Sir William, for your handling of affairs of State. And,' she added, 'your tact.'

An hour later one of the guards returned to the cellar where Walsingham was still playing cards and Gardiner, in desperation, had joined the other bishops in sending up fervent, if unaltruistic prayers to the Almighty. After a whispered consultation with Walsingham, the guard withdrew – leaving the door wide open.

Walsingham put the cards back in his pocket and walked over the bishops.

'I apologise for interrupting your devotions,' he drawled, 'but you are now free to go if you wish.'

'If we wish?' spluttered Gardiner, breaking off from prayer with unseemly haste. 'Do you think we *wished* to be here in the first place?'

'No. But I repeat that you are free to go.'

Belatedly, Gardiner realized why they were being released. Above them, he could hear the sound of hundreds of footsteps as the members of the House filed out of the Great Hall. 'They have voted?' he gasped. 'Already?'

'Indeed they have. And it seems that your presence was sorely missed.' Walsingham was grinning from ear to ear. 'The Act of Uniformity is now law. It was passed by two votes.'

'Two votes?' screamed the apoplectic bishop as the implications of the narrow majority sunk in. 'This is . . . this is monstrous! It is illegal. What you have done is . . . '

'What I have done,' said Walsingham, 'is as nothing compared to what you have done.'

'What do you mean?'

Walsingham didn't reply, merely noted the extra-ordinarily defensive tone of the reply. Then he turned to leave. 'And I would be very careful about what you are planning to do, my Lord Bishop,' he said over his shoulder.

Walsingham didn't turn back to see the effect his words had on Gardiner. He didn't need to: he knew perfectly well that the bishop had turned a deathly shade of white. Intelligence, for Sir Francis Walsingham, was never too dear. And the intelligence he was gathering on Bishop Gardiner was most illuminating indeed. And not even very expensive.

Elizabeth heard the news shortly after she returned to her quarters in the Palace of Whitehall. 'Your Majesty,' said the sombre messenger who was ushered into her presence. 'I bring news from the Parliament.'

One look at his face told Elizabeth all she wanted to know. With a sinking heart, she reached out for the proffered letter. What now, she thought? Ridicule?

Disgrace? It would surely only be a matter of time before her authority was completely undermined. After all, she had started the process herself, had led by example. That thought nearly made her laugh. 'Follow me!' she envisaged herself crying out. 'For I know the best way to ruin and damnation!'

Aware that the messenger was looking at her in a most peculiar manner, she tried to quell her rising hysteria. I have tried, she told herself. And I have failed. That is the start and finish of the matter.

'God's death!' she shrieked as she read the single sentence. 'I have succeeded! The Act of Uniformity is passed!' Her triumphant cry carried to the far end of the room where her ladies had been busying themselves with embroidery. Most of them had also been trying their best to sink through the floorboards. Elizabeth had not been in the best of moods since her return from Parliament.

Now she was gripped by euphoria. 'Thank you!' she shouted at the startled messenger. 'Thank you so much for being the harbinger of such glad tidings. Kat!' she shouted, 'ensure that this fine fellow is rewarded for his gallant efforts!'

The messenger departed with a bemused expression, a shilling in his pocket and the opinion the Queen Elizabeth was the kindest creature who had ever lived.

Queen Elizabeth herself collapsed on a divan near the window. Several thoughts raced through her brain. One was that she had cured England of the cancer that had been gnawing at her very fabric for many years. Another was that Sir William Cecil needed taking down a peg or two. A third was a resolution to follow her instincts in the future. It also crossed her mind that Walsingham was a very fine man indeed and that she was glad she had listened to him on the subject of detaining Gardiner at her pleasure.

The last thought that came to her on the subject of the Bill of Uniformity was that it negated all objections to her marrying a Protestant. Robert Dudley was a Protestant.

The news spread through Europe more quickly than the Black Death. And it was greeted by some with the same shocked disbelief.

Others had made preparations for such an eventuality. Distasteful though it was for him to contemplate, the Pope had not been idle on the subject of Elizabeth's Bill of Uniformity. And he had known about it from the beginning.

'You did well, Father Ballard,' he had said to the blond English priest, 'in informing me of this proposed heresy.'

He changed his tune when Ballard informed him of the outcome of the vote. 'You did not do well enough!' he shouted.

'I . . . I had no time to make sufficient preparations', stammered Ballard. 'Her Majesty surprised us all by rushing the Bill through the house.'

'She is not a Majesty!' The Pope waved a piece of paper in front of the cowering priest. 'She is the bastard daughter of a whore. And she is no longer the Queen of England.'

'Father?'

'Not in the eyes of God. This,' voice rising to a high-pitched scream, he waved the document again, 'is the proof.'

'Yes, Father.' Ballard didn't have a clue what the man was on about. Ballard's knowledge of his religion was, at best, sketchy. His knowledge of clandestine international affairs, however, was infinitely greater. And far more useful to his paymasters. His paymaster-general was Cardinal Ruffirio, with whom he sought an audience after his meeting with the Pope.

'What,' he asked as he walked into the Cardinal's room, 'did the Holy Father mean about the Queen not being a Queen? Has he taken leave of his senses?'

'Insolence!' screamed the Cardinal. 'Such insolence will not be tolerated!'

'I'm sorry, Father,' responded Ballard, not sorry in the least. But as he bowed his token apology, he noted out of the corner of his eye the presence of a third man in the room. His eyes narrowed and his brow furrowed as he tried to place him. 'I don't believe that we have . . . '

'Had the pleasure?' The other man laughed. 'Oh but we have, Father Ballard. Once. In England. Don't tell me you have forgotten already?'

Ballard *had* forgotten. He hadn't the faintest idea of the identity of the flamboyantly dressed, smirking individual sitting opposite the Cardinal. 'Of course,' he replied blithely, 'of course I remember you. We discussed our . . . our mutual interests, did we not?' Given the circumstances, the guess was a fairly safe one. He was here to discuss many things with Ruffirio – among them espionage, treason and murder. The other man was hardly likely to be a casual visitor with a different agenda.

He wasn't.

'His Holiness,' said Ruffirio as he bade Ballard to sit down, 'has issued the Papal Bull. *That*,' he added with a disapproving look at the Englishman, 'is what he meant by Elizabeth no longer being Queen. The Bull of Excommunication deprives her, the pretended Queen of England, of her throne. It also declares that her subjects are absolved of their allegiance to her.'

'Praise be to God', chorused Ballard and the other man in unison.

'And it means,' continued the Cardinal, 'that our work will now be much easier.'

'How so, Father?'

Ruffirio's lower lip curled. The gesture, Ballard knew from experience, constituted a smile. 'Because His Holiness also decrees that any man who should undertake the assassination of Elizabeth will be welcomed by angels into the Kingdom of Heaven.'

Ballard nearly fell off his seat. This was a far more extreme reaction than he had ever dared hope – and proof as far as he was concerned that the Pontiff had taken leave of his senses. Yet what Ruffirio said was true: it would make his job a lot easier.

'You,' continued the Cardinal, turning to the other man, 'will have to be careful at court. News of the Bull will soon be widespread and Catholic ambassadors will be under suspicion.'

'Catholic ambassadors,' countered the other man

in a laconic drawl, 'are always under suspicion. Myself in particular. Elizabeth has never forgiven me.'

Ruffirio brushed that one aside. 'She never will.' Then he laughed. 'She won't have time. I feel in my bones there is precious little time left to her.'

Ballard was now thinking furiously. He was foreign. A Catholic ambassador. But for the life of him, Ballard still couldn't remember who he was.

'And you don't have much time either, my friend. You must persuade our friends in England to act soon.' Ruffirio leaned across the desk to the ambassador. 'Give my blessing and hope to those friends, Excellence. And give my particular good wishes to our friend the Duke of Norfolk. You,' he added to Ballard, 'will also go back to England. But you shall have no contact with Monseigneur Alvaro de la Quadra.'

Alvaro de la Quadra.

'You shall have no contact with the English court at all. No, Father Ballard, you will stick to the streets. Stay with the common people. For that is where you will find those who will try to foil us. That is where you will find the spies of Sir Francis Walsingham.'

Then Ruffirio stood up, signalling that the audience was over. De la Quadra and Ballard followed suit. To the former's surprise, Ruffirio picked up a packet of letters on his desk and handed them to Ballard. 'But you shall take these letters, Father Ballard. They are too inflammatory to risk being seen at court. And you shall see that they are delivered into the right hands. You may,' he finished, 'have to wait some time.'

De la Quadra would have been exceedingly surprised, and not a little concerned to know that the letters were addressed to his greatest friend and ally in the English court – the Duke of Norfolk.

Chapter 13

'I must confess that I am rather enjoying his Grace's visit.'

'But you have only met him once, Madam.'

Elizabeth giggled. 'Yes. And a highly memorable occasion that was too. Did I tell you what he said to me?'

Kat turned pink. 'Indeed you did. And you say you enjoyed his company?'

'I found him tolerably amusing.'

'I don't think he meant to be amusing, Madam.'

'No.' Elizabeth stood still as Kat put the finishing touches to her elaborate head-dress. 'I don't suppose he did.'

Elizabeth had confounded her court with the expensive and exacting arrangements she had ordered for the Duke of Anjou's visit. Immediately after the passing of the Act of Uniformity, she had turned her attention to his impending arrival. 'We must ensure that his Grace enjoys every possible comfort and every courtesy we can afford him', she had declared. 'He must leave our shores with the fondest possible memories, with an indelible impression of our greatness and of the extent of our regard for him.'

This was a far cry from her original attitude. Cecil had been convinced that after the success of the Act of Uniformity, she would change her mind about Anjou and rescind her invitation. Instead she had gone to great lengths to ensure that he would be welcome. To most people, her attitude was puzzling in the extreme.

Not to Robert. His hurt and annoyance about the visit had turned to amusement when Elizabeth had informed him of the reasons for her enthusiasm. 'Don't you see?' she laughed. 'If I show a high regard for Anjou, if I feign interest in his proposal, it will keep them quiet on the subject of my marriage.'

Robert wasn't so sure. 'Not for long.'

'Yes, for long. For as long as I can keep them guessing. It is a woman's prerogative,' she said with a wicked smile, 'to vacillate on the subject of marriage, to consider a proposal most carefully before accepting it, to dwell at length on all aspects of the man she might marry.'

'I thought there was only one man on whose aspects you wished to dwell.'

'Robert! I do believe you are being crude.'

'Me? Never!' But Robert's lascivious grin was at odds with his protestation. So, a moment later, was the movement of his body under the bedclothes.

The events of the day at the hunting lodge were now, by tacit consent, distant memories. Since then, the relationship between Elizabeth and Robert had continued as before; loving, constant – and the subject of ever more scurrilous rumours. Only the imminent arrival of the Duke of Anjou, and Elizabeth's constant and enthusiastic references to it kept her other councillors from haranguing her on the subject of marriage. Like Cecil, they considered the Duke to be entirely suitable: the marriage would put an end to the troubles in Scotland and, furthermore, would be a fitting postscript to the Act of Uniformity. It would unite a Protestant with a Catholic on the throne of England.

And then, two weeks after the passing of the Act, Anjou had arrived with a splendid, gilded entourage and began to press his suit.

'I can scarcely believe,' said Elizabeth as Kat fastened the last jewels in her hair, 'that anyone could have thought him a handsome fellow.'

'No. Nor indeed tall.' Then Kat too began to giggle. 'Never have I seen such an unprepossessing little man. And his poor pock-marked face!' She clicked her tongue. 'Heaven knows what treatments they use for smallpox on the Continent.'

'Probably none', ventured Elizabeth. 'Still,' she remembered with a smile, 'he was very complementary about my own complexion.'

'And about your other attributes.'

Elizabeth burst out laughing. Anjou had been in her presence for precisely one minute when he had leered at her and whispered the words that Elizabeth would never forget. 'I dream of the moment', he had rasped in his lisping French, 'when we are naked together, and I can caress your thighs.'

Elizabeth had been so stunned that she had been unable to summon a reply. She had merely stared in open-mouthed amazement. Then she had started to giggle.

Anjou had been astonished – and not a little upset. He had been led to assume this was the sort of talk Elizabeth wanted to hear. 'You would not like me to do that, no?'

'Perhaps,' replied Elizabeth, struggling to keep a straight face, 'but I am very religious, your Grace.'

'Ah!' Anjou had been delighted with that. 'Me too, Your Majesty. Me too.'

No one else had heard the exchange, but Cecil, looking on, had been delighted that Anjou had been able to bring a smile to Elizabeth's face so quickly. A meeting that he had secretly been dreading appeared, after all, to be highly propitious. The rumours about Anjou, he concluded, must be just that. Wicked and unsubstantiated gossip.

'His Grace,' said Kat as she stepped back to admire her handiwork, 'will be in raptures.'

'So, I hope, will someone else.'

Kat didn't reply.

'So.' Elizabeth moved over to the window. 'All augurs well for the pageant?'

'Indeed, Madam. They are already saying it will be the finest yet seen in London.'

'Good. I aim to please. And I do love a party.'

Elizabeth had – literally – pushed the boat out for the pageant in honour of the Duke of Anjou. The huge pageant was to take place on the river; a glittering tableau involving dozens of barges, hundreds of musicians, a dazzling display of fireworks and, for the benefit of the Londoners themselves, free feasting on the illuminated banks of the Thames. Cecil had been deeply disapproving, claiming that not even Anjou merited such extravagance. Elizabeth's reply had been to accuse him of being a pedant and a killjoy. Then she had further goaded him by ordering the State barge to be refurbished. 'A canopy of red and gold,' she stipulated, 'under which I shall sit on a throne scalloped into the shape of a shell.'

Cecil had been livid. 'But his Grace the Duke of Anjou has his own barge!'

'Indeed he has – and I have mine.'

The point needed no elaboration. And nor did Cecil find it necessary to ask who would have the pleasure of Elizabeth's company in her vessel. 'Madness', he mumbled under his breath when she had gone. 'Sheer folly. She will undo all the good she has done, disporting herself like some wanton Cleopatra.'

The analogy was cruel but, in the event, not inaccurate. Later that evening, as the haunting music of the lutes floated through the warm night air, a stately fleet of barges shimmered down the Thames. Revellers on Tower Bridge looked on in awe as the procession glided towards them. Few could identify the nobles in their various craft, but none could mistake Elizabeth. Clad in brilliant scarlet, glittering like an opalescent jewel, she reclined on silken cushions at the rear of the State barge. The drapes of the canopy had been drawn back, opening the barge to the stars. But nothing in that heavenly constellation shone so brightly as the Queen of England.

Elizabeth wouldn't have been surprised to be told she *was* in heaven. She had never been so happy in her life. Water, her favourite element, surrounded her; music soothed her; the gentle laughter of her people cheered her and the attentions of her courtiers flattered her. But they were not with her in the barge.

Like a cluster of less valuable jewels to complement her lustre, they were grouped round her in other magnificent barges. Her ladies, as protocol demanded, were with her. But they were at the front of the barge.

Robert Dudley was her only companion at the rear.

Both were intoxicated. Not on the wine they were quaffing but on each other's company, on the glory of the night and on the attentions of the crowds on the riverbank. As they floated down the river they were serenaded with cries of affection, deluged with flowers thrown from the water's edge, and illuminated in their finery by the blazing torches around them.

Yet where the people were in raptures of delight, Elizabeth's court was quietly seething. They had never seen such a blatant display of wantonness, such an overt declaration of love. For there could be no mistaking the signal Elizabeth was sending out. She was snubbing the Duke of Anjou – and succumbing to the charms of the snake in their midst.

Anjou himself seemed to find the whole display amusing rather than insulting. The French Ambassador to England, however, was practically foaming at the mouth. De Foix had envisaged this evening as the culmination of all his dreams; he had entertained fond and confident hopes of Elizabeth and Anjou supping wine together in the State barge. He had visualised the Duke's increasing ardour and the Queen's compliance. Most of all, he had marked the evening out as the nadir of the diplomatic career. He, de Foix, would be recognized at the engineer of this glorious match. He would surely be rewarded as such. He would be recalled to France and elevated to a Dukedom.

Instead, he sat in Anjou's barge and watched the Queen of England giggling with a *parvenu* plaything who was, to add insult to injury, only an earl. The shame was intolerable.

Anjou was watching as well. 'The Queen,' he mused, 'seems most familiar with her companion – does she not?'

'Yes,' replied de Foix through pursed lips. 'Lord Robert Dudley – only *recently* created the Earl of Leicester.' Then he remembered that it was Anjou, not himself, who should have been in Dudley's place. He turned to the Duke and adopted the obsequious manner of his calling. 'Your Grace must understand that she is a woman! And . . . and that women are strange and irrational creatures. They say one thing,' he added with a sidelong glance at the State barge, 'but they mean another! They flatter one man only because they are really in love with another. No man,' he finished with impressive conviction, 'can unlock their secrets.'

'Unless,' laughed Anjou, 'he was a very large key!'

Dutifully, de Foix laughed with the Duke. Inside, he was still seething. The Duke, he thought, was even more of a fool than he had been led to believe. A mere cipher for the ambitions of his aunt. He didn't even know why he was bothering to make excuses for Elizabeth; Anjou didn't seem to care. And his jokes weren't even amusing. De Foix took another gulp of wine and rued the day he had been sent to the Godforsaken backwater that was England.

But for others, England was an enchanted isle. In the State barge, Elizabeth and Robert were revelling in its delights. And, now, its poetry.

'Say those lines Robert. Say them to me softly.'

Robert's hand brushed against Elizabeth's. 'Which lines, my love?'

'You know . . . "I wonder by my troth . . . "'

'Ah!' Robert looked up to the stars. When he looked back at Elizabeth it was through eyes that carried the loving message of his words.

'"I wonder by my troth, what thou,
And I did, 'till we loved?
Were we not weaned 'till then,
But sucked on country pleasures,
Childishly?
Or snorted we in the seven sleepers' den?
'Twas so, but this,
All pleasures fancies be.
If ever any beauty I did see,
Which I desired, and got,
'Twas but a dream
Of thee."'

Elizabeth herself was dreaming by the time he finished. She dreamed that she was floating on an ethereal plane high above the water. A luminescent light bathed her body and her soul, cosseting her against the cares of the world. She felt safe, protected – and blissfully happy. For the light was that of Robert's all-consuming love.

Then she felt touched by something else. On the

cusp between waking and dreaming, her eyes flickered and a small frown furrowed her brow. When she opened her eyes she found that the touch was that of Robert's hand on her cheek. Oblivious to everything except each other, they stared deep into each other's eyes.

Robert traced the delicate line of her lips with his fingertips. 'Marry me', he said.

The words seemed not to register with Elizabeth but to drift past her into the warm night air.

'Marry me.'

Elizabeth *had* heard. She heard nothing but the soft, urgent entreaties and the rapid beating of her own heart. 'Robert . . . '

'Marry me.' It was a command now.

Elizabeth had never seen him look so serious. Suddenly she was afraid; frightened that she may still be dreaming and that the moment would end with a thundering intrusion of reality. She would open her eyes and find that she was staring at Cecil or one of her courtiers and that they were discussing affairs of State. Worse, she would find that her suitor was Anjou and that she was staring with cold indifference into his pock-marked face.

She leaned back and stared up at the stars. They were real enough. So were the other sights around her, and the sounds of merriment from the barges close by. Then she looked back at Robert and knew that neither he nor his words were illusory.

'On a night such as this,' she whispered, 'could any woman say no?'

'Ah! But could a Queen say no?'

'Does a Queen,' teased Elizabeth, 'not sit under the same stars as any other woman?'

'You do not take me seriously, Madam.' Robert was grinning as he spoke, but there was an element of doubt behind his comments. She thought he was playing games. He wasn't. Suddenly he leaped to his feet and called across to the barge beside them. Almost as grand as Elizabeth's it was somehow ostentatious where hers was stately; vulgar where hers was sumptuous. It was Norfolk's.

But it wasn't to the grim-faced Duke that Robert called out. It was to Norfolk's guest of honour – Alvaro de la Quadra.

'Monseigneur de la Quadra!' he cried. 'Monseigneur! I beg you, a word in your ear!'

More than a little surprised at being called into the Queen's presence, de la Quadra had no choice but to obey the summons. Elizabeth's hostility to him was no secret, she could hardly even bring herself to look at him. Yet as he made his way to the edge of Norfolk's barge he saw her, barely five feet away, reclining on her cushions and smiling at him in a languid, lazy and distinctly friendly manner. Then he looked more closely and suspected that she was drunk. No one could look that delirious on the elixir of life alone.

De la Quadra bowed. 'Your Majesty . . . my Lord.' The greeting to Elizabeth was unctuous, that to Robert was uttered through pursed lips.

But Robert appeared not to notice. 'Tell me,' he said, 'as well as an ambassador, are you not also a bishop?'

De la Quadra addressed his response to Elizabeth. 'Indeed I am, your Majesty.'

Elizabeth's eyes gleamed with barely suppressed excitement. It couldn't, she thought, be true.

It was. Robert clapped his hands and let out a great bellow of delight. 'Then you can marry us!'

De la Quadra reeled back as if he had been hit. 'M . . . *marry* you?'

'Yes!' Elizabeth was laughing now. 'Here and now! This very night!' She could barely contain her delight. Robert was serious in his proposal, but not in his request to ask the Spaniard to marry them. De la Quadra was being teased, was having his nose rubbed in the bitterest irony of all. Elizabeth would not marry his King, but her own courtier.

De la Quadra took himself far too seriously even to contemplate that others might not. He stood with his mouth wide open and his hands flapping comically at his sides. 'I . . . I . . . '

'Perhaps,' giggled Elizabeth, 'he does not know enough English to perform the ceremony!'

De la Quadra did not find that amusing. Nor did see anything funny about Elizabeth's intention to marry Robert Dudley. But now something else was preying on his mind. On this, of all nights, he had no desire to step any closer to Elizabeth. He had no wish to be on her barge. He was desperate to keep his distance. He took his refuge under the mantle of his calling. 'Madam', he said with another, rather stiff bow. 'I would gladly play your priest – if you would rid yourself of all the heretics in your party.'

'Oh fie, Monseigneur! You know that cannot be!'

'Then, alas, I can be no help to Your Majesty. Forgive me.' With palpable relief, de la Quadra turned on his heel and returned to the sanctuary of the stern of Norfolk's barge.

Still laughing, Robert settled himself beside Elizabeth again.

'You shouldn't have done that', she said with mock severity.

'Oh why not? It was only a game.'

'Was it?' There was a faint hint of dejection in Elizabeth's voice.

Robert touched her cheek with exquisite tenderness. 'Only partly.' Then his eyes locked with hers. '*Will* you?' he whispered.

Again Elizabeth was oblivious to everything around her. The tinkling laughter, the ripping water and the lights that flickered all around receded into the distance. Only Robert was real – and the answer that was forming on her lips. She knew she was no longer dreaming, that nothing of the brutal world outside this enchanted moment could intrude on her happiness.

She was wrong.

Later, Elizabeth would recall the episode in slow motion. She would remember how Robert's loving expression changed to mirror her own, how the shock turned to horror and how her response died on her lips to be replaced by a terrified scream. The blinding flash as the pistol was fired seemed to illuminate the entire sky; the sharp crack of the report resonated loud and long. But it was the whine of the bullet and sound of the splintering wood above their heads that she would remember most vividly.

'God's death!' Elizabeth's first instinct was to leap to her feet. 'Robert! What is happening?'

'Majesty!' The word lashed at her like a whip. The soldier behind it, appearing from nowhere, threw himself against her, pinning her down on the cushions.

He was only just in time. Another flash; another bang – and a truer aim. A low moan from the soldier as his body jerked on top of her in a macabre mockery of love. Then a wetness, a cloying stickiness as his life-force left him and his blood ran through to his Queen.

Then pandemonium. Beside her, paralysed with shock, Robert was aware of terrified screams and shouts, of the heavy tread of soldiers as they leaped across the barges. But it was the man in black he remembered. Materializing out of the darkness, he appeared beside him, pushed him roughly to one side and bent down to the soldier. With a strength that belied his slight frame, he heaved the dead man aside and bent down to Elizabeth. 'Madam . . . '

But Elizabeth couldn't reply. Breathless and rigid with shock, she found herself unable to move. All she felt was a numbness and then a terrible chill. Her face was like a death mask, but above her was a mask of concern. 'Robert . . . ?'

Then she fainted. It was only much later that she learned that Francis Walsingham had swept her into his arms and had not let her go until she was safely inside the Palace.

She never knew of, and no one had seen, the look that had passed between the Duke of Norfolk and

Alvaro de la Quadra as the bullet meant for her had taken the life of another.

Once Elizabeth was safely back in her Privy Chambers she was quick to recover her spirits. She had to be. Sir William Cecil had swung into action and he wasn't going to be deflected by womanly vices of swooning.

'From this present danger,' he said, 'I pray your Majesty may be well delivered.'

'How so, Sir William?'

'If you will only heed my advice.'

Elizabeth didn't reply. She was familiar with that advice and with the grim look that heralded it. She was only thankful that, at the moment, she couldn't see that look.

'Madam?' Cecil stepped closer to the screen that had been placed round Elizabeth.

'I am still here, Sir William. I think to spare you the sight of me until my ladies have finished.'

'Hush, madam,' soothed Kat. 'If you will remain still for a moment I could just . . . '

Elizabeth remained still. Kat began to sponge the dried blood on her face. Around her, the other ladies helped divest her of her blood-soaked dress.

But Cecil's distress and anger were greater than his realization that his timing was off. For the Palace was in turmoil, the royal entourage was in shock and Privy Council in panic.

Where Walsingham had taken charge of Elizabeth, Cecil had commanded the situation. He had organized the carriage to take Elizabeth back to the Palace under armed guard, he had sent soldiers to scour London for the assassin and he had decided who would – and who would not – be allowed into the Privy Chamber. Robert Dudley was not allowed. In Elizabeth's wake until they reached her apartments, he had been barred by the guards from going any further.

Sir William Cecil had been pushed beyond the limit of endurance and now he was going to act.

'Madam', he pleaded. 'You must heed my advice to marry . . . and to save your reputation from this . . . this woeful scandal.'

Behind the screen, Elizabeth's eyes flickered in alarm. 'What scandal?'

'You and Lord Robert!' shouted Cecil. 'It is said that he visits your chambers at night!' Then he lost control altogether. 'It is said that you fornicate with him – and even that you already carry his child!'

The women behind the screen didn't know where to look. No one had ever heard Sir William Cecil utter such words. Their effect was almost as shocking as the crack of the shots that had pierced the stillness of the night. And for Elizabeth, they were doubly shocking. Someone had betrayed her. She glanced at Isabel Knollys. The other woman lowered her eyes.

A terrible sense of loneliness gripped Elizabeth.

'Sir William', she said, steeling herself to remain calm. 'I do not live in a corner. As you see I am constantly surrounded by my ladies. Since my life is so open, I do not understand how so bad a judgement can have been found of me.'

Those words were intended to shame Isabel as

much as to placate Cecil. They worked with the former. Not with the latter.

'Madam,' said Isabel, not looking at her mistress. 'If you would remain still for one moment more . . . '

'Oh very well!' Allowing Isabel to fasten a new dress around her, Elizabeth stood impatiently as she fastened the hooks. Then, pale but composed, she appeared from behind the screen.

'You! Elizabeth stopped in her tracks and glared at the man beside Cecil. 'What . . . ?'

'Madam.' De Foix bowed low. 'The Duke of Anjou would know of your answer to his suit. The patience of princes,' he added with a smirk, 'is not infinite.'

'The Duke cannot love me so much,' spat Elizabeth, 'if he demands my answer so precipitously!'

But de Foix appeared totally impervious to Elizabeth's rage. It was the rage of another woman, of Mary of Guise, that he feared more. 'Perhaps,' he suggested, 'your Majesty will not answer because your heart is already set upon another.' Then, feigning regret, he shook his head. 'But, alas, you cannot marry Lord Robert.'

Elizabeth stiffened. So, beside de Foix, did Cecil. Suddenly he was no longer angry with his Queen. Instead he felt terribly sorry for her. First an attempt on her life – and now this. In a way, this was going to be worse. Monarchs were under constant threat from pistols fired by unknown assailants. Few of them lived in fear of blows of this magnitude.

With a supreme effort, Elizabeth threw the question as casually as she could to de Foix; as if she were only politely interested in his response. Inside, she was quaking. 'Why do you say I cannot marry Lord Robert?'

'Because,' answered de Foix, 'he is married already.'

Chapter 14

Elizabeth stayed in bed for a week. Cecil had been accurate in his summation that the second blow would cripple her. She refused to see anyone other than her ladies. To Kat, it was as if she had reverted to childhood: when she wasn't raging in fury, she clung to Kat and cried until she exhausted both herself and her tears. Kat herself was appalled that she herself had not known of Robert's marriage. She had known of his increasing arrogance and his outrageous flirting when Elizabeth's back was turned – but not about *this*.

Relentless grilling of the other ladies revealed that she was not alone – only Isabel Knollys had known of Robert's clandestine marriage.

'And you didn't *tell* anyone?' Kat's anger was quick to find an outlet.

'I was not aware the matter was of any great importance.'

'*Importance?* You do not regard Her Majesty's happiness as a matter of importance?'

Aware that she was in danger of digging her own grave, Isabel lowered her eyes. 'I . . . I did not know that the . . . the liaison between her Majesty and Lord Robert was of a serious nature. Anyway,' she added, forestalling Kat's disbelieving response, 'Lord Robert was ashamed of his marriage. He had been forced into it by his father. He . . . he was trying to end it.'

Kat felt faint stirrings of unease welling within her breast. 'How come you know so much about it?'

'I know his wife, Amy Robsart. She is the daughter of a Norfolk landowner. She too was averse to the marriage.'

'Why so? Lord Robert is attractive, and his family was powerful.'

'She was only sixteen at the time. Robert was the fifth Dudley son but heir to none of the Dudley money. Amy,' finished Isabel with a look that verged on the contemptuous, 'was very wealthy.'

'Why is none of this known at court?'

'Amy never wanted to come to court. She lives quietly in Oxfordshire. She is quite opposite in nature to her husband.'

Still Kat nursed a vague suspicion that Isabel was keeping something from her. A woman who lived quietly in Oxfordshire and who hated court life didn't sound much like a friend of the gregarious Isabel. 'Children?' she asked. 'Don't tell me they have children?'

'Oh no. It is but a marriage in name only. I told you, Lord Robert has been trying to end it almost since it began.'

Kat snorted. 'He doesn't seriously think he could divorce her and marry the Queen?'

'I don't know', said Isabel. 'I am not privy to his innermost thoughts.'

The court could talk of little other than Robert Dudley's marriage. But no man talked to Robert himself. Never popular on account of his looks, his skills, his background and his special place in the Queen's heart, he was now shunned wherever he went. The words 'traitor' and 'coward' echoed down corridors in his wake and, like his few real friends, wafted into the breeze. No man wanted to associate with him. Until Elizabeth chose to broadcast the extent of her wrath, no one dared be seen with him.

That, at least, was the public reaction. In private, there were several people who wished to have business with Robert Dudley. One of them was Monseigneur Alvaro de la Quadra.

He had been very busy since the night on the Thames. His initial fury that Elizabeth had emerged unscathed from the assassination attempt melted away in the face of the new sensation at court. De la Quadra saw an opportunity to pursue a new, more subtle yet equally incendiary course of action. One that would damage Elizabeth as surely as an assassin's pistol. And one that would be sweet revenge for the indignity he suffered that night on the barge.

For three days de la Quadra busied himself with plans. On the fourth day he lay in wait for Robert as he went about his increasingly solitary business.

Robert was startled and not a little unnerved when the Spanish Ambassador sidled up to him in the lower Privy Corridor. 'A word, my Lord,' he whispered.

Robert whirled round. 'What? What about?'

De la Quadra's only response was to beckon him with a finger as he slunk back into the shadows. Robert shrugged and followed him. Nothing, he reasoned, could be worse than his present predicament.

'I see it is true', said de la Quadra with a glint in his

232

eye. 'The Queen still favours you above all others. And yet, there is this . . . this impediment to your marriage.'

She favours me still? thought Robert in surprise. Still. Then there is hope . . .

'Yes.' De la Quadra shook his head. 'This impediment. And then there is the unfortunate matter of your position at court. Many enemies: no friends. But,' he added after a moment, 'it could be otherwise.'

Warning bells began to ring in Robert's mind. 'How so? How do you mean – otherwise?'

De la Quadra moved closer. 'If you would be prepared, in secret, to renounce your heresy and embrace the true faith, then you might find many new, powerful friends which you had not before. And,' he finished with a triumphant leer, 'the impediment would be . . . removed.'

Robert's flesh began to crawl. He stepped back and eyed the other man with lip-curling distaste. 'You are most mistaken, Monseigneur,' he snapped, 'if you think I might so easily be persuaded to act against my conscience – and my love.'

'Ah!' De la Quadra seemed not in the least offended. 'But what will a man not do . . . for love?' He smiled, and was still smiling as he walked away. He was sure that it would only be a question of time. It was always the same with men like Robert Dudley: vain, ambitious and weak, they always came round in the end. And if he needed a little persuasion . . . well, de la Quadra would see to that.

*

The death at Cumnor Place took place on the day of the Abingdon fair. No one was there to witness it and, for that very reason, there were countless people who swore they knew exactly what had happened. Had the deceased been someone of little importance, then the word 'accident' would have been attributed to the unfortunate event and the matter would have ended there. Had the servants not been given leave to attend the fair then there would surely have been witnesses – and a little less suspicion surrounding the event. And had the staircase been steep there would have been no doubt that someone could meet their death by falling down it. Even if the deceased had been old or infirm a reasonable explanation for the fall and the resultant broken neck could have been offered.

But the lady who was found dead at the foot of the shallow staircase after the Abingdon fair was only twenty-four. She had been in radiant good health. Only the fact that she was alone in death seemed fitting. For she had also been alone in life. For while she lived quietly in Oxfordshire, her husband lived at court.

'Murderer!' thundered the Duke of Norfolk.

Robert reeled back in horror.

'Hah!' Norfolk gestured to Robert's sombre clothing and ashen countenance. 'We see you prefer to act the part of the grieving widower. And a good performance too. But,' he sneered, 'we know better, don't we, Sussex?'

Undecided as to whether he should look supercilious or disgusted, Sussex wavered somewhere in between – and ended up looking stupid. 'And we are amazed,' he added, 'that you show your face at court!'

Looking at their smug expressions, Robert felt the dread hand of reality settle on his shoulder. He castigated himself for being blind, cursed himself for not having realized the truth. For three days he had been wandering round in a daze, first at Whitehall where the news had been brought to him, then in Oxfordshire where he had looked upon the corpse of his wife, bowed his head – and felt accusatory looks of her servants descend on him.

It was the same when he returned to London. The coincidence was too great: Amy Robsart, invisible in life but notorious in death. Amy, the hidden impediment to Robert's union with Elizabeth. Amy – deceased. The finger of suspicion pointed from behind walls, from far-flung corners of the rambling Palace, and the voices whispered and gloated by day and haunted Robert by night. 'Guilty!' they choroused.

Robert Dudley was guilty of many things, but not of the murder of his wife. Now, as he looked at Norfolk and Sussex, he recalled his conversation with Alvaro de la Quadra. He remembered the night on the river when the Spanish Ambassador had sat cosseted with the two nobles on Norfolk's barge. And he realized with horror that Norfolk's ambition knew no bounds. He was bent on toppling Elizabeth from her throne. And he would take Dudley down as well.

'You . . . you know that I,' stammered Robert, 'you *know* that I am not a murderer. It was *you!* You . . . '

Norfolk laughed and shook his head. 'Poor, sad,

buxom, country Amy! Who else can we blame but you?'

'Look in a mirror!' roared Robert. 'Look in a mirror, your Grace!'

'Pah! Me? I would not wet my finger on such a wench. But you? You rut with anything! You see, Lord Robert, I *know*.' Stepping closer, he looked deep into Robert's eyes. 'There is nothing you can hide from me. Nothing!'

Then, with his magnificent cape billowing behind him and the complaint Sussex at his side, he turned on his heel and marched down the corridor.

Robert was left with the distinctly uneasy feeling that Norfolk *did* know; that Norfolk knew everything. It wasn't just the cold of the windswept corridor that made Robert shiver. It was the realization that he was slowly being sucked into a vortex of deceit from which there would be no escape.

Then some unknown force impelled him to look upwards, towards the first floor of the Palace and the apartments where Elizabeth had lain in bed for more than a week. There had been no word from her; no sign. He wondered if she had already cut him completely out of his life.

He would have been extremely surprised that Elizabeth was no longer angry with him. Nor had she decided to cut him out of her life. While the news of Amy's existence had cut her to the quick, the fact of her death had made her look deeper into her heart. What she had found there disturbed her at first. Then she remembered that she was Queen. Her findings still disturbed her, but to a lesser extent. Walsingham, she found herself thinking, would liken what she found to a card in a pack. He would say that you played the hand you were dealt. For the first time in days, she found that she was smiling.

Behind her, Kat Ashley was frowning. Kat was not accustomed to dealing with moral dilemmas and this one disturbed her greatly. Wrestling with her conscience, she decided that she must tell Elizabeth. Then she concluded that she mustn't; that she would be lending credence to court gossip and should keep quiet instead.

'Kat?' Elizabeth noted her worried frown in the mirror. 'Is there anything wrong?'

'No, Madam. On the contrary. I am delighted that you have decided to make an appearance tonight.'

'Mmm', Elizabeth responded without much enthusiasm. 'I cannot stay hidden for ever. I have not been in Council for over a week, I am ruling over a country that is now more precarious than ever, and people will think me frightened of assassins if I stay here much longer.'

'Nonsense, Madam. Everyone knows that you needed quiet to recover from the shock of the attempt on your life.'

This wasn't strictly true, and both Kat and Elizabeth knew it. The official line for Elizabeth's protracted absence from court was that she was recovering from the trauma of the assassination attempt. Everyone knew better: Elizabeth was recovering from the news of Robert Dudley's marriage – and the untimely death of his wife. No one had dared say a word, but those who thought Robert guilty suspected that he had a partner in crime: Elizabeth.

Suddenly Kat couldn't bear the thought of her mistress appearing at the evening's festivities and trailing a cloud of suspicion in her wake. 'Madam,' she said. 'I must speak of it. I cannot stay silent any longer.'

'Speak of what?'

'They say . . . that is, some people say that . . . that it was you who ordered Mistress Dudley's death.' The words came out in a rush and, when she had finished, Kat drew back instinctively. She knew what Elizabeth's reaction would be, she could see it in the eyes reflected in the mirror: a cold, intense fury.

Elizabeth made to rise, to round on Kat and shout at her to get out of her sight and remain there for ever. Then, with supreme self-control, she checked herself and took a long, deep breath.

'Kat,' she asked in a surprisingly calm voice, 'do you really think that of me?'

'No, Madam.'

'Really?'

'No, Madam.' This time Kat responded with feeling – and no little relief. She realized that she hadn't asked herself the question. Had she done so before, she would never have delivered a verdict of 'guilty'.

'Thank God!' sighed Elizabeth. 'Thanks be to God. You who know me best in the world; if you had thought me capable of such a thing . . . '

'But,' said Kat with a vigour that surprised her, 'I fear for you. If you marry Lord Robert, I think he is like to prove unkind.'

To her even greater astonishment, Elizabeth simply smiled. 'Yes', she sighed. 'You need not tell me his faults, Kat. I know him too well. I know his vanity . . . I know how he flirts with other women. But . . . but in this world, Kat, I have had so much sorrow and so little joy . . . ' She turned round and looked Kat in the eye. 'He makes me laugh, Kat. He knows me better than any man.'

'I know.' Kat reached out and put a hand on Elizabeth's shoulder.

'Is it such a crime to . . . to have someone near me who makes me laugh?'

'No, Madam. No, it is not.' But Kat couldn't help feeling that where Robert Dudley used to laugh he would now make her cry. Again and again.

'Now,' said Elizabeth in a firmer voice, 'finish my hair and we shall descend to the dance. Poor old Anjou will be thinking that I am most remiss as a hostess. I wonder that he is not bored of pressing his suit!'

He was. Anjou had danced attendance outside Elizabeth's chambers every day for a week and had quite given up hope that she would ever deign to see him again. He cared not a whit for himself, but he was deeply concerned on account of his aunt. If he didn't marry Elizabeth soon then he would be at the receiving end of the wrath of Mary of Guise. He had been there many times before and had not found it pleasant.

It was a surprisingly affable de Foix who informed Elizabeth that the Duke was not present. 'Unfortunately, his Grace is indisposed', the Frenchman winced and patted his stomach. 'He has some bad pains of the stomach.'

'Ah! You French – always succumbing to the *mal de foie*.'

De Foix roared with laughter. 'Madam, a fine jest indeed! I had not likened by name to the name of the . . . what is it you call it in English?'

'Liver.'

'Yes.' De Foix began to look doubtful. Perhaps it hadn't been such a funny joke at all.

'But my jest was in poor taste', said Elizabeth. 'I am very sorry to hear that his Grace is indisposed.' Then she held out her left hand and, with her right, began to slip a ruby ring off her finger. 'I had intended to give him this ring. As a token of my love.'

'Oh.' *Love?* De Foix began to look hopeful. 'Well,' he said, reaching for it, 'perhaps if I relay the message and give him the ring . . . '

'No.' Elizabeth replaced it on her finger. 'We will give it to him ourselves.'

De Foix blanched. 'Madam . . . I should not . . . no . . . his Grace is . . . unprepared to meet Her Majesty.'

'Then we shall surprise him!' In high good humour and followed by an equally ebullient Kat, Elizabeth turned and headed out of the room. She failed to notice that nearly everyone present was staring at her. All were dumbfounded by the casual manner she had appeared at the dance, smiling and laughing as if nothing had happened. Those she had already greeted were further stunned by her conversation: she had chatted merrily and had not even asked one astonished courtier if Lord Robert had arrived yet.

She seemed blissfully unaware that the entire court was waiting on tenterhooks for her opinion and verdict on the scandal of Dudley's wife – and equally ignorant of the fact that some of those present already had her marked down as a murderess.

But de Foix's reaction to his exchange with Elizabeth had nothing to do with Dudley. Thrown into a blind panic, intent on stopping Elizabeth, he rushed after her. 'Your Majesty!' he panted as he hurried down the corridor. 'I really don't think now is the time . . . '

'That,' interrupted Elizabeth, 'is what my friend Sir William Cecil is given to saying.' She waved a dismissive hand at the hapless Ambassador as they reached the staircase leading to Anjou's apartments. 'And I am bored of that particular refrain. Kindly desist from interrupting me, Monsieur de Foix. I am sure that a visit from me will lift the Duke's spirits.'

Behind her, de Foix cringed and then crossed himself. He was quite sure that the visit would do no such thing. On the contrary, it would herald the abrupt termination of Anjou's visit, the end of Mary of Guise's hopes for his marriage to Elizabeth – and possibly de Foix's career.

'God's death!' exclaimed Elizabeth as they reached the door to Anjou's chamber. 'It would appear that he has visitors already. It sounds like a veritable party in there.' Frowning slightly, she listened to the raucous screams and the high-pitched laughter from the other side of the door. 'It would appear that you are wrong, Monsieur de Foix. Now *is* the time.' She turned and smiled at the ashen-faced Frenchman. Then, again, she frowned: de Foix was making no attempt to step forward. 'Monsieur de Foix?'

'Your Majesty?'

'The door is closed.'

'Yes, Your Majesty.'

Elizabeth looked pointedly at the offending obstacle. 'It will not open by itself, monsieur.'

'Ah! No ... no.' Reluctance writ large on his unhappy face, de Foix stepped forward and opened the door. As Elizabeth and Kat passed over the threshold, he rolled his eyes and crossed himself again.

Elizabeth progressed precisely two feet into the room before she stopped dead in her tracks. 'Good God!' she whispered. 'What ... what is ... ?'

'Majesty!' The man nearest to her turned bright red and tried to scramble out of her way. At the same time he tried – unsuccessfully – to cover his naked chest. Then he ran for cover behind a tapestry screen.

Most of the other young men in the room lacked such presence of mind and merely stared in horrified disbelief as Elizabeth stood before them. The only sound – the same high-pitched laughter audible from the corridor – came from next door.

Several of the young men began to shake with fear as they looked at their sovereign. 'Your Majesty,' one of them mumbled as he leaped to his feet. Then, remembering himself, he bowed low. Too late he remembered that he was naked from the waist down. Too scared to look at Elizabeth again, he remained bent double, willing the floor to open up and swallow him whole.

Elizabeth remained completely impassive. Beside her, Kat was fighting the urge to giggle. And behind them, de Foix was praying.

At last Elizabeth spoke. 'Goodness', she said to Kat. 'I had no idea there were so many pretty young men at court. How fortunate England is.' Then, for all the world as if she had just expressed admiration of a bunch of innocuous flowers, she walked towards the inner chamber.

The young men were, if anything, even more shocked than before.

But if England was fortunate France was not. Elizabeth didn't wait for de Foix to open the other door for her, she wrenched at the handle and walked into the most embarrassing moment of the Duke of Anjou's life.

Again the room was full of beautiful young men in various states of undress. Some of them were caressing each other, others were laughing at the antics of the only woman in the room. In sharp contrast to the men, she was fully clad in a voluminous scarlet dress bedecked with glittering jewels. Her face was heavily painted, her head sported a fantastic wig piled high with more jewels and, to crown it, she was wearing a tiara. The tiara, like several of the tresses of hair, appeared to be making a bid for escape and lurched drunkenly downwards.

The edifice that was the Duke of Anjou was magnificent, gaudy – and quite grotesque.

Elizabeth burst out laughing. So did Kat. De Foix covered his face with his hands. And like their counterparts in the antechamber, the young men turned to stone.

But Anjou was indignant. 'You laugh, Madam', he

asked Elizabeth. 'Why?'

Elizabeth couldn't speak for laughing. At last she managed a gasp. 'You are wearing a dress, your Grace!'

'Good God!' shouted Anjou. 'I only dress like this when I am alone!' He gestured towards his finery. 'Always in private! It is not important!' He glared at Elizabeth. His huge ear-rings appeared to mirror his outrage and quivered furiously.

It was too much for Elizabeth. Bent almost double with laughter, she fell back against Kat. 'Not important, perhaps, for *you*! But for me . . . oh! . . . this is too much!' She let out another great peel of laughter.

By now Anjou's indignation had given way to fear. Belatedly he realized that this was not furthering the cause of his marriage. His mother would be livid. 'Madam,' he wailed. 'Madam . . . !'

De Foix cut him short. 'Madam. This can be explained . . . I will explain exactly . . . '

'There is no need, Excellency.' Elizabeth held out an imperious hand. 'Only . . . only do not speak to me any more of marriage . . . or,' she added with a sly grin, 'conversion!' Then, still giggling, she left the room.

By the time she rejoined the dance her hysteria had subsided and, while still highly amused, she was greatly relieved. The Anjou problem had solved itself. She would not have to marry the degenerate nephew of Mary of Guise.

It was only later that she remembered the likely alternative to marriage was war.

But for the moment she was intent on enjoying her-

244

self. Still seemingly oblivious to the strange atmosphere as she joined the dance, she took Lord Sudeley's hand for her favourite dance – a volta.

A minute later the partners changed and she found herself face to face with Robert. He took one look at her and turned white.

But Elizabeth just smiled. 'I am sorry,' she said, 'about your wife.'

Robert didn't reply – there wasn't time. He swung her round in time to the music. As they passed back to back he recalled Alvaro de la Quadra's words. *Still her Majesty's favourite.* Could it *still* be true – even after Amy's death?

'Why did you not tell me?' whispered Elizabeth as they joined hands again.

'I could not . . . I . . . I was afraid that you . . .'

'That I what? Would not love you any more? Do you think so little of me, that you would not tell me the truth?'

Her remarks threw Robert into total confusion. Unable to summon a reply, he stared at her in panic.

Elizabeth wasn't the only person who noted his expression. Norfolk and de la Quadra were watching intently from the other side of the room. So, at the far end, were Cecil and Walsingham.

'This,' whispered Cecil, 'is too much. She *cannot* carry on that liaison.'

'She won't.'

Cecil cast a suspicious look at the other man. 'How can you be so sure?'

'Robert Dudley,' replied Walsingham, 'is about to get himself into a very pretty pickle. And anyway, I think Her Majesty has changed her mind about him.'

'Huh!' Cecil was scathing about that one. 'You suppose she thinks he murdered his wife?'

'No. She's not stupid. She knows that someone is trying to set him up.'

'Then she will remain his champion.'

'That,' said Walsingham, 'depends on whether he can resist temptation.' Then, before Cecil could ask him what he meant, he took his leave. There was work to be done. Work following on from the unfortunate episode in Anjou's apartments.

For Walsingham knew all about that. Thanks to de Foix.

On the dance floor, Elizabeth and Robert had changed partners. Now they met again – and Robert had had time to think.

'What does it matter that I didn't tell you the truth?' he protested, holding her in a fierce grip. 'I am free to love you!' Then he bent towards her. 'Marry me!'

'No.'

'*What?*'

'No!'

'For God's sake!' Robert eyes flashed with sudden anger. 'You are still *my* Elizabeth!'

Something snapped in Elizabeth. She wrenched herself away from Robert and, eyes blazing, rounded on him. The movement ruined the formation of the dance. Half-heartedly, with eyes and ears only for Elizabeth and Robert, the others stumbled on.

'I am *not* your Elizabeth! I am no man's *Elizabeth!* And if you think to rule here, you are mistaken!'

The entire court fell silent as Elizabeth shouted. The dancers stopped in their tracks. Even the music faded and, finally, died.

Elizabeth's next words resonated throughout the entire room. 'I will have one mistress here', she screamed. 'And *no* master!' Then she stormed out of the room.

The next day the words began to echo throughout the entire kingdom.

PART THREE

Chapter 15

'Sir Francis – let us be honest with one another.'

'Very well.'

'Your Queen is weak. She had no army and no friends. She only has enemies.' Mary of Guise spread her hands in an eloquent Gallic shrug. 'What possible terms can she propose?'

Walsingham took a deep breath and smiled at the Queen Regent of Scotland. Smiling at her, he had to admit, wasn't difficult. She had a fine, strong face, huge dark over eyes and a wide, curvaceous mouth. The jet black hair, he supposed, was dyed. For Mary had to be nearly fifty yet her body and her spirit belied the passage of time.

'Her Majesty,' he began, 'was too hasty in rejecting the Duke's proposal of marriage. She will be prepared to reconsider.'

The other man in the room banged his fist on the table. 'How can I marry such a woman? She is frigid! They say she is really a man!'

Mary looked at her nephew with barely disguised contempt. 'You must forgive my son, Sir Francis. He speaks when he should not.' Then, to Walsingham's great amusement, she turned to Anjou and, in French, told him to go to bed.

Anjou briefly considered rebellion but, seeing the expression on his aunt's face, kissed her goodnight and left the room. As he did so, Mary gestured to the courtiers in attendance. 'And you may leave us too! Sir Francis and I have something to discuss in private.'

When they had left, Mary turned her attentions back to Walsingham. 'More wine, Sir Francis?'

'Please.' Walsingham leaned back in his exceedingly uncomfortable chair and watched the elegant Frenchwoman pour out more wine. The fine clothes and air of sophistication were at odds with the room – indeed with the whole of Edinburgh Castle. And, he thought, the whole of Scotland. How Mary put up with living here he couldn't imagine. The contrast between the French court and that of Scotland couldn't be greater. Yet the widow of James V of Scotland had chosen to stay and rule over this wild, unruly and barbaric country for the sake of her daughter. She had chosen to take on the unwieldy and unpredictable Scottish nobles and to quell their resistance to French rule.

And now, again in the name of her daughter, she planned to do the same with England. Walsingham looked over to the standard above the stone fireplace. It bore the coat-of-arms of Mary's daughter, the sixteen-year-old Mary Queen of Scots. And on it was quartered the arms of England.

Mary followed his glance. 'Yes, Sir Francis. My daughter's father-in-law had already claimed the throne of England on her behalf – on account of the illegitimacy of your supposed Queen.'

Walsingham smiled. 'I know. And there are many in England who would like to see her usurp Elizabeth.' That, he knew, wasn't strictly true.

Norfolk and his cronies wanted Elizabeth off the throne and would tolerate Mary Queen of Scots if only one of them could marry her and become king. But there was what de la Quadra would call an 'impediment' to that solution. Mary was already married to the heir to the French throne.

Happiest when speaking of her daughter, Mary of Guise's eyes always clouded over when she referred to her nephew – the gross disappointment that was Anjou. 'My nephew,' she said with vigour, 'is a fool.' Then she leaned towards Walsingham and smiled. 'Most people are fools – do you not agree?'

Sir Francis responded with a dazzling smile of his own. 'There is some truth in that.'

'You and I, on the other hand, are both creatures of the world.' Mary held his gaze over the rim of her wine goblet. 'We understand its ways.'

'Indeed.' Walsingham spread his hands in a gesture of supplication. 'I have no illusions. I know it is only a matter of time before the Queen is overthrown.' Then he too picked up his wine and looked over to his companion. 'In such circumstances, a wise man would be careful not to put himself in the way of harm.'

Almost skittish now, Mary leaned closer. Her beautiful hands curled round and tapped against her goblet. 'And how would a wise man do that?'

Walsingham didn't waver. 'He would change his allegiance. There are only two choices: he would get into bed with either Spain . . . or France.'

Mary tasted the rim of her goblet with the tip of her tongue. Her eyes remained fixed on Walsingham's.

'And which would you prefer?'

'I have always found France the more beautiful.'

'Really?'

'And more seductive.'

Mary stood up. 'And you think her comforts would keep you warm against the chill of the night?'

'Undoubtedly.'

Mary walked over to his chair and curled a coquettish arm round his neck. 'The nights in Scotland,' she whispered, 'are very cold indeed. A great contrast to France.'

'Yes.' Walsingham reached for her hand. 'I have always found France to be a passionate place.'

'What about England?'

Now Walsingham stood up. 'Oh ... England. England can be a very hot-blooded place. Rough, sometimes.' He bent towards her, his lips searching for hers. 'But tender. And, like France, passionate.'

''Tis a pity they are so divided.'

'Not tonight. Tonight they shall be united.'

Walsingham's seduction, like everything else he practised, was consummately professional. And Mary was more than willing to be seduced. Half an hour later, they lay entwined and naked in her bed, each spurring the other to greater heights of lust. Their lovemaking had a feral, almost combative element to it, an extra frisson borne of the fact that neither believed the other. Mary knew Walsingham's reputation too well to believe that he would betray his Queen and country. And she was highly suspicious of his request for a clandestine meeting in Scotland. Yet she was only too happy to have him in her bed tonight. Tomorrow she would deal with him.

But there would be no tomorrow for Mary of Guise. As Walsingham's dextrous fingers roused her to orgasm, she cried out with an ecstasy that bordered on pain.

She didn't make a sound when the real pain came; when he plunged a dagger into her heart.

'Your Majesty,' thundered Cecil, 'must deny that you ever sanctioned such an act!'

'Of course I shall deny it!' Elizabeth delivered her response with equal vigour. 'I never *did* order it.'

The Queen and Secretary of State stood facing each other in the former's Privy Chamber. This was not the first heated exchange in the weeks since Elizabeth had made her extraordinary statement to Robert Dudley. It was merely one of many. Cecil privately thought that the Dudley scandal had unhinged her. Elizabeth was of the opinion that it had made her stronger – and that it was Sir William Cecil who sought to weaken her. Privately, she held him responsible for the disasters that had befallen her since that night. And there had been many of those.

The brutal murder of Mary of Guise was but the latest. The shock-waves were still reverberating throughout Scotland, England and France – and the suspicion centred on England.

But England's Queen hadn't sanctioned the death. 'I really do not know,' she fumed, 'how you could imagine I had anything to do with it. No matter that Mary had committed monstrous and wicked acts against me, I would never stoop to such barbarity.'

An uneasy silence descended on the room. Elizabeth and Cecil continued to stare at each other – mainly because neither wished to look at the other man present. In the wake of Elizabeth's impassioned denial, neither felt comfortable about looking at the man whom they both knew was responsible.

Cecil broke the silence by changing the subject – to another disaster. 'You must also make conciliatory noises to the Spanish,' he counselled in a more business-like tone. 'For your dependence on their goodwill is now greater than ever. I must advise you that . . . '

'Sir William!' Elizabeth had heard enough. 'You have been a true and faithful councillor, but it seems to me that your policies would make England nothing but either a part of France or Spain!' Then, eyes blazing with anger, she repeated the now-familiar refrain. 'I will have no King to rule over me, nor any country to rule over mine!'

'But Madam, you are only a woman! You can never succeed!' Cecil didn't mean it as an insult – merely a fact.

'I may be a woman,' snapped Elizabeth, 'but if I choose, I have the heart of a man. I am not afraid of anything!'

In the corner, Walsingham was failing to suppress a smile. Elizabeth was a changed woman – something Cecil clearly couldn't cope with.

Cecil tried a more conciliatory tactic. 'I regret that I have caused Your Majesty such offence, though God knows all my advice has been in order to secure Your Majesty's throne.' He wondered if Elizabeth remembered the letter she had written him from Hatfield on her succession, urging him to advise her even if the advice was contrary to her will. He suspected a selective memory on that score.

Then, to his surprise, Elizabeth mellowed and offered him a sweet smile. 'I am not angry with you, Sir William. No. Quite the opposite. I am going to reward you. I have decided to create you Lord Burghley, so you may enjoy your retirement in greater ease.'

'I beg your pardon?' Cecil hadn't heard her correctly.

'Your *retirement*.'

Cecil *had* heard correctly. 'Madam!' he gasped. 'I . . . I . . . '

But as he reeled with shock, Elizabeth's mood changed again. 'Lord Burghley, I have no further need of you!' To illustrate the fact, she offered him her hand.

The hand seemed to swim before Cecil's eyes. He looked at the delicate bejewelled fingers and then back up at Elizabeth. Her gaze was steely, unwavering – and authoritarian. Cecil bent down and kissed the hand. 'Your Majesty . . . ' he stammered.

'Goodbye, Sir William.' Without looking at him again, Elizabeth turned her back on him and walked to her desk.

She waited until she heard the door close behind him before she turned back to address Walsingham. When she did, her face was an inscrutable mask. There was no trace of anger, none of regret, nothing to suggest sadness. And there was no indication that she knew she was addressing a murderer.

'What is *your* advice, Sir Francis?'

Walsingham was as adamant as Cecil had been, but with advice to the contrary. 'Madam, forgive me, but . . . you have no choice now but to act against those who threaten you.'

'I will not countenance war!'

'No, Madam. That is not what I am saying. You . . . you have been forgiving to your enemies, but since they do not fear you, such virtues will only harm you. I know it would be better if a prince exhibited all those qualities people say are good . . . but that is not the case.' He paused, trying to gauge Elizabeth's reaction. Her face remained set, but in her eyes he saw an understanding – a tacit acknowledgement of the necessity to abandon the princely qualities of goodness.

'In truth,' he continued, 'a prince should not flinch from being blamed for vices which are necessary for safeguarding the State – and their own safety.'

'Go on.'

'Madam, your kingdom buzzes with priests and spies – and the nobles who wish to harm you are becoming ever more powerful. There is even now a priest abroad in the land – by the name of John Ballard. It is said he carries messages from King Philip and the Pope, to those who wish to harm you.'

Elizabeth's response was as curt as it had been to Cecil – but infinitely more positive.

'Find him,' she commanded.

Walsingham bowed in acquiescence. He was smiling as he did so – for the command had already been obeyed. Thanks to Christopher Marlowe, he knew all Ballard's movements. What he had yet to find out was the whereabouts of the incriminating letters.

Elizabeth watched him depart and, with a weary sigh, settled herself at her desk. Normally she set this time of day aside for reading, for furthering her quest for self-improvement. Already considered by many to be overeducated for a woman, she had considerable knowledge of physics, astronomy, mathematics, botany and a host of subjects in between. Her command of languages, too, was remarkable, and her linguistic prowess had earned her many a complement. Yet she was always dismissive about her achievements. 'No marvel to teach a woman to talk', she had once remarked to de Foix. 'Far harder to teach her to hold her tongue.'

And Elizabeth had learned the hard way. Since that fateful night at the dance, there had been much to talk about, but Elizabeth had kept her counsel. She hadn't even confided her inner feelings to Kat. For if one of her trusted ladies had betrayed her, then why shouldn't another? It was little comfort to Elizabeth that Isabel Knollys had paid dearly for her betrayal.

Isabel's terrible accident was still the talk of Whitehall. 'They say,' declared one gossip with spurious yet convincing authority, 'that she endured the greatest agonies known in Christendom.'

'Apparently,' declared a particularly ghoulish interpreter, 'she screamed for hours before anyone heard her.'

But that view was not widely held. Although Isabel was found alone in her room, the popular theory was that she had been with a lover when the tragedy had occurred. Why else, said the gossips, would she have been wearing the Queen's dress? She would hardly have purloined the new and glittering gown in order to parade alone in her bedroom.

For Walsingham's fear about poisoned dyes being applied to Elizabeth's dresses had proved well-founded. A week after Elizabeth's highly public renunciation of Robert Dudley, a gown of gorgeous French silk had been sent to her. Even before Elizabeth had seen it, Isabel had taken it upon herself to borrow it, to wear it in private – and to nearly die in agony from the poisoned fabric. The physician who had been called to her room corroborated – did the gossips but know it – that Isabel would be lucky to survive, that her agony had been protracted and excruciatingly painful. When he examined the barely-conscious woman, he found blood under her nails – her own blood. She had scratched and clawed at her own skin in a desperate attempt to ease her agony and calm the suppurating blisters. 'It is as if,' he told Walsingham, 'she has been boiled.'

But Walsingham hadn't been looking at Isabel: instead he had eyed the rumpled bed with suspicion. Isabel had dressed herself as a queen for the night: who had been her king? Who had witnessed the terrible event, panicked, and left Isabel alone?

Walsingham had his theories. So did the court gossips. Robert Dudley, they declared, had always had an eye for a pretty lady. Spurned by his Queen, he had sought sweet revenge by seducing a lady prettier than she.

The only problem with that theory was that it contradicted an even more tantalizing and incendiary story – that Robert himself had sent the dress to Elizabeth.

Elizabeth herself chose to ignore the gossip. Like Walsingham, she equated the silk dress with its country of origin. The dress had come from France.

And now France was up in arms because of the murder of Mary of Guise. A murder doubtless engineered by Elizabeth in retaliation.

'Oh God,' sighed Elizabeth, throwing Seneca to the floor and sinking her head into her heads. 'What am I to do?'

Then she remembered Walsingham's words. She was going to act against those who threatened her. And she knew exactly who they were.

'My master, the King of Spain, commends himself to you, as a brother in Christ and the true religion.'

Norfolk didn't bother to reply. He regarded it as entirely fitting that Philip should praise him. After all, everyone else did.

'But,' said Alvaro de la Quadra, 'he is not altogether content.'

'Oh?' Norfolk looked at the Ambassador with lofty disdain. 'Why so?'

'Some English privateers are attacking our ships. His Majesty had hoped you might have acted already, so such unfortunate actions would be prevented by our alliance.'

'I am not the King of England', said Norfolk. 'I cannot stop such attacks.'

'No – but you are more powerful than England's Queen.'

That, thought Norfolk, was true. As Elizabeth's power waned, so the court was rallying round him. All in good time, he told himself. All in good time.

When he turned back to de la Quadra he was smiling. 'Everything in nature must take its proper course, Excellence.'

But de la Quadra was convinced that Norfolk, not nature, was dictating the direction of that course. And neither he nor his master were happy about that direction. 'It is rumoured,' he said, 'that your Grace has made contact with the French, and Mary of Scots, in order to promote your ambitions.'

Norfolk burst out laughing. 'Do you suppose me an idiot? Your master is the most powerful man in the world. I would not cross him for my life.'

But De la Quadra was unconvinced. He felt a certain disquiet around the great Duke. Norfolk, he was sure, was keeping his options open. The Papal Bull authorizing the removal of Elizabeth from her throne was all very well for the sake of Catholicism, but what about the good of Spain? For a Catholic England would ally itself to either Spain or France; an alliance that would be dictated by the most powerful man in the country. And de la Quadra suspected that Norfolk would turn to France. He had far more to gain from that country than from Spain. The French husband of Mary Queen of Scots was now gravely ill. If Mary were to be widowed, who better for a husband than Norfolk? He would then become the power behind the thrones of Scotland, England and

262

Spain's enemy France.

As Norfolk left him and swaggered down the corridor towards the Great Hall of the Palace of Whitehall, de la Quadra cast his mind back to his audience at the Vatican with Cardinal Ruffirio. His master the Pope was canny enough to know that the English problem was about more than Catholicism. Which did he favour: Spain or France?

Then de la Quadra remembered the English priest and the letters the Cardinal had given him; the letters that were 'too inflammatory' to risk being found at court. But why had the Pope given them to Ballard, what was he going to do with them – and what did they contain?

Thomas Elyot was wondering the same thing. Months ago, Walsingham had entrusted him with the surveillance of the mysterious priest. 'Do not approach him yourself,' Walsingham had cautioned, 'but let some of your men become known to him. Find out to whom he talks, what he says, how often he goes to Rome – and wait for an exchange of letters.'

But Ballard had exchanged no letters. Elyot's men had shadowed him through the streets and taverns of London, struck up his acquaintance, one of them had followed him on his trips to Rome – but no exchange of letters had taken place with anyone in England. Elyot had begun to think that Walsingham must be mistaken, that there was nothing suspicious about the priest with the dyed blond hair. 'The only crime he has committed,' reported one of his spies, 'is sodomy.'

Elyot hadn't even bothered to report that to

Walsingham. If they arrested every priest in the land for that sort of crime then neither the Protestant nor the Catholic Churches would last for long.

Then, a few days previously, they had struck gold. John Parry, one of the men who had made Ballards' acquaintance, had been approached by him on a 'matter of great delicacy'. Did Parry know, he asked, of a gentleman of high standing who could be trusted with the delivery of some letters?

Ballard had already confided his Catholicism to Parry – there was no need to question the nature of the delicate matter.

Parry did know someone in such a position: Thoms Elyot himself.

'Elyot?' Ballard had frowned. 'Is he not a poet?'

'He is. But he is also known at court . . . and he is a Catholic.'

'And he can be trusted? Implicitly?'

'Implicitly.'

Ballard had been delighted. 'I cannot tell you,' he said with a cryptic smile, 'how long I have been waiting for this.'

He didn't have to wait much longer. On the same evening as the Duke of Norfolk and Alvaro de la Quadra's relationship began to fall apart, his own association with Thoms Elyot began.

As arranged with Parry, the meeting took place in a crowded tavern. Despite the throng and the raucous, drunken laughter, the two men had no trouble finding each other. Ballard, as Parry told Elyot, was an unholy looking priest with died blond hair. And Elyot, as he had told Ballard, was an exceptionally handsome man with a finely-turned calf.

Ballard went straight to the point. 'What makes you want to help me?'

'My faith,' whispered Elyot.

'You are a Catholic?'

Elyot crossed himself. 'Yes. I speak to you with complete honesty, as if I were before God, as if I were about to die. I am a Catholic, Apostolic and Roman.'

Ballard smiled. 'And do you know who I am?'

'Yes, Father.' Elyot affected an even more reverential look. 'You are John Ballard. I have heard much about you.'

'Good. And you are willing to serve me? You are willing to deliver letters that may endanger your life?'

'I will serve you with all my heart. For I would rather serve God,' he said with sudden passion, 'than a heretic!'

Ballard smiled again. Then he rose to his feet and leaned over the table. Taking Elyot's head in his hands, he kissed him on both cheeks. Then he smiled and looked deep into his eyes. 'You are lying,' he hissed. 'You belong to Walsingham.'

Elyot didn't even flinch. 'Who?'

Ballard still had his hands on Elyot's head. Now he moved them to his neck. 'You poor fool. You think to speak to me before God, with all your heart – as if you were about to die? Well you *are!*' With frightening speed, Ballard released his hold on Elyot, delved into his pocket and whipped out a dagger.

But Elyot, too, was quick to react. As soon as Ballard let go, he sprang to his feet and lunged at the other man.

265

He was too late. As his own momentum carried him forward, he realized that he had made the wrong move. The dagger was there, before his very eyes. The next second it had embedded itself in one of them.

A moment later it pierced his brain and the scream of agony died on Elyot's lips before anyone even knew that a murder had been committed.

Ballard was gone by the time anyone noticed that the man sitting with his back to the room was dead. He was still upright in his chair; his ale was still warm and so was his blood. It was still gushing forth from the eyeless socket in a face contorted with agony.

Chapter 16

'These privateers who are attacking the Spanish fleet. Have they weakened it?'

'Not yet, Your Majesty.'

'Would they, if they were to continue?

'Undoubtedly, Madam. The captains of these vessels are the most fervent opponents of Catholicism. And,' added Walsingham with a meaningful look, 'they are your Majesty's most loyal supporters.'

'That,' said Elizabeth, 'is as may be. But I find myself unable to reciprocate that support. We are not at war with Spain, Sir Francis.'

'We have not *declared* war against Spain, Madam. Nor has Spain officially declared war on England.'

'Dear me', said Elizabeth with a disingenuous smile. 'Declare. Official. Anyone would think there are princes who would . . . what were the words? Oh yes . . . "not flinch from being blamed for vices which are necessary for safeguarding the state".'

Walsingham grinned. He had forgotten quite how acute Elizabeth's memory was. 'When I said "blame", Madam, I was merely anticipating the worst possible outcome of any . . . any intervention.'

'And what would be the best possible outcome?'

'Oh . . . that your people would see how close you are to them, how much you support them. That you are seen to encourage the people whose help you need most.'

'My nobles, you mean?'

'No Madam. I mean your sea captains.'

Elizabeth stood up. 'Good. I was hoping you might say that.' Then she turned to look out of the window. 'It is nearly dusk, Sir Francis. Shall we wait until it is dark? So many good deeds are best done in the dark, don't you think?'

For once, Walsingham was lost for words. The twinkle in Elizabeth's eye was extremely unnerving, and highly suggestive. He had no doubt whatsoever that she was referring to his murder of Mary of Guise.

Elizabeth was in high spirits and good humour by the time they arrived at the docks. Subterfuge, she was beginning to realize, was a hugely rewarding game. And it was extraordinary how easily people were fooled. Creeping out of the Palace under the cover of darkness – and that of a heavy cloak – she had run straight into the Duke of Norfolk. His appearance was never deceptive: Elizabeth had nearly died of fright. Norfolk, on the other hand, had gave not the slightest flicker of recognition. But he had spoken to her. 'Mind where you're going, you bloody woman!' he had shouted.

Highly amused, Elizabeth had curtsied low. In a meek voice, she had begged his Grace's pardon before hurrying away into the night.

But now she was sanctioning a different and far more dangerous kind of subterfuge. In the State room of the boat they were now boarding were the twelve sea captains who, Walsingham assured her, would risk anything for Queen and country.

'Anything?' queried Elizabeth as she clambered down the gangway.

'Anything rather than be ruled by Catholics.'

Privately, Elizabeth still bitterly regretted the awful religious divide. Yet she now knew that she must use it to her best advantage. And this evening could prove highly advantageous.

When they entered the oak-lined State room the captains bowed low and, with touching informality, beckoned for her to sit down on an old stool. 'It ain't much, your Majesty,' said the captain whose vessel this was, 'but it's the best there is.'

Elizabeth thanked him, sat down and immediately addressed the room at large. 'My good captains, it makes me very happy to be among you, for I know you to be loyal and steadfast in your attachment towards me.'

'Aye, Madam', they chorused. 'As true as any men now living.'

'You are men of the sea', she continued. 'You speak with salty tongues, honest and direct. So let me be direct with you.'

Faintly disconcerted by the change in her tone, her audience shifted on their own, even more uncomfortable seats.

'You have no licence from me,' Elizabeth stated, 'to act as pirates and privateers to rob and steal from Spanish ships.'

'But your Majesty!' The captain of the ship, articulating the murmurs of protest, looked at her in alarm.

This was not the sort of talk Walsingham had led them to expect.

Elizabeth silenced then with an authoritative hand. 'I said I could not give you licence! I did not say,' she added with gusto, 'that you should not do it!'

The mutterings of discontent turned to cheers. Suddenly everyone in the room, Elizabeth included, was grinning broadly. 'The Spanish fleet,' she continued, 'now controls the world. Their ships carry the riches of its empire, without hindrance, from the Indies to the Dutch lowlands ... rich pickings, my captains!'

It took a moment for the meaning implicit in her words to sink in.

And even then, the captains were doubtful. 'You would not call it ... piracy?' asked one.

'And,' said his most acquisitive colleague, 'what would happen to the catch?'

'It will henceforth be divided. One quarter for you, the rest for my Treasury.' Waad, she thought, would be ecstatic. But some of the seamen looked dubious. 'If ... if ... '

'If the Spanish protest to me?' Elizabeth looked at them in wide-eyed innocence. 'I shall say it was nothing of *my* doing, that you are privateers, and do not obey my will.'

'Aye – but if they should desire us captured and punished?'

Elizabeth had thought long and hard and, she reckoned, justly about that one. 'For the sake of appearance, I will have you arrested and housed in the Tower, for a little while, and at my own expense.

270

There,' she added with a conspiratorial grin, 'you can write poems – and meditate on your sinfulness.'

As the captains burst out laughing, Elizabeth leaned forward. There was a different, more fervent look in her eyes, and a new passion in her voice as she spoke again. 'With some of the wealth from the catch I will begin to build a fleet that will make England proud again – and the master of her fate!' Then she looked, one by one, at the weatherbeaten seamen. 'If you will serve me in this way, for the glory of England, say "Aye"!'

None of them hesitated for so much as a second. 'Aye!' they chorused, almost raising the roof of the small cabin.

With a radiant smile on her face and a warmth in her heart, Elizabeth rose to her feet. 'Then I bid you good fishing, my brave captains!

Behind her, Walsingham turned and opened the door. 'I see that you fish too, Madam', he whispered.

'I? Fish?' Elizabeth looked at him in alarm.

'Yes Madam. For the souls of men!'

Elizabeth was smiling as she swept out of the room. Yet behind the smile there was a sadness. Why, she wondered, could her courtiers and her Council not support her like this? Why did they not respond to her with fire in their eyes and conviction in their voices?

Then she remembered. The answer was simple – and deadly. Norfolk.

Norfolk's influence at court had always been strong. Now it was immensely powerful – and increasing daily. The crises that plagued Elizabeth were not only

271

undermining her throne but bolstering the ego of its pretender. Norfolk made no secret of the fact that he thought Elizabeth weak, foolish and incapable of ruling. In public he was never anything but courteous to her, but every time they met he looked at her with a strange expression which sent a shiver down her spine. When he had mistaken her for a maidservant on the night of her speech to the captains he had called her a 'bloody woman'. And that, Elizabeth knew, was exactly what he thought of her as a queen.

A week after Elizabeth's secret nocturnal visit to the shipyards, the court began to buzz with yet another scandal – the murder of Thomas Elyot. As with the poisoning of Isabel Knollys, there were many theories about how he had come to his untimely end. That a refined poet who had regularly graced court festivities with his gay presence should have died in a tavern brawl was strange enough. That the poet had been Elyot was infinitely more gossip-worthy. For it was well known that Elyot had a darker side, that he had kept his private life swathed in secrecy. Several people – mainly the ladies who had failed to attract his merry eye – opined that he was a sodomite, notorious in the seedier streets of London. Others claimed that he was a member of a sinister cult of necromancers. But the most widely held belief was that Elyot had been a spy.

Alvaro de la Quadra had always refrained from joining in the speculation about Elyot's life. And now he distanced himself from the gossip about his death. For he had always known Elyot to be one of Walsingham's agents. Under normal circumstances,

De la Quadra would have welcomed the poet's death: it would have meant one less player in the game of espionage; one less threat against the Vatican – and another strike at the foundations of Elizabeth's throne.

But these, thought de la Quadra as he watched the Duke of Norfolk sweep into court, were not normal circumstances. He was now certain that Norfolk meant to side with the French. For de la Quadra had his own gatherers of intelligence – and they informed him that John Ballard, the man with the letters de la Quadra was so suspicious about, was currently in hiding at the house of the Catholic Earl of Arundel. Arundel was known to be vehemently opposed to Spain – and he was Norfolk's lackey.

De la Quadra's lip curled as he took in Norfolk's regal swagger, the huge entourage that followed him into the room and the great hunting dogs at his side. And he watched in disgust as people flocked around him, eagerly welcoming him to the evening's festivities. Everything in their manner echoed Norfolk's own unspoken words: he was a king in waiting.

On the other side of the room, Walsingham was also watching the performance with increasing worry. He noted that many people present – even Protestants – were sporting something yellow in their costume. Norfolk's colours. He noticed the obsequious manner in which Norfolk was greeted. And his eyes narrowed as he saw that even those who had sworn loyalty to Elizabeth swarmed around the Duke. The Earl of Derby, Nicholas Throckmorton – and Robert Dudley. So, thought Walsingham, Dudley has found friends at last. And he's following in his father's footsteps.

Walsingham felt a great heaviness descend as he took in the scene before him. Only a few evenings previously, Elizabeth had dealt so magnificently with the Spanish threat, pitching her own vessels in a secret war against Philip's. But the French threat remained. And, he didn't doubt, it was gathering momentum in the shape of the Duke of Norfolk. For the husband of Mary Queen of Scots was now the King of France – and he was on his deathbed. Her next husband would be Norfolk. And her next kingdom would be England.

Walsingham was well aware that the only way to stop Norfolk was to arrest him for treason – and the only way to do that was by finding John Ballard and the letters he carried.

He was also well aware that John Ballard had murdered Thomas Elyot. And that he had disappeared.

Lost in contemplation of the disaster that had ruined his carefully laid plans, Walsingham stood, even heavier of heart, and wondered how to tell Elizabeth. She had put all her trust in him, and he had failed her.

He was jolted out of his reverie by a soft, familiar, and unwelcome voice. 'How pensive you are looking tonight, Sir Francis.'

Walsingham whirled round, angry that he had not noticed the Spaniard sidling up to him. His anger gave way to suspicion when he saw that he was also smiling at him.

Then de la Quadra gestured in Norfolk's direction.

'You are looking, I see, at our regal friend.'

'The Queen,' said Walsingham stiffly, 'is not yet here.'

De la Quadra laughed. 'No, indeed she isn't. And nor is Thomas Elyot.'

Warning bells rang in Walsingham's head. So, he thought. That's why he's here; an elliptical little conversation about espionage. He thought de la Quadra knew him better than to think he could elicit any information on that subject.

But de la Quadra hadn't come to elicit anything. He had come to divulge. 'Mmm', he said, still looking at Norfolk. 'Poor old Elyot. Such a good poet – devoted to his craft.'

Walsingham cast a sidelong glance at de la Quadra. The Spaniard's cryptic smile left him in no doubt as to which particular craft he was referring.

'And 'tis a pity,' he continued, 'that he never found those . . . those words he was looking for to complete his last work.' At last he turned to look at Walsingham. 'I gather the work would have been of great benefit to her Majesty. Not a ballad – more of a *Ballard?*' Amused by Walsingham's shocked reaction, de la Quadra burst out laughing. Then he leaned closer. 'Sometimes, Sir Francis, intelligence is not too dear to share.'

'Why would you wish to share intelligence with me, Excellence?'

'I think you know the answer to that one, Sir Francis.' Again de la Quadra turned in the direction of the Duke of Norfolk. 'We would not want our regal friend getting *too* regal, would we?'

Walsingham smiled. So it was true: Norfolk had aligned himself to France, not Spain. No wonder de la Quadra wanted to stop him.

'But what method,' he asked, 'would you recommend to divest him of his finery?'

'Ah . . . you'd have to ask Ballard that.'

'The elusive Ballard.'

'Not so elusive, my friend. I think you will find that he is lodging with the Earl of Arundel.' Then, without another word or even a glance in Walsingham's direction, the Spanish Ambassador melted into the throng.

Walsingham was a past master at disguising his feelings: no observer would have been able to guess that the encounter had left him nothing short of elated. Alvaro de la Quadra, of all people, was voluntarily leading him towards Ballard. True, he was not moved to do so out of the kindness of his heart, but out of malice against Norfolk. Walsingham's elation was nevertheless tinged by what was to him a most unfamiliar sensation: guilt. He had already repaid de la Quadra, in advance, by authorising piracy against the Spanish navy. Poor old de la Quadra, he thought – always destined to be the loser. Then, as he watched the Spaniard weave his unctuous way through Elizabeth's supporters, Walsingham felt his guilt evaporate – to be replaced by suspicion. De la Quadra knew too much: if he knew of Ballard's whereabouts, then what else did he know? And *how* did he know about Ballard? From whom had he gleaned his intelligence? Suddenly Walsingham was gripped by a new resolve: after he had concluded the more urgent business towards which de la Quadra had just led him, he would deal with de la Quadra himself. It would, after all, be most improper to flinch from a vice necessary for the safeguarding of the nation.

Without telling Elizabeth, Walsingham acted on the urgent business that very evening. He knew that she regarded the Earl of Arundel with great affection almost as an uncle and, that she would vacillate and waver about agreeing to a raid on his house. He knew that she was also fond of his young Countess and the three Arundel children. And he knew that she would have great difficulty in believing that the Earl could plot against her. But most of all he knew that Elizabeth would balk at the methods he would employ in his urgent need to find Ballard.

He arrived with twelve armed guards precisely half an hour after Arundel had returned from the festivities at court. As he anticipated, there was a delay before his furious knock at the door was answered. He imagined the scene inside the house as he waited: a servant alerting his master to their arrival; the hasty rearrangement of whatever room they were using as a makeshift chapel; the hiding of Ballard in the priest's hole. All, he thought with a grim smile, would be in vain.

At last the door was answered by a liveried servant who tried, and failed, to disguise the fact that he was out of breath. 'May I ask . . . ?' he began.

But the time for niceties was long over. Walsingham brushed the man aside and, with the soldiers in his wake, stormed into the house.

Arundel himself was standing in the hallway. 'Sir Francis!' His surprise was clearly genuine. And so was the fear behind his kind, compassionate eyes. 'How come you so rudely enter my house in this fashion?'

'Because I think a priest is hidden here.'

The eyes flickered. 'No. No. There is no priest here.' But even as he spoke, Arundel registered defeat. Sir Francis Walsingham was quite capable of sending soldiers on a whim, but he would never arrive himself unless he was sure, beyond a shadow of a doubt, that his suspicions were well founded.

He looked with regret, even compassion, at the elderly Earl. 'I regret to inform you, my Lord, that your denial obliges me to order that your house be searched.' He turned to the soldiers and nodded.

Arundel watched as they dispersed. The three of their number who stayed in the hall laid down their swords and, with ruthless efficiency, began to tear the room apart.

Walsingham looked almost pained as he watched the scene of destruction. Then he turned in sympathy to the horrified Earl. If only it had been Norfolk, he thought, rather than this good, kind, misguided man. 'Perhaps,' he suggested, 'you would like to wait with your wife and family?'

'My wife and family are not . . . '

' . . . Oh but they *are*, Lord Arundel. Shall we go and join them?'

The Countess and her three terrified children were huddled in a small parlour at the rear of the house. As her husband reluctantly led Walsingham into the room, she flinched, closed her eyes and crossed herself. Then she realized what she had done and looked, if anything, even more fearful.

But Walsingham's sympathy was genuine. Rather than comment on her overt display of her religion, he merely smiled and addressed the Earl again. 'My Lord – it would be better for you . . . and your family . . . if you would just tell me where he is hidden!'

Arundel missed the slight emphasis on the word 'family'. 'I have told you! There is no one hidden here!'

Walsingham sighed and, to the sound of loud crashes above them as the house was ransacked, he walked towards the Countess and crouched down beside her eldest child. An angelic boy of around ten, he stiffened and reached for his mother's hand as Walsingham tousled his hair. '*You* know!' said Walsingham in a playful manner. 'You know, don't you? Tell me where he is.'

With slow but exaggerated movements, the boy shook his head from side to side.

Abruptly, Walsingham changed his tone – and with it the rules of the game. 'You would not like your father to be hurt, would you?'

The little boy shook his head more vehemently.

Then Walsingham reached for the boy's arm and held it in a vice-like grip. 'And your mother wouldn't . . . '

'No!' screamed Lady Arundel. Beside her, her son went rigid with fear. Then, as Walsingham watched intently, he looked towards the fireplace.

Lady Arundel burst into tears.

Walsingham let go of her son and rose to his feet. 'In here!' he called to the soldiers. Rather than sounding triumphant, he appeared wearily resigned. Then, as the soldiers stormed into the room, he walked towards the enormous fireplace. The hearth and mantelpiece were of solid stone. The walls on either side were bare plaster. But above was a large expanse of linen-fold panelling.

'Bring me a sword!'

One of the soldiers stepped forward and handed his weapon to Walsingham. He took it by the blade and, reaching up, tapped the hilt against the panelling.

The dull echo reverberated around the small room. And the sound was quite hollow.

A minute later he located the mechanism, hidden in one of the folds of the panelling, that opened the door. It swung open to reveal John Ballard. He was shaking like a leaf. And he was clutching a bundle of letters.

Chapter 17

Elizabeth was vacillating, pacing the length and breadth of her Privy Chamber, running over in her mind the multitude of problems that beset her. By her own admission, she was 'not a morning person', and this morning in particular, after a restive night, she was in a particularly tetchy mood. In the small hours she had resorted, as she often did, to requesting Kat's company in her bed to help her sleep. The ruse hadn't worked. Quite the opposite: she had kept Kat awake for most of the night with the result that her Mistress of the Bedchamber was in as foul a mood as she.

It was her fatigue that made her question the recent decisions she had made. Not the decisions to tackle her enemies head on – that resolve remained intact. Rather she was beginning to doubt what she now regarded as her peremptory dismissal of Robert from her inner circle, and her bed. Had his concealment of his marriage been such a terrible crime? She knew now that he had been forced into it by his father many years ago and that he had never loved Amy . She also knew that he had had no part in her murder: Robert could be rash and impetuous, but he wasn't *that* hotheaded. Nor that cruel.

Elizabeth still found it hard to think any ill of Robert. She dismissed outright the rumours that he had been with Isabel Knollys on the night she had suffered such terrible disfigurement from the poisoned dress; she simply couldn't believe that he could be so duplicitous.

So Elizabeth paced and fretted, wondering how best to restore Robert to favour without losing face. The poor man was, she knew, still unpopular at court: if she made him her friend again then so would others.

Only on one point did she remain resolute. She would never marry him.

'Madam?'

'Oh! Kat – how you startled me!' Elizabeth paused mid-stride and turned, frowning, towards the door. 'I do wish you wouldn't creep in like that.'

'I'm sorry, Madam,' said Kat without a trace of contrition. As far as she was concerned, she had thundered, not crept into the room.

'Well? What is it?'

'Sir Francis Walsingham is here to see you Madam.'

'So early? Walsingham of all people knows I do not receive anyone at this hour.'

'He says it is a matter of great urgency.'

Elizabeth sighed. 'Oh very well. Show him in.'

Walsingham looked even more strained than Elizabeth. He could barely manage a smile as he bowed and wished her good morning. Elizabeth suppressed a smile of her own: seeing Sir Francis looking so drawn had the peculiar effect of cheering her up somewhat. It was refreshing to know that she wasn't the only one who had had a bad night; reassuring to see that even he, who always looked the same, could look ghastly at this hour.

'Sir Francis. To what do I owe the pleasure at such an early hour?'

'To a priest called John Ballard, Madam.'

Elizabeth stiffened and stopped in her tracks. 'Ballard? You have located him?'

More than that, thought Walsingham. I have located him, incarcerated him in the Tower, interrogated him, and tortured him.

'And?' Elizabeth gave him a piercing look. 'He is talking?'

Not any more, thought Walsingham. He could still hear Ballard's agonised screams as he was stretched on the rack, as his every muscle and sinew shuddered and protested, as his bones creaked and finally snapped under the strain. And he could still visualize the great spurt of blood as, when it was over, the torturer plunged the crude butcher's knife into his stomach.

'Yes, Madam,' he said. 'He has talked. It is . . . it is not good news.'

'In what way?'

'He had letters, Madam. From the Pope.'

Elizabeth frowned. 'But that is what you had hoped, isn't it? Surely it is good news that you have uncovered a conspiracy.'

'The contents of the letters are . . . offensive to your person.'

Elizabeth brushed the protestation aside. 'I think,' she said with a bitter smile, 'I can cope with an offensive letter. Let me see.'

Walsingham reached into the folds of his cloak and

extracted a scroll of thick, expensive paper. As Elizabeth took if from him she saw the Pope's seal on the outside. On the inside it bore his coat of arms, and an inscription in Latin.

To legitimize his claim to the throne, it read, *His Holiness proposes that his Grace, the Duke of Norfolk, should take as his bride Mary, Queen of Scots, cousin to* . . . Elizabeth blanched as she saw the words in black and white . . . *the illegitimate and heretical woman who now sits upon the throne of England.*

Elizabeth shuddered and handed the scroll back to Walsingham. 'It is offensive,' she admitted, 'but it is what I expected. More to the point,' she added, 'it is not incriminating of Norfolk himself.'

'No. It was expedient to intercept it and verify its contents before he signed it.' Walsingham looked over to Elizabeth, wondering how she would take the next piece of news. 'And it was necessary to . . . to extract from Ballard the names of those to whom it was to be sent.'

Elizabeth raised an eyebrow. 'And? I take it you succeeded in doing that?'

'Yes, your Majesty.' Walsingham shuffled and looked down at his feet.

Strange, thought Elizabeth. 'Well?' she prompted.

'Norfolk himself, of course. And Sussex. And Bishop Gardiner.'

Elizabeth pursed her lips. Gardiner. At last.

'And,' added Walsingham, 'the Earl of Arundel.'

'*Arundel?*' Elizabeth was horrified. 'No! And I thought him to be . . . to be my friend.' Visibly upset, almost moved to tears, she sat down and put her head in her hands. 'I thought him to be loyal to me. And his wife . . . I . . . his wife and I . . . Oh! this is too bad . . .'

Walsingham maintained a tactful silence while Elizabeth sought to compose herself.

When at last she looked up again her eyes were dry and her mouth was set in a firm, resolute line. Then she saw the expression on Walsingham's face. 'There's someone else, isn't there?'

'Yes, Madam.'

'Who?'

'Robert Dudley, the Earl of Leicester.'

'Soon,' whispered Norfolk, 'you will be the mistress of a king!'

Lettice smiled into the eyes that burned into her own with a lust that had nothing to do with their coupling. Norfolk was crazed: but with power not passion. And he was gripping her so fiercely that she derived no pleasure from him – only pain.

'When?' she gasped. 'When shall you become king, my Lord?'

'Soon, Lettice. Soon. When I am married to the Queen of Scots I shall have the power and might of both France and Scotland behind me.'

Lettice looked up at the cold, arrogant face and shuddered. 'The letter,' she whispered, trying not to wince. 'You have received the letter from the Pope?'

'Today! And now it is signed.'

'Why did it take so long, my Lord?'

'Long?' Norfolk began to laugh. 'My poor woman, these months have not been long. These things take time: time to plan, to marshall resources and gather forces. Oh no, Lettice, it has not taken long.' Then, his appetite sated, he rolled away from her.

'Leave me now Lettice. I shall sleep alone.'

Lettice shot him a furious glance. She wondered if he had any idea how much he humiliated and hurt her; how much she resented being treated like a chattel to be used, abused and then cast aside. But as she looked at the strong, arrogant face on the pillow, she realized that he hardly knew she existed. And when she saw him close his eyes, she knew he had already forgotten about her. She had served her purpose for the night. Wearily, she slipped out of the bed and reached for her gown. *Mistress of a king.* No, she would no longer be Norfolk's mistress – and Norfolk would not be king. She had seen to that.

Soon, she thought as she padded out of the room, it would all be over. She would no longer have to endure Norfolk's brutal advances. And neither would she have to act out her other, clandestine role.

Walsingham had promised that he would release her from her duties as soon as Norfolk was incarcerated in the Tower.

As she closed the door behind her, she turned back to take a last, lingering look at the room she so hated. The great bed where Norfolk was already snoring; the foul hounds sleeping beside it. They, she thought with a wry smile, would no longer plague her. Then she saw the rich tapestries and the voluminous, vulgar draperies emblazoned with the Norfolk colours and crest. And, in the corner of the room, the desk from where she had stolen the letter from the Pope.

Lettice smiled again. She had, she realized, derived some satisfaction from her liaison with Norfolk: she had duped him completely. She had played the awe-struck ingenue with total conviction. It hadn't been very difficult – for that was what she had been when she first became Norfolk's mistress. And then he had beaten her so badly that she had taken to her bed for a week. That was when the worm had turned.

As she crept down the corridor to her own quarters, Lettice cast her mind back to the day when, fearing for her own life, she had confided in Sir Francis Walsingham: the day that had changed her life. He had offered her a way out – but at a price. And now she had paid that price: the letter, now signed by Norfolk, was back in Walsingham's hands.

Lettice reached her own room, entered, and bolted the door behind her. She would sleep soundly tonight. Norfolk would not.

'Wake up, your Grace!'

Norfolk felt the hand at his shoulder, the rough shake that sought to rouse him from his slumbers. He brushed it away. 'No', he mumbled. 'Leave me alone, Lettice.'

Walsingham leaned closer. 'Your Grace?'

'What . . . ?' Norfolk opened his eyes. Yet he was slow to come to his senses. He saw, but did not register, a man in black bending over him. He saw armed soldiers surrounding his bed. Refusing to believe his eyes, he sat up and rubbed them with vigour. Dreams, he told himself. Always unsettling.

But the scene before him was more than unsettling.

Nor was it illusory. When he opened his eyes again he saw Walsingham.

'Your Grace', the man in black repeated. 'You are arrested for treason.' Then he gestured to the soldiers. 'You must go with these men – to the Tower.'

Norfolk stared in wide-eyed disbelief. Shock registered on his face. Then anger. Then, finally, amusement. He burst out laughing. 'Little man!' he scolded as he climbed out of bed. 'Little man! Do you not know that you do not say "must" to princes? I,' he sneered as he shrugged into his magnificent yellow robe, 'am Norfolk!'

'You *were* Norfolk.' Walsingham's lip curled with distaste. 'But now you are nothing. Dead men have no titles. You are a traitor!'

'Am I? And where is your proof, little man?'

Walsingham reached into the folds of his cloak. 'Here . . . your Grace.'

The colour drained from Norfolk's face as he saw the letter he had signed only hours previously. 'No!' he whispered. 'No . . . it cannot be . . . I . . . ' Then, as his shoulders slumped and his features sagged, he saw, out of the corner of his eye, his hunting dogs. They were lying quite still, undisturbed by the intruders. And there was blood at the corners of their mouths. Norfolk let out a low, agonized moan. Then, as Walsingham watched, the towering edifice of his vanity crumbled where he stood; his knees gave way beneath him and he sank back on to the bed. 'No,' he repeated in a disbelieving whisper. 'No, this cannot be.' Then he put his head in between his hands and began to rock back and forth.

Walsingham looked at him in contempt. 'You were the greatest man in England', he spat. 'You could have been even greater still – but you had not the courage to do it.' He shook his head, almost in sorrow. 'You are all show . . . nothing more.'

But there was still something of the old Norfolk in the quivering wreck before him.

'No', he said, raising his head. Then he stood up and gathered his cloak around him. 'Say what you will. Here stands Norfolk. For ever! Norfolk!'

The defiant stance and pitiful delusion served him well: he maintained them until he reached the Tower. But there, days later, they would crumble in the face of brutal reality as he was led to the scaffold.

Elizabeth had been quite precise in her instructions. Walsingham was to arrest Norfolk, Sussex and Gardiner as and when he saw fit. She wanted no part in the proceedings, would derive no pleasure from their downfall. She would not abase herself by sinking to their standards of overt and gleeful satisfaction. She never wanted to see them again. Arundel, however, was to be brought to her. Elizabeth didn't ask – and Walsingham did not volunteer any information – about de la Quadra's involvement in the conspiracy. The fact that the Spanish Ambassador's name didn't feature in the equation suited his purposes. And de la Quadra himself, sensing that discretion was his best tactic, was remaining out of sight – another bonus as far as Walsingham was concerned. For a week after the conspirators had been arrested, but while all attention was still focused on them, Alvaro de la Quadra was found dead. The verdict was suicide; the implication was that he was involved in the conspiracy. The black-clad figure who visited the Ambassador's house in the dead of night knew better. But then he had always known the best, and most ruthless ways of safeguarding the nation.

Two days after Norfolk's arrest, he was brought to Elizabeth in chains. Pale and drawn, dishevelled and dirty he looked infinitely older than his fifty years. He sank to his knees in front of her. 'Your Majesty', he mumbled.

'Look at me, my Lord.'

Arundel looked up. He saw no anger in Elizabeth's eyes. Nor was there any pity; and no grief over his portrayal.

But Elizabeth saw much in Arundel's face. There was contrition, guilt and sadness. And there was also a certain defiance.

'Your Majesty,' he whispered as if reading her thoughts, 'knows that I did it only for my faith, nothing more.'

Yes, thought Elizabeth. I know.

Arundel saw the weary resignation in her face. And, now, the compassion. 'I do not suppose,' he stammered, 'that . . . that for the sake of my children . . . ?'

Elizabeth looked down into the pleading eyes. 'I remember all your kindnesses to me . . . '

'So you will . . . ?'

'No.'

The flicker of hope died in Arundel's heart.

'But,' added Elizabeth, 'you must not think that I

have not a care for your children. They will not be punished.'

But they will grow up without a father, she thought with regret. And they will never be allowed to forget they were spawned by a traitor. They would have to live with that for ever. Then again, they may turn traitor themselves. It had happened before.

Elizabeth had been equally precise in her instructions about Robert's arrest. 'I will come with you', she had told Walsingham.

'But your Majesty . . . !'

Elizabeth had been adamant. 'I want to see his face. I want to see what is there. I don't want him to have time to compose himself. I . . . I want . . . '

'Yes, your Majesty.' Realizing that she was on the verge of breaking down, Walsingham had made a tactful withdrawal.

Elizabeth *did* break down at that point. She cried all the tears that had refused to flow when Walsingham had informed her of Robert's treachery. Then, her reaction had surprised her. She had frozen. Some innate sense of self-preservation had numbed her every sense, had shuttered the part of her brain that made her want to scream, to cry out in disbelief and then to wallow in a grotesque orgy of pity.

Walsingham, too, had been surprised by her reaction. All she had done was to look at him, tell him to ensure that Norfolk be given the Pope's letter without delay, and that 'it all be done and finished with'.

But the breakdown prior to Robert's arrest was terrible. And private. She let no one witness her distress; Robert's name never passed her lips in public.

291

But in private she made another resolution. Her previous attempts to banish Robert from her heart had failed. They would not fail again. She would never again leave herself open to hurt, humiliation, despair and deceit. She would never be vulnerable again.

For love equated with vulnerability – and Elizabeth would never love again.

When one of Walsingham's men came to inform her that they had found Robert Dudley, she was calm, composed, almost icily regal. Walsingham's man, in contrast, was extremely uncomfortable. 'Lord Dudley is . . . well, he is in the cellars, your Majesty.'

'Indeed?' Elizabeth seemed only politely interested. 'And what would he be doing there?'

'Drinking, Madam.'

'Ah!' Elizabeth turned and smiled. 'Drowning his sorrows?'

The manservant grinned weakly. Elizabeth's expression, while friendly enough, was somehow unnerving. It was as if only part of her was behind it; as if the other part was hidden somewhere in the depths of her soul.

'If your Majesty would follow me . . .'

Elizabeth had never been to the cellars before. She had never had any call to descend to the dank, dark bowels of the Palace. Nor would she ever again. She was only here, she told herself as she followed Walsingham's servant, out of curiosity. Nothing more. And a detached curiosity at that. She felt unreal, wandering through the warren of barrel-vaulted rooms in the light of flickering torches. Not like Elizabeth at all but like some half-forgotten creature from the dim and distant past. She wondered vaguely if that was how she would view Robert.

It wasn't. The servant showed her into a cellar at the end of a long corridor and there, slumped on a table in the middle of the room, clutching a bottle of wine and clad only in breeches and a dirty white shirt, was the man she had once sworn to love for all eternity. He looked exactly as he had when Elizabeth had seen him in the Tower of London all those years ago: strong yet strangely vulnerable. Innocent yet irresistible. Elizabeth fought to quell the urge to run to him as she had done then, to fling her arms around him and seek succour from his strength and his love.

And then Robert lifted his head at the sound of her footsteps. Elizabeth gasped as she saw his face. Pale, strained and unshaven, it was the face of a man who had lost the will to live. And the eyes, bleary and unfocused with drink, were not those of the man she had known and loved.

It took Robert a moment to focus on her. When at last he managed, he smiled drunkenly and hauled himself to his feet. 'Your Majesty', he slurred. 'I . . . I thought you to be . . . ' Attempting to bow, he swayed and fell back against the table, knocking over the bottle of wine. It spilled its contents all over his white shirt and then went crashing to the floor.

'Hah!' said Robert after a moment. Then he steadied himself and looked back at Elizabeth. 'I thought you to be Walsingham. I have been waiting for him.'

'And not in vain, my Lord.' A grim-faced Walsingham emerged from the shadows of the corridor. Behind him stood twelve armed guards. But Robert was still looking in awed disbelief at Elizabeth. 'Why,' he whispered, 'have you come?'

Elizabeth stepped forward. 'To look a traitor in the eye.'

Robert flinched and lowered his eyes.

'They are all gone to the Tower', said Elizabeth. 'Your friends.'

'Yes. I . . . I . . . '

'Tell me. How should I serve *thee*, Robert?'

Still Robert refused to meet her eye. He lurched groggily, swinging one arm in the direction of the guards. 'Tell them to kill me!' he yelled. 'Why not? I would rather die now. My course is run.'

Elizabeth stepped even closer. 'Just tell me', she whispered. 'Why?'

At last Robert met her eyes. She saw no shame, no contrition – merely anger. They were not the eyes of the man she had loved.

Then Robert laughed at her – a bitter, humourless sound. 'Why? You ask why, Madam? Is it not plain enough to you? Hah!' he laughed again. 'It is no easy thing, to be loved by a Queen! It would corrupt the soul of any man!' He pointed an accusatory finger at Elizabeth. 'Especially . . . 'specially if he . . . if he were . . . '

'If he were what, Robert?'

There was no more anger left in Robert; no more bluster. There was not even any belief in his own self-pity. He slumped back into his chair and put his head in his hands. 'If he were vain, ambitious . . . and weak.' Then he began to sob.

Walsingham looked at Elizabeth. Her face was still deathly pale. Her eyes were blank. Only by the almost imperceptible quivering of her lower lip did she betray any sign of the agony she must be feeling.

'For God's sake!' screamed Robert, lashing out again towards the guards. 'Let them kill me, and be done with it! There is nothing more now that life can show me, that is not already spoiled.'

Spoiled, thought Elizabeth. That was it. He's spoiled. He has never had to strive for anything: all his gifts were God-given – and he threw them all away. 'No,' she said, 'I think rather to let you live.'

Robert's befuddled brain took time to process the information. Walsingham's did not. 'Madam!' he protested. 'That is not wise.' He moved closer to Robert and looked down at him with contempt. 'He is a traitor, like his father. He must be made an example of.'

'And I will,' said Elizabeth 'make an example of him. He will always remind me,' she continued as though he were not there, 'of how close I came to danger!'

It was only when Robert looked up again that her vituperative, violent anger overcame her. 'And I know he will be loyal from henceforth,' she spat, 'knowing what manner of man he is!'

Then she reached into her sleeve and pulled out a silver chain. Only fleetingly did she remember the Robert who had given it to her: he was not the same Robert at whom she now threw it. As the medallion of the bear and staff formed an arc in the air and landed at Robert's feet, she bent down and hissed in his ear. 'Only remember, my Lord: my dogs wear *my* collars!'

Robert flinched and looked away; down at his family emblem on the wine-soaked floor beside the shards of broken glass. He didn't look up as Elizabeth turned and walked away. Instead he gazed with unseeing eyes at the shattered fragments on the ground. '*I wonder*,' he whispered in a broken voice, '*by my troth, what thou and I did – 'till we loved?*'

When he finally looked up it was to discover that Elizabeth, Walsingham and the soldiers had left. The flickering torches, too, had gone.

The light and the life had gone for ever.

Epilogue

'Lady Knollys, Madam, has been sent to the Tower.'

'I know.' Elizabeth's voice was cold; her manner disinterested. Then she raised her head and locked eyes with Kat in the mirror.

She knows, thought Kat with a sharp intake of breath. Then she caught the expression on her mistress's face and realized that Elizabeth didn't just *know* about Isabel's fate – she had ordered the arrest herself.

So she knew about the other matter as well.

Kat lowered her eyes, steeling herself to relay the request that the hysterical Isabel, still horribly disfigured from the poisoned fabric of Elizabeth's dress, had made of her as she had been dragged from the Palace. 'She is . . . she requests that . . . I mean . . . Madam, she is with child.'

Yes, thought Elizabeth. Robert's child. 'I know', she said as she picked up a pair of scissors. 'In future,' she snapped as she handed them to Kat, 'all my ladies will be virgins! I will have none about me who secretly belong to another! Now . . . begin!'

With a trembling hand, Kat took the scissors and began her work. Reluctance was writ large on her face, palpable in her every movement, yet the expression on Elizabeth's face forced her to continue. A heavy silence hung in the room – broken only by the snip of the scissors and, as the last tresses fell, a low moan from Kat. 'Why, madam?' she sobbed. 'Why do you do this?'

Again their eyes met in the mirror. Elizabeth's were softer now, betraying a trace of her old gentleness. 'Do not weep for me, Kat', she whispered.

'No, Madam.' But Kat did weep. Unable to stop herself, she cried as she looked at Elizabeth's hair; at the beautiful auburn tresses that had been her crowning glory. They were all lying on the floor now; nothing remained on Elizabeth's head save the cruel, jagged and close-cropped helmet that she had forced Kat to create.

Elizabeth stared fixedly at herself in the mirror, willing herself not to cry as well. She failed. As the tears welled in her eyes she swivelled round and held her arms out. 'Hold me, Kat!' she pleaded. 'Hold me tightly!'

For a moment the two women clung to each other in silent mourning. Then Elizabeth turned back to the mirror and glared at her reflection. Her metamorphosis was not yet complete. 'And now,' she sighed, 'the rest!'

Still tearful, with every sinew in her body crying out against the travesty required of her, Kat reached for a pot on the dressing-table. Then, with slow, reluctant movements, she began to smear the paste of ground alabaster, beeswax and asses' milk on Elizabeth's face.

A minute later the face she knew had disappeared. In its place was a mask of polished marble; a smooth, utterly characterless carapace. Only the eyes betrayed emotion. Then, as Kat applied red ochre and cochineal to Elizabeth's lips, transforming them into a vivid slash of red, a veil descended over the eyes.

Elizabeth had disappeared.

'Look,' she said to Kat. 'I have become a virgin.'

Kat didn't reply. It was all she could do to stop herself bursting into tears.

'The rest, Kat', commanded the woman in the mask. 'The rest!'

'The Queen!'

A hush fell upon the Great Hall as the Chamberlain threw open the doors and banged his staff on the ground. Everyone present turned towards the door; some in apprehension, others with eagerness – all with curiosity. For this was Elizabeth's first appearance at court since the execution of her enemies; the first time she would walk into her own court as the true mistress of her realm.

And then a collective gasp of amazement filled the room; a great involuntary exhalation of astonishment. Followed by an awed silence.

Elizabeth was standing in the doorway. For a moment she remained quite still. Then she moved slowly forward; a magnificent, stately figure only recognizable by its majesty. But not its humanity. This was a goddess: both beautiful and frightening to behold. Seemingly propelled by sheer force of will, it moved into the centre of the room and drifted forward, gliding slowly down the aisle the courtiers had created. For as they had sank to their knees, so they had instinctively drawn back.

Half-fascinated and half-repelled, they watched as the woman who was their Queen descended into their midst.

Elizabeth betrayed no emotion whatsoever. The porcelain mask moved from side to side, nodding acknowledgement of those present. But there was no movement in the eyes; no smile on the lips.

The apparition floated towards Cecil. Open-mouthed in amazement, he willed his senses to recognize this creature, at once dazzling and dangerous, that was his Queen. The transformation, he realized, was total. The hair was gone, replaced by a magnificent wig encrusted with jewels. Hundreds of them, he noted. Ropes of diamonds and pearls the size of pears. And each more brilliant than the next. But nothing shone as brilliantly as the dress. Gorgeous and glittering, catching the light as it moved towards him, it epitomized the woman who was wearing it: breathtaking beyond words; fabulous in its richness; mesmeric in its display of power. But not human.

'My good Lord Burghley.'

Cecil looked up. The hand, seemingly more white and more beautiful, more ethereal in appearance, was extended towards him. He grasped it in his own and, stumbling over the words, greeted his 'most gracious and Sovereign Lady'.

Elizabeth moved on, pausing now and then to let other awe-struck courtiers kiss the jewelled hand.

Then she stopped beside the man standing apart from the rest of her courtiers. 'Lord Robert.'

Robert had been rigid with shock from the moment Elizabeth had entered the room. Now, obeying the command implicit in her voice, he bent to kiss her hand. He was shaking all over, but Elizabeth's hand was quite still. And deathly cold.

As was the frozen mask when he steeled himself to look up at her. There was nothing there. And nor was there anything in the hidden depths of Elizabeth's soul. For she had been true to her resolution. She had cut out her heart.